Fatima Tate
Takes the Cake

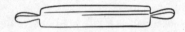

KHADIJAH VANBRAKLE

HOLIDAY HOUSE   NEW YORK

HOLIDAY HOUSE is registered in the U.S. Patent and Trademark Office.

Printed and bound in April 2023 at Maple Press, York, PA, U.S.A.

www.holidayhouse.com

First Edition

1 3 5 7 9 10 8 6 4 2

Cataloging-in-Publication Data is available from the Library of Congress.

ISBN: 978-0-8234-5485-3 (hardcover)

To those teens who are viewed as not

Black enough while at the same time

judged for not being Muslim enough,

I tell stories for you. You are seen here.

WELCOME.

one

I, Fatima Noor Tate, do nothing without parental approval.

Today is no different.

Zaynab's speeding will get me to the soup kitchen in time for my shift, but my homemade spice cupcakes might be DOA.

"Can you please slow down?" My left hand grips the cake carrier while my right is fused with the door handle.

"Stop complaining, Fatima, I got you. You won't miss a minute of flirting with your Muslim Prince Charming." Zaynab smirks in my direction before merging her Mini Cooper into an exit lane— without using her signal.

"Raheem is not my *anything*." The wind from her half-open window doesn't stop a wave of warmth from spreading across my face. "He's nice to *all* the volunteers at the Shared Table."

My best friend's box braids sway in the merciless Albuquerque sun as she brakes hard at a stoplight. "Nah! You're busted. I've seen you sneak glances at him—and I've seen him watching you, too."

My palms dampen. I only wish it was true. "You've only been there *once* when he and I were both serving food. Raheem is friendly and he likes my desserts. It's really nothing personal."

She speeds past the masjid, then a minute later swings a sharp right into the soup kitchen's parking lot. Whipping her car into the first open space, Zaynab scolds me. "We've known each other *way* too long for those weak denials to fool me. You just think you're not good enough for a guy like him."

The knot in my stomach confirms her opinion is closer to the truth than I want to admit, so I keep my mouth shut.

"And yeah, he's okay, but he's got nothing on Amber." Zaynab winks at me. "Although she doesn't like green chile. How can I be dating a girl who doesn't like green chile?"

Before I can think of a snappy response, Raheem parks his dark gray sedan right beside us. My mouth dries up; I struggle to pull my eyes away from him.

My BFF cracks her gum, filling my nose with cinnamon. "Or maybe you're scared a college student who drives an eighty-thousand-dollar Lexus might actually be interested in you?"

A brief silence surrounds us.

"Spend more than a few seconds talking to him," she presses. "You'll see—what I'm saying about him liking you is true."

Rather than agreeing with her, I escape out the passenger door.

Raheem is already out of his vehicle. Smooth brown skin; six-foot-tall frame; perfect face. He's my weekly distraction while volunteering. "*As-salaamu alaykum*, ladies. Let me get those, Fatima."

I pass him the cake carrier. "*Wa alaykum as salaam.*"

He flashes me a smile. I tear my eyes away.

Zaynab hops out and opens her rear door to grab my second tray of cupcakes. "*Salaam*, Raheem." She glances at me. "Here, Fatima. I'll be back to pick you up by six-thirty at the latest."

I recognize the *I told you so* in her voice.

I grab the aluminum sheet pan from her. After a quick wink,

she gets in her car and drives away, leaving me alone with Raheem.

Steady, Fatima.

Forcing myself to take one step after another, and avoiding the deep cracks in the concrete, I walk with him toward the front door.

"So what did you make for me today?" He asks me the same question every time we're together at the soup kitchen. It's almost like our own private joke.

I can't hide a teeth-baring grin. He knows he can only have some if there are leftovers. "Spice cupcakes with cream cheese frosting. But they're not for you—they're for the people we're feeding!"

Raheem is already holding open the door. "Can't blame me for trying. Everything you bake is so delicious. Now I'm ruined for store-bought desserts, and it's all your fault."

Should I say "*Sorry*"? Or "*You're welcome*"?

Heat travels up my limbs as I slide past him into the lobby and head for the dining hall. Rows and rows of tables are set up there, including buffet tables, and we leave my contributions at the dessert station.

"See you after the food service," he says.

Watching Raheem unfold a couple of chairs, I wipe my sweaty hands down the sides of my jeans. After stopping by the supply closet to grab a clean apron and stash my bag, I head into the kitchen to help with dinner prep.

Head Chef John nods at me as he slides a tray of seasoned chicken thighs out of one of the big commercial ovens, his stained apron tight under his beer belly. The aromatic smell of garlic and rosemary makes my mouth water.

"Hey, Fatima. How are you today?" he asks, smiling.

I sneak a peek at the empty stainless-steel sinks, already dreading having to wash all the pots and pans after tonight's meal. "Hi. What're my assignments today?"

"Well, one of the new volunteers called in sick twenty minutes ago, so first I need you to make the salad. Then you can organize the dessert table, replenish the slotted spoons on the food line, and put a new box of disposable gloves out for the servers. I need it all done right away—dinner service starts in thirty minutes."

"That's a lot! Let me get started."

Grabbing two huge silver bowls, I dump a couple jumbo bags of prewashed salad mix in each. Even with gloved hands, tossing the ingredients with half a bottle of salad dressing takes me no time. After covering both bowls with plastic wrap and setting them in the fridge, I change my gloves and leave the kitchen.

Raheem is in the far corner of the dining hall, wiping down the tables. His gaze meets mine and he waves.

Damn. He caught me looking—he always does.

I give him a weak wave back and focus on my tasks, ending up at the dessert table cutting two dozen Costco muffins in half. I'm putting the serrated knife back in its place when someone deposits four trays of decorated sugar cookies in front of me.

"Hi. Can you tell me where John is?" It's a tall brunette dressed in a light blue sweatshirt and jeans, an expensive black leather purse slung across her chest.

"He should be in the kitchen." I point toward the door to the left of the serving line. "Do you want me to get him for you?"

"I know the way," she says, the sweet tone of her voice soothing. After patting the top tray of cookies she brought, she adds, "Been here many times."

My eyes land on her donation: the cookies are delicate heart-shaped creations piped with red and white icing. "These are beautiful."

"Thanks. My students worked hard on them. I should introduce myself: I'm Erica."

She has students? We exchange smiles. "I'm Fatima."

"Nice to meet you." Erica heads toward the kitchen. "I shouldn't keep you from your job. A long line of people is waiting outside."

She's not wrong. The instant the doors are unlocked, there's a surge. The crowd rushes in to pick up trays, hungrily circulating from station to station. Before volunteering here, I had no idea so many people were food insecure in Albuquerque.

The hour goes by in a blur. The dessert station is popular, and I hand out everything we have. Helping here is my small contribution to the community.

Once the dining hall has emptied out, I go to stash whatever leftovers we have in the fridge—and almost run straight into Chef John standing in the kitchen's doorway.

"This is for you." He hands me a single sheet of paper.

"What is this?" I ask, taking it.

John rubs his chin. "I hope you're not mad. You don't like us to make a fuss over your goodies, but when Erica stopped by today, I asked her to try one of your cupcakes."

Huh? Why would I be *mad*? He's not making sense. "I don't mind if you share my cupcakes."

A sly grin creeps onto his face. "She's not just anyone, Fatima. Her name is Chef Erica Newsome, and she's the head pastry chef at Central New Mexico Community College's culinary program. A couple of times a semester she brings us her students' baked goods."

I blink three times before whispering, "You gave one of my cupcakes to a *head pastry chef*? Why?"

He frowns. "You never believe me when I say how talented you are, Fatima. I thought if Chef Erica tasted one and liked it, you'd finally see what a gift you have. And I was right—she loved it! She asked me to give you this flyer."

I look down. The words TEEN BAKING CHAMPIONSHIP sear into my eyeballs.

My heart rate quickens.

The grand-prize winner and a parent (if the winner is under 18) will be invited to the Culinary Institute of America campus closest to their home. Once there, the winner will spend three days learning and baking under the supervision of some of the country's premier pastry chefs.

Okay, no joke: the CIA is my dream culinary school.

John's still staring at me when I focus back on his face. "Take some time to think about it." He points toward the back of the kitchen. "I'll wash the dishes today. Go."

I can take a hint, so after folding the flyer into my back pocket, I drop my dirty apron in the storage room laundry and grab my empty cake carriers and bag. But when I walk outside, Zaynab's Mini Cooper isn't there.

Instead I see Raheem leaning against his car, absorbed in his phone.

Where are you? My texting fingers work fast. **I finished my shift. Did you forget about me?** 😆 I press send and wait.

"Hey, Fatima." Raheem's deep voice makes my insides flutter. "Isn't Zaynab picking you up?"

I shuffle toward him, unsure if my voice will crack. "I don't know. She's never flaked on me before."

His eyebrows bunch up, but he doesn't say a word. Instead, he opens his passenger door. "It's almost dark—I can't leave you here. Hop in and I'll give you a ride."

"You don't have to! I can wait until she texts me back." The longer I stare at his face, the harder it is to breathe.

The corners of Raheem's mouth turn downward. "I promise to drive you straight home." He holds up three fingers. "Scout's honor: you can trust me."

The early March night quiets around us. I'm so tempted. My parents would be pissed if they knew . . .

. . . but who's going to tell them?

This is probably my only chance to ever talk to him. And I want to take it.

"Hand those over, please." He shifts his gaze to the empty cake carriers I'm gripping to my chest like a life jacket.

My fingers glide against his as I pass them. *Zap!*

My skin is still tingling as I ease into the shotgun seat. Right after he closes my door, he races around to the driver's side and gets in. The woodsy scent of his aftershave surrounds me.

"What part of town do you live in?" Raheem asks as he backs out of the parking space and turns north toward the freeway.

I tuck my hands underneath me. "Northeast Heights, near Tramway and Montgomery." To force myself to stop staring at him, I focus on all the tan leather around me. Growing up as a mechanic's daughter, I've always heard about the high-quality materials used in luxury cars—Dad goes on and on about them—but I've never actually *seen* them.

This leather is like softened butter. I get it now.

While we wait at a red light, I pull my phone and the flyer out of my back pocket. I send Zaynab a selfie, then shoot my mom a quick text: **Ma, I got asked to compete in a baking competition for teens. What do you think?**

"*Idiot!*" Raheem yells at a driver who cuts him off. "Learn how to drive!" Out of the corner of my eye, I catch his quick look in my direction. "Sorry. I'm usually more chill than that."

I believe him: he's always calm at the soup kitchen. It's no big deal. I cross my legs at the ankles and hope he doesn't expect me to come up with witty conversation.

"Where do you live?" That's all I have.

He's focusing on the traffic around us, but still answers my question. "In one of the High Desert subdivisions, right off of Tramway Boulevard."

We're almost neighbors. My brain turns to mush.

Except . . . my parents could never afford the million-dollar price tags for houses in that development.

The next few minutes of silence remind me how bad I am at this. Flirting. Making small talk of any kind with the opposite sex. So, so bad.

"What's in your lap?" he asks, a curious eyebrow raised.

I forgot to put the flyer away. Crap. *What do I say to not sound stupid?*

"Chef John gave it to me. It's from another volunteer. Chef Erica Newsome—she's the head pastry chef at CNM." I bite my lip, not sure if I should keep talking.

The car speeds down I-25 North. Raheem glances from the road to me more than once. "And . . . I'm waiting for the rest of the story."

I blow out a small breath. "Ever since I started volunteering at the soup kitchen, Chef John's been telling me how much he likes my baking. Today he gave one of my cupcakes to Chef Erica." I refold the flyer. "She suggested I enter this teen baking competition in April at the convention center."

Do I sound dorky? Baking isn't, like, *the thing*.

"Well, all the stuff I've tasted has been fantastic," he says, a grin spreading across his face. "You should definitely enter!"

I giggle inside. He thinks I should go for it?

Too bad, nothing in my life is that simple. I can't do anything without my mom's permission—but I'm not telling him that.

We're already at my exit, so he veers the car right onto Montgomery Boulevard. "How long have you been baking, anyway?"

"When I was eight and fasting during Ramadan for the first time, my dad distracted me from being hungry by showing me how to make chocolate chip cookies." The tension in my shoulders releases a little. "That was it for me. Ever since, baking has been my passion."

"You should do it, Fatima. I bet you'll win the whole competition."

His support is a gift he doesn't know he's giving me. I hold onto the armrest between us.

We don't talk the rest of the way home. As we pull up to my complex, I give Raheem the gate code and he turns into the visitors' lot. I get a new notification and open the text from my mom.

Wonderful opportunity. Not for you. Nursing is more stable and friendlier on the waistline.

Angry tears well up in my eyes, but I refuse to cry in front of Raheem.

My mom doesn't care about what I want—only what she thinks I should want. But maybe it's a blessing in disguise this time. My baking skills are all self-taught—cooking shows, TikTok, YouTube—and probably not good enough.

He reaches over and touches my shoulder, bringing my attention back to him. "I'll walk you to your door."

My feet tingle as I step out of the car. It's surreal that the guy I've been crushing on for months is right here beside me. He's been the main character in my daydreams since we met, and now he's in front of my condo.

"Th-thanks for giving me a ride home." I struggle to get the words out. "You don't have to walk me the rest of the way. I'll be okay."

"I insist," he says, his straight white teeth on full display.

He follows me through the courtyard. I walk super slow—now isn't the time to trip over my own feet. Standing in front of our door, I turn toward him. "Here safe and sound. Thanks again for the ride."

Raheem takes a single step into my personal space. "Fatima, would it be okay if I come in and pray *Asr*?"

A big *YES* teeters on the tip of my tongue, but I force it back down my throat. Being too eager isn't the best look.

"I could head back across town to the masjid," he offers, after a moment of silence. "But I'd miss it."

I nod. How can I say no to another Muslim who's asking to make salaat? "Of course."

With shaky hands, I fish my keys out of my purse and let us

into the apartment. The automatic timer turns on the living room floor lamp: my parents aren't home from work.

Raheem and I slip off our shoes.

After sinking onto the closest couch cushion, I point down the hall. "If you need to make wudu, the bathroom is the last door on the left."

"Thanks."

Once the bathroom door closes, I breathe out.

This morning's *Albuquerque Journal* is spread out on the dining table at the far end of the room. Other than that, the only furniture in our open living-and-dining space is the couch I'm sitting on, a loveseat, and a side table beside me.

Maybe he won't notice that we have, like, four possessions.

My fingers nervously adjust my hijab, and then Raheem reappears. "The prayer rugs are in the basket beside the TV." Pointing toward the northeast corner of the room, I add, "The qibla is in that direction."

After snagging one, he lays it down in the correct direction, then raises his hands to his ears. "Allahu Akbar."

I try to stare at the drab beige wall-to-wall carpet. But—holding my breath—I can't help but sneak a quick peek as he prostrates right in front of me.

That's it.

I'm going to Hell for ogling Raheem while he's fulfilling one of the pillars of our faith.

Minutes later, I look up and watch him fold his rug and drop it back into the basket.

Then he sits beside me.

And wraps my hand with his.

My whole body trembles. I can't help but stare at our joined hands. His smooth skin reminds me of milk-chocolate baking squares, while mine is closer to a well-used wooden mixing spoon.

"Are you okay, Fatima?" Raheem's gentle words pull me from my silent panic.

"Uh. Yes. Fine." I blow out a small stream of air.

Hints of earthy cologne tickle my nose. *Damn, he always smells good.* Should probably let go of his hand and force myself off the couch, away from him.

But I'm not that strong.

Raheem grins, then pulls his hands back, breaking our physical connection. "If you *do* enter the baking competition, you'll need a taste tester. I volunteer as tribute—we'd make a good team."

My eyebrows bunch together. *Wait, what? Team?*

I can't stop my gaze from wandering across his body. I've seen him in those dark-washed jeans before; they must be one of his favorite pairs. His biceps are amazing. I start imagining running my fingers along his strong jaw and . . . no, this isn't like me.

And I know my parents wouldn't approve of my new "friend"; the only time two single people get to know each other in my community is when the families agree marriage is a possibility.

That's my future.

"You can't leave . . . without a couple of my homemade spice cupcakes," I manage.

My conservative mom would *flip* if she knew Raheem was here with me alone. I'm less than two months away from getting my high school diploma, yet I've never been alone with a boy—EVER. But I don't get it. How will I ever know if a parent-approved

Muslim guy is the one for me if I've never even had a friendly *conversation* with someone who has a Y chromosome?

That's all this is. Conversation. Right?

He scoots forward, closer to me.

Breathe, Fatima, breathe. But I've got nothing to focus on. Except him.

"Are you nervous?" Raheem whispers. When all I do is nod, he says, "I like you, Fatima Tate."

Shock floods my body, but I can't hide a wide smile.

But being here with him, hearing this, letting him touch me— and liking it—is so wrong. *This can't be happening.* He is perfect. His body is perfect. This is quickly getting beyond *conversation*, and I know it.

"Fatima? Did you hear me?" Raheem asks. I realize he's been talking.

Nope.

Not.

A.

Word.

After another pause, I dare to meet his deep brown eyes. "But why?"

Raheem chuckles. "Isn't it obvious? We've gotten to know each other at the Shared Table, haven't we? You've got a quiet strength, and I like that. Remember last month when that man insisted your parents force you to cover your hair? You didn't even react. Both of our moms would've made it a huge deal." He reaches out and holds my hand in his again. "We're both mature. We'd be good together."

What does that mean, exactly?

"Before I go, I'd like to kiss you. Are you okay with that?"

All the cells in my body come alive. *Kiss?*

But before I can respond, Raheem abruptly gets up and walks toward the door. "I'm sorry, Fatima. I shouldn't have asked you that."

The next second I'm on my feet. Without thinking, I blurt out, "I've never been kissed before."

He moves back toward me, closer and closer, until the heat of his body mixes with mine. "You mean I'd be your first?" His hushed voice is almost impossible to hear.

We're almost touching, body to body. The answer gets stuck in my throat.

He leans even closer. His lips brush the shell of my ear. "So . . . can I kiss you?"

My faith tells me I shouldn't—but the truth is my body wants to know what it's like.

I know what my mom would say . . . what Islam says . . . but right now I don't care. Adrenaline courses through me. No one needs to know.

"Y-yes."

With one finger, Raheem lifts my chin up. And just like that, I'm lost.

Raheem presses me against his chest and wraps his powerful arms around my waist. I drink in his scent, every nerve ending in my body ablaze as I melt into his embrace. The moment our lips touch, my doubts dissolve. I never want this feeling to end.

A couple of delicious minutes later, he breaks our connection, a huge grin on his face.

"Are you okay, Gorgeous?"

I press my fingers against my mouth. No one's ever called me that before. ". . . Yeah."

Raheem's thumb traces the outline of my lips. "Fatima, you're special to me."

My breath hitches. "I am?"

"Do you think I kiss every female I meet?" he scolds, frowning, and my mouth grows dry. But then his stern expression softens and he runs his hand along my cheek. "Relax . . . it was a joke. Now, where are those cupcakes you promised me?"

Leaving him, I rush into the kitchen and come back with three cupcakes in a disposable pie pan.

"Thanks." He accepts my homemade desserts, leans in, and plants another quick kiss on my lips. "See you soon, Gorgeous."

Once he's gone, I press myself against the back of the door. Other than my next bake, it feels like Raheem—and kissing?!?!—suddenly occupies all the free space in my brain. Nothing can stop me from dreaming about what will happen the next time we're alone, even though I know there shouldn't *be* a next time.

I can imagine myself addicted.

I.

Salaam Fatima. Are you awake?

It's him. The sun is barely up, meaning I'm barely alive but talking to Raheem is something I want more than sleep. At least he can't see me in my oversized Hershey's shirt and messy hair.

Salaam, I'm here!

Just wanted to check on you after . . . yesterday

My thumbs hover over my Samsung keyboard. **I'm okay.** ☺
How are you? It's our first time texting—and after the kiss, it
feels loaded. I'm so NOT okay.

I can't stop thinking of a certain high school baker. The
blinking dots show up for more than a minute. **Is this a good
time to reach you in the mornings?**

He wants this to be a regular thing? **Sure. Yes.**

I have a personal training client soon, but we'll talk tomorrow.
We will?

**Salaam Sunshine. This nickname fits you since we're wak-
ing up together . . . in a halal way** ✺

Salaam Raheem!

I stare at my phone screen until the sound of footsteps pushes
me out of my own thoughts. Tomorrow morning can't come fast
enough.

II.

Salaam Fatima

This time I'm already sitting up, ready for this—no more
sleeping after *Fajr*.

Salaam Raheem. Are you always up at this time??

**Daily. I usually have a client before my first class. Bake any-
thing new lately?**

Why, you hungry? Kinda early for any sass. It's a risk.

If it's something you made, I'm starving.

My cheeks warm, and my brain can't find any words.

He rescues the conversation. **So. Decided about the
competition?**

Damn. He didn't forget? Not really . . .

Tell me. If you DID get a culinary degree, what would you do with it?

Finally, an easy answer.

I'd like to work in a bakery. Become a pastry manager. My dream job! 🍰

Then that's what you should do.

Maybe. But it's just more complicated than that in my family.

What about you? College senior & a part-time personal trainer. That's a lot.

Been going to the gym since HS. I need to keep busy.

Why? *His body is already perfect.*

. . .

Tbh, I don't like being alone.

He's lonely???

I'm an only child. So are you. Ever felt that way?

All the time. My arms are dotted with goosebumps.

Knew you'd understand.

100% on the same page.

Heading to the gym now. Salaam Sunshine ☀

Salaam Raheem

His support is the sweetest thing I've ever tasted.

III.

Salaam Fatima

Seeing these two words every morning makes my day.

Salaam Raheem

I was thinking. Only a few months left, then you're done with high school forever

He hasn't seen the crossed-out days on my Dollar Tree calendar, has he?

Can't waittt. Charter school is the worst. Having all online classes sucks. Super lonely. Everybody keeps to themselves 1000% of the time. Sitting in a huge computer lab in a silent daze, surrounded by strangers trying to hurry up and finish their last semester—well, that about sums up my senior year experience.

Be positive. I see good things in your future.

Easy for him to say—he's already in college.

What things?

Silence.

Sorry to run but I've got to go. Until tomorrow Sunshine. Salaam ✴

Salaam Raheem

I don't need cryptic texts to reel me in.

I'm already hooked.

IV.

Salaam Fatima

The corners of my mouth pull high, ready for our daily conversation.

Salaam Raheem. Gym this morning?

No, I won't have any clients for a few weeks. I got an internship in Northern NM.

What kind?

It's a program in Santa Fe for college seniors headed to law school, meeting with state legislators about NM issues. Encouraging us to practice here. I'm leaving tomorrow. Our texting might have to stop until I'm back in ABQ.

Oh . . . okay.

Now that I've put "Morning Chat" into my phone's calendar, we're all done. Super.

What's that answer? Is there something wrong?

Nope. I add: Thanks for telling me! 👏

Fatima I'll be back. InshaALLAH. Are you going to miss me?

Maybe . . . Idk

I'm going to miss you. It's not that hard to say.

Maybe for him. But I've got nothing.

InshaALLAH we'll talk soon. Salaam Fatima ✋

Salaam Raheem

Enjoying something and wanting to hang onto it is normal. Right? Having that something yanked away . . . it blows. Raheem has paid me more attention than anyone ever, aside from my mom and dad.

Right now, my greatest wish is that we talk again. Or maybe that we talk forever. Whichever.

two

It takes me more than a week, but I find the courage to take matters into my own hands.

My hand shakes as I complete the baking competition's online application. I don't know where this bravery came from; I'm *not* someone who breaks the rules. You know, generally speaking. But this chance is just too amazing to pass up—Raheem certainly thinks so, and he's been pushing me to do it for a reason. (I even set up a new secondary email account for this. Rebel!)

So this is probably why I've woken up sweating in the middle of the night, guilt seeping from every pore. All I can do is stare at my popcorn ceiling until the 5 a.m. alarm on my phone goes off.

I move my eyes slowly around the room. It's nothing special. My mom found each piece of furniture at the biggest consignment store in town, and they all represent her taste. Only my dream board, crammed with pictures of desserts I plan to make one day, is 100 percent me.

After Fajr prayer, the first of the five daily chances Muslims have to communicate with *ALLAH,* the sun still hasn't risen, so I manage a few more hours of fitful sleep before my second alarm at 8.

Should I have asked forgiveness for an action I'm not actually convinced is wrong?

Mom will be home from her Friday-morning workout soon, and—despite her insistence that I can only bake for fun—she likes volunteering me to make homemade desserts for different events at the mosque. I have to whip one up this morning.

I don't complain, though. Baking is baking is baking. From the first time I baked a batch of cookies by myself, my future was set: I *know* this is what I want to do. The fact that I can mix together some raw ingredients and make something gooey and delicious and warming is like magic to me.

I send Raheem a quick text before starting my day. **How's it going?**

Not sure if we're maybe . . . possibly . . . on our way to becoming a couple. He hasn't said anything sure about that. And it's not like we can be alone together in public, anyway.

Down in the kitchen, the knot in my stomach loosens as I organize everything I need to bake a pineapple upside-down cake. After setting the oven to 350 degrees, I sift all the dry ingredients, then add pineapple juice, eggs, and canola oil to make the batter. After that, I get out my favorite baking dish, put a stick of unsalted butter in it, and plunk it in the oven. Five minutes later, that butter is a pool of melted gold.

With the baking dish out of the oven, I sprinkle a cup of brown sugar on top of the butter, lay two rows of pineapple rings in the pan, then pour in the batter. Pop it back in, and thirty-eight minutes later, I take a finished cake out.

A small smile creeps across my face.

After it cools, I flip the cake out of its baking pan and onto the bottom of the cake taker, the delicious aroma of caramelized sugar filling the air.

Okay, I can check my phone now. I race upstairs with my fingers crossed, hoping Raheem answered me. I grab my phone off my desk and—

No new notifications.

The front door slams shut. My mom's presence, like the heavy air that comes before a thunderstorm, closes in around me. "*As-salaamu alaykum*. Where are you, Fatima? It's after ten—are you still in bed?"

With a huff, I meet her downstairs. She's putting her sneakers on the wooden shoe rack.

"Before you ask," I begin. "I've been awake long enough to finish the cake you're taking to *Jumaah*."

She smirks. "Alhamdulilah. I hung two new party dresses in your closet yesterday. Please choose one." My mom points to the stairs behind me. "I'll wait here."

Ugh. We've already had half a dozen arguments about this. I don't want to go to tonight's *Walimah*. I don't even know the bride or the groom.

"Ma," I say. "Why does it matter? I could've worn something I already have." It's the *sunnah* to attend a wedding if invited, but honestly, without Raheem there to see me, to be honest, I really don't give a damn about what I'm wearing. Zaynab certainly isn't going to judge me either way.

"It's a religious obligation to go, and it's a good idea to put a little extra effort into your appearance tonight. This could be the start of great things for you—you never know who you'll meet. It's not like your dad and I could ever afford such an expensive wedding party." My mom's intense gaze slices into me. "You're going. And you'll dress up, too."

"Are *you* wearing a new abaya?"

She folds her arms across her chest, her neck and jaw tightening.

I don't know why it's so important I attend this *Walimah*, but it doesn't matter. She wins, as usual. "Fine," I say, blowing out a huff. I know when a discussion is over with my mother.

Sharifa Tate's will is as strong as platinum . . . while mine is more like tin.

But maybe tin has some strength, after all. I did send that application in.

Five minutes later, I'm standing in front of her, wearing a shiny dark gray dress.

"Satisfied?" I ask her.

"It's a deeper V-neck than I realized—you can wear a white tissue tee under it. And I have a light gray hijab you can borrow that will match perfectly." My mom beams. "Maybe you'll catch the eye of a young man. Wouldn't that be nice?"

Alhamdulilah, she doesn't know a thing about my *friendly* interactions with Raheem. I'd never be able to see him again.

"Ma, please stop. No one in this community is interested in me." I look down at my feet for a nanosecond. It's not a lie, exactly, since no one has ever approached either of my parents about marriage. It's *technically* true. This flirtation between me and Raheem is a risky thing, anyway, and far from secure—if it got out we shared my first kiss, mine and my family's reputation would be ruined. "Are we done? Don't you have to leave for *Jumaah* soon?"

"A decent young man could make your life so much easier, Fatima." The hope in her eyes covers me with guilt all over again.

She drones on about marriage, and I hug my elbows, counting

the seconds until she's done. I've told her a gazillion times I want to be a pastry chef and *wait* to get married, but she thinks that's too risky a plan. My mother likes everything to be as orderly as her patients' charts: triple-checked and certified.

Eventually, she finishes her lecture. "Please hang the dress back in your closet and, inshaALLAH, after I return from the masjid, I'll get you the accessories."

I leave her in the middle of the living room and take the stairs two at a time to my bedroom. Once I'm safe behind my door and the dress is a pile on the floor, I throw myself down on my hospital-cornered bed.

Thirty minutes later, a loud "*Fatima*" rings in my ears.

I go out and stand at the top of the stairs. "Yes?"

"I'm leaving. Did you hang the dress back in your closet?" I did not. Her pursed lips tell me she knows the answer. "Go do it now, please. *As-salaamu alaykum.*"

I spend the whole afternoon tucked in my comforter texting Zaynab and rewatching one of my favorite baking shows on Netflix. Two episodes in, I already have five notebook pages full of hints and ideas.

Then—a new notification—my prayers are answered: I get a text from Raheem.

Hey Gorgeous. Sorry I didn't reply sooner. This law internship is keeping me busy. How are you?

A giggle slips out. Hi. I'm okay. But let's talk about you. Do you like what you're doing?

It's okay. All these meetings with legislators are boring, but great for my resume. Thinking about you is a very nice distraction . . .

My body warms. I wish I knew how to ask him what cologne he wears without sounding like a creep.

Bring up that baking competition with your parents yet?

I get up from the bed and check my bedroom door is closed all the way—just in case. Paranoid much?

Not yet ☺

Admitting to him that I forged Ma's name on the application . . . that's not easy to drop into normal conversation.

The unexpected sound of the front door opening lifts the baby hairs on the back of my neck.

"Fatima! We should pray *Asr*, then get ready for the wedding party—it's past four o'clock!"

I type **gotta go**, then turn off and drop the phone on my bed— just as my mom barges into the room.

"Are you ready for *salah*?" She studies my darkened screen as if she suspects something, then searches my face.

Stay calm.

"Sure. Yes." Grabbing a waist-length prayer hijab from the closet, I slip it on and follow her downstairs.

The rugs are already side by side, facing northeast in between the couch and the mounted television. After we're done praying, she removes her prayer scarf and motions toward the stairs.

"InshaALLAH be ready in an hour."

We head out right after six o'clock. Off to spend a couple of hours pretending I'm happy this will be my fate.

"Fatima, we need to talk about your future."

She's been driving for less than five minutes, so I know I'm in for it. My mom has that look in her eye.

"I wouldn't keep pushing if I didn't want the best for you. You could have a comfortable life if you'd listen to me! You know your dad and I got married when we were nineteen, right after we converted to Islam. Our parents kicked us out and cut us off, so we struggled . . . still, Alhamdulilah, our thirtieth wedding anniversary is next year."

A heartbeat of peace is all I get between this sentence and the next.

"If you were married to a good young man with a promising future, it would be much easier for you. You'd struggle less than we did. Raising a family is expensive. Don't you want kids?"

"Today? No, I'm good." Children?! I can't even decide which flavor of buttercream is my favorite.

She grips the steering wheel tighter. "Fatima, you need a stable career. With a nursing degree, you'll be able to get a job anywhere."

"But Ma, you *know* there's an oversupply of nurses in the market right now! There aren't enough jobs to go ar—"

"And I've told you before that there's a nursing *shortage* in rural New Mexico. You could help so many out there! There will *always* be work for a nurse."

WHAT ABOUT WHAT I WANT????

I want to scream it all the way down the freeway. But of course I bite my tongue.

"I know you love to bake," my mom continues, unaware my breathing is becoming shallow. "But it doesn't mean you should chase this dream of becoming a *pâtissière*. It's a challenging and expensive profession to break into. And it's not like medicine— you'll never be guaranteed work."

How the Hell does she know *pâtissière*? Someone's been on Google.

"Also—working around decadent desserts all day every day isn't the best thing for your figure." Her hidden insult hits me hard.

No need for me to obsess over every calorie. My mom does that enough for both of us. I understand she doesn't want me to get Type 2 diabetes like she did, but having a dad with a serious sweet tooth, I've been surrounded by desserts my whole life—I think I can handle it.

The tightness across my shoulders increases, so I count the cars we pass out of the passenger-side window.

"Sometimes I think you make the wrong decisions just to go against me." My mom checks the rearview mirror, then pats my hand like she always does when reminding me I'm wrong. "Would that state lottery scholarship even cover culinary classes at CNM?"

I shift in my seat, my shiny gray dress doing nothing to protect me from her questions. "Yes, it does! I asked my career counselor in the last senior meeting, and it covers *'any accredited educational program after high school in any public New Mexico university or community college.'*" I memorized that just to answer this question. I knew it would come.

If I can get my culinary degree without any debt, what's the problem?

She brakes hard. "Then it will pay the costs to earn a nursing degree, too—such an amazing opportunity! Go ahead and apply. Fatima, remember, I push because you refuse to do what's best for your future."

"Ma, I can make like twenty-five dollars an hour once I'm a pastry manager in a bakery. It might take a few years after culinary school, I admit, but it's what I love." My teeth sink into my bottom lip. "After that . . . after that, the next step could be becoming a pastry chef. And running my *own* bakery."

"Just twenty-five dollars? As an RN, you could make double that."

Staring out of the window, I whisper, "What good is more money if I hate my job?"

She switches on her favorite public radio station, ending our conversation.

Finally, we reach our destination. My mom parks in one of the hotel's visitor spots, and then it's only a second until we're out, my black wedge heels moving across the dry pavement. My fingers clutch my purse tight against my hip as we follow the signs in the lobby to the ballroom.

My mom's shoulders are back. She strides down the hallway with a confidence I just didn't inherit.

The ballroom's double doors are wide open. Right outside, a table with a crisp white tablecloth sprinkled with red rose petals holds a gold-trimmed guest book on a black pedestal. We're early, and there are only a few entries.

"These Montblanc pens are beautiful," my mom says as she picks one up.

I shrug. "Which costs more, those or a KitchenAid stand mixer?"

My question is ignored.

She puts her well wishes inside the book, and then we step into the actual wedding venue. My breath hitches.

"MashaALLAH, Fatima, you need to see this!" she gasps. "It is gorgeous!"

All around us are circular tables covered in shimmering gold tablecloths, a slender vase blooming with long-stemmed white and pink roses on top of each one. Small votive candles in crystal holders sit at the base of every centerpiece. Even the silverware is shiny and gold.

"Do you like the table settings and linens?" Ma asks. "We might be planning your wedding soon enough!"

I'd rather eat store-bought oatmeal raisin cookies.

I step away from her. Down a verbal sparring partner, she goes to inspect the roses, but I'm more interested in the five-tier wedding cake. Right behind the long dessert table, a temporary wall separates the men's and women's party spaces. (So glad this family decided to have separate party spaces so the hijab-wearing Muslim women and teens, like me, can take off their scarves.)

"These desserts are too perfect to eat." I'm talking to myself, but I don't care. After snapping a couple pictures of the wedding cake's delicate lattice work, I inspect the large platter of petit fours covered in a shiny chocolate mirror glaze, and then the huge tray of traditional baklava. More entries for my baking journal.

My mom returns to my side. "Such a beautiful piece of furniture."

I follow her gaze to the raised stage, a set of stairs running up each side. In the center, a golden damask-patterned loveseat with gilded legs stands alone. The curved arms are decorated with matching sunbursts. It's so elegant, but it can't be comfortable.

"Let's find a place to sit—and not too close to the dance floor."

Other than the two marked *Reserved,* every other table in the horseshoe pattern is empty. By the time my mom chooses the best vantage point and we sit, about a dozen women have joined us in the ballroom.

"Someone's trying to get your attention." She points behind me.

I pivot toward the double doors. Imani is heading my way, waving. Her all-black overgarment has dainty silver embroidery cascading down the front. I can't stare too long or she'll assume I like her abaya.

"*As-salaamu alaykum*, Sister Sharifa," she says when she reaches us. "Fatima, your outfit is nice. I like the silver flowers stitched on the sleeves, and the dress is fancy without revealing too much skin. You know how some girls will show up tonight—like they're going to a club and not a wedding party." Imani scrunches up her face.

Gossip is Imani's favorite drug, and I want absolutely no part of it. Especially now that I have secrets of my own. She can't tell just from looking at me, can she? Gulping down my nervousness, I reply, "*Wa alaykum as salaam.*"

Thankfully, she doesn't start prying—or saying anything else judgmental. "My mom loves to remind me that the first time Dad's mother met her was at a *Walimah* like this one in Beirut. She loves them! It's the *best* place to find a match. But she doesn't like to sit this close to the tower speakers." Imani points to one side of the raised stage. "We've got room at our table—Fatima?"

And then my savior appears.

"*Salaam.*" Zaynab points to the chair on my left. "Is this empty?"

Relief washes over me. "*Wa alaykum as salaam!*" I cry, the greeting falling out of my mouth.

Zaynab's mid-thigh fuchsia top is full of gold swirls and sits on top of black dress pants. Her box braids are flawless, and her gold clutch is the perfect accessory. Compared to my shapeless floor-length dress, her outfit shines.

"Sit," I continue, "I saved you that seat."

The one Imani's standing in front of.

My BFF glares at her. "Am I interrupting?"

"Nope." Imani sneers at Zaynab's uncovered hair. "We were talking about how *some* Muslims will show up dressed like they're on their way to stroll Central Avenue after dark."

I swear the whole room gets quiet.

Zaynab keeps a straight face. "Then it's a good thing you're here to talk to them about their wardrobe choices."

After a quick "*Salaam*," Imani storms off.

As soon as Zee sits down, I slug my best friend's arm and double over in my chair, barely holding in a belly laugh. Her confidence to face girls like Imani who judge her for not wearing hijab is impressive. It's reputation suicide in this community. At least my choice to wear it has never affected our friendship.

Zaynab rubs her forearm, the sides of her mouth inching up. "What? Imani had it coming. She acts like she's the morality police."

"Hush." She's not wrong.

Before I can say anything else, an Arabic wedding song erupts throughout the oversized ballroom. I don't understand the words, but I know it's a wedding party favorite—that strong, rhythmic beat is irresistible. The female DJ will be busy tonight.

"And now the spectacle begins. Very cool." Zaynab's words drip with sarcasm.

I laugh behind my hand. "Shhh."

Everyone—me and Zaynab included—comes out of their chairs, clapping to the beat as the bride and groom join us in the ballroom. They're followed by every male member from both of their families. For some silly reason, I search the crowd of men for Raheem.

You know *he's not here.*

After the first song is over, the men leave. Now, with only female relatives surrounding them, the couple move to the dance floor. During their first dance, they never touch, but they move their bodies together to another bass-filled song.

"How come you're here?" I ask Zaynab, sitting back down. "I can't remember the last *Walimah* you showed up to." I move my chair closer to hers since the decibel level could now shatter glass.

Zaynab snorts. "Someone has to keep Imani away from you."

The newlyweds finish dancing, ascend the stage, and sit on the fancy golden loveseat, where everyone can see them. For half a second, I picture Raheem and me in their places.

My body tingles at the thought. *Traitor. I shouldn't be imagining being his wife.*

A woman dressed in a burgundy floor-length gown—and dripping in diamonds—floats onto the dance floor, a wireless microphone in her hand. "*As-salaamu alaykum,* sisters," she says to the crowd. "I'm Naima, the groom's mother. Before my son leaves, he and his bride will cut one slice from the cake. Please join us."

"Are you coming?" my mom asks from her seat on my right side. Her navy-blue abaya with its sequined collar and coordinated hijab shines in the subdued golden lighting of the ballroom.

"No, I'm good here."

She shakes her head at me, but I sink defensively into my chair as she joins all the women and girls rushing toward the elegant five-tier creation. Once they feed each other a bite of cake, the groom plants a kiss on his bride's forehead and exits the ballroom.

Zaynab has her head down, so I lean toward her. She's got a book open on her phone.

"*Are you reading a book right now?* We haven't hung out all week, and you're *reading?* At a *wedding party,* no less?"

"Sorry. Why?" Zaynab raises her eyebrows at me. "Do you have a problem with books without recipes in them?"

We bust out laughing.

What Zaynab doesn't mention is that her pretty face and effortless style brings a ton of unwanted popularity. She always looks amazing: tonight her bright red lipstick is perfect, but my mom calls that kind of makeup "face paint," so I'm only allowed to wear clear lip gloss and kohl.

Why Zaynab has been friends with me since elementary school is a mystery. She's always in the light; I'm always in the shadows, pressing myself firmly against the wall.

We spend the next hour eating tasty food from the elaborate buffet. Zee even lets me keep a couple extra spinach pies on her plate, away from my mom's calorie-counting gaze.

All of a sudden, my theme song bursts out of the speakers: Beyoncé's "Single Ladies." The lyrics speak to my heart—and almost every other woman's, too, apparently, because everyone in this fancy ballroom rushes to the dance floor in their designer dresses.

I settle deeper into my chair. With so many people here watching and judging my every move, I am *not* dancing.

Before the end of the first verse, however, Zaynab is hauling me up. "It's time to show these women how it's done!"

"But . . ." I protest in a whisper.

She puts her index finger to my lips. "No excuses!"

All around us, women and teenage girls start yanking off their hijabs and overgarments. Here come the stilettos, bulging cleavage, and lots of short dresses.

Welcome to the real lives of Muslim women.

At least some of us.

Zee and I join the other brave souls on the dance floor. Dancing is a balance. Muslim teenage girls can't be "too much" in how they gyrate, or the rumor mill will take over. According to my mom—and I quote—"No future mother-in-law wants to watch a potential wife for their precious son grinding in public." But several girls and women dance like they want a scarlet letter anyway.

Mouthing every lyric, the beat infects me, and I focus on the music. A semicircle of teen girls has formed around Zaynab. She swivels her hips, perfectly mimicking the newest dance routine. The girls' cheers fight with the music to be heard.

Nothing in my own dance arsenal can compete, so I go back to the table. A tiny seed of jealousy sprouts inside me.

Zaynab and I have always been different from each other. In fifth grade, I helped her study for the school spelling bee. We both aced the practice sessions, and she wanted me to enter the contest with her, but getting up in front of the entire school would've been terrifying for me, so . . . I didn't.

She made it all the way to the state competition that year. Could I have, too?

As the song fades out, I eye my mom whispering to a Muslim sister I don't recognize. They both gaze in my direction for such a long time that I return to the table without Zee and gulp down half a glass of water.

After that, I retreat into my phone. My Pinterest dessert board has my full attention when Zaynab finally plops down into her chair and snatches my cell right out of my hands.

"Hey! What are you doing?" My irritation is half sincere. "I just pinned a lemon zucchini bread recipe I want to try."

I haven't heard anything from the baking competition yet, and not knowing is about to drive me crazy. It would be a dream come true to have professional pastry chefs taste and assess my creations.

Maybe . . . if I made it into the final round . . . or *won* . . . my parents would agree culinary arts is the best career path for me . . .

"What happened?" Zaynab holds the phone away from me. "I turned around and you were gone."

The new-text sound dings from my phone. Zaynab glances at it, then glares at me.

"Why is *Raheem* asking you if you're having fun at this *Walimah* without him?"

Oh shit. I am so busted.

three

"Are you two dating in secret?!"

Zaynab scoots her chair closer to mine, waiting for an answer. I don't know what to say. Kissing Raheem was the best-worst decision of my life. But soon he'll figure out he's too good for a pastry geek like me. *Won't he?*

Since I don't know what to say, I stay silent.

After what feels like forever, Zaynab hisses, "I can't believe you didn't tell me." The hard edge in her tone is a bad sign. She's actually mad.

"Zee, there's not a lot to tell. We're just . . ." But I'm not sure *what* we are—if me and Raheem are anything at all. Just for something to do, I unpin my hijab and free an ocean of black curls. My throat tightens while I avoid her gaze.

She drops my phone in my lap. "Fatima, you've been keeping this from me. *Why?*"

My temples throb. The beat of the next Arabic song is loud as a jackhammer.

"Raheem and I are just . . . friendly." A sin of omission. We're friends who've kissed. "You know how traditional my parents are," I begin again. "They'd never allow me to have a boyfriend. It's marriage or nothing for them."

"So if he *did* ask, what would you say?" Zaynab demands.

I grab my wineglass filled with water, draining half of it. Why won't my girl let this go? Her eyes latch onto mine—and she knows.

"You really like him. Why won't you be honest with me?"

My eyes wander from table to table—and I discover my mom's eyes are on us from across the dance floor. "Can we talk in the bathroom?"

"Let's go." She's up and moving within seconds.

Wrapping my hijab loosely around my head, I race to catch up. We leave the ballroom and stride down a long hallway. She reaches our destination first and holds the door open.

"Thanks." Inside, my hands shake as I bend down and check each stall.

Zaynab cuts in front of me. "Okay, spill!"

I lean on the solid granite countertop to steady myself. One, two, three . . . here goes nothing. "Remember the day you forgot to pick me up from the soup kitchen?"

She lifts a single eyebrow at me.

"Raheem took me home. And, well, we . . . we sort of connected . . . on the drive to my house." I'll keep the kissing part to myself. For now. "He's . . . nice."

"*Nice*. Okay. Let me understand this. On the same day a head pastry chef invites you to enter her baking competition, you and Muslim Prince Charming start some kind of secret 'friendship'"— she makes bunny ears—"and you don't *tell* me? You had the biggest day of your life and only told me *half*?"

I rip my gaze away from her scowl. "I'm sorry, Zee. It's not like I'm used to guys paying attention to me. I just . . . didn't have the words." My full stomach is in knots.

"Fatima, I apologized over and over again for not picking you up. Amber and I, we had our first argument as a couple—it was stupid, and I'm sorry I forgot you. But you could've come over *that night* and I would've listened to you rave about Mr. Tall, Dark, and Handsome!"

I check and her frown lines are gone.

"Speaking of. Did your mom change her mind about the competition?" she asks.

My fingers adjust the loose hijab around my head. "Well, no. The truth is . . . I forged her name on the application."

Before I can say anything else, the bathroom door bursts open and my mom rushes in.

"Good! I found you. There's someone here I want you to meet." She doesn't ignore Zee, but I don't miss how her gaze lingers on every inch of Zaynab's uncovered braids. "*As-salaamu alaykum.* It's good to see you at a wedding party. You should come to more of these community events."

Zaynab peeks at herself in the mirror, her poker face intact—a public parental confrontation isn't her thing. "*Wa alaykum as salaam*, Sister Sharifa. Maybe I will."

"I need to borrow my daughter for a few minutes. InshaALLAH, she'll be back at your table soon."

Sorry, I mouth to Zaynab.

After giving me a quick once-over, my mom leads me back into the ballroom. The bride and groom are standing on the raised stage again. The groom's mother holds a large wooden box open while her son takes out piece after piece of twenty-two-karat gold jewelry—gifts for his new wife—to the delight of the all-female audience. By the end of the night, this bride will be dripping in expensive jewelry. Things the Tate family could never afford.

It's strange. My mom doesn't even stop for a second to watch what's usually her favorite part of the Muslim weddings we attend.

"Fatima, this is Sister Jameela," my mom says, abruptly sitting at an empty table.

Still standing, I pivot, looking for this lady. "*As-salaamu alaykum.*"

The woman in front of me is tall, maybe five-nine. She's wearing a beautiful black and silver beaded gown with a matching hijab. But her piercing, judgmental gaze hits me like a slap across the face.

"*Wa alaykum as salaam.*" She sits in the chair on my mom's right, while I slide into the left.

"Fatima, I wanted you to meet Jameela because her son is single and he's interested in you."

For a brief moment, I can't speak.

"Ma, I don't think I know her son." My heartbeat speeds up. "Did he say he knows me?"

"Fatima, he first mentioned you to me last Ramadan when you served food at the community iftars," Sister Jameela answers. "It was one of the Friday nights our family donated the meals."

I gasp. On a normal Friday night, at least four hundred people show up to break their fast at the masjid. Sister Jameela paid a *ton* of money to whatever restaurant catered that dinner.

My eyes drift to the stage, where the bride and groom are now posing for pictures with the female guests. Is that *really* supposed to be me soon?

"Ma, I know high school graduation is coming," I whisper, "but I'm not ready."

"Her son is a senior in college. MashaALLAH, he's graduating a year early. On his way, InshaALLAH, to law school right here at the University of New Mexico. There's no harm in meeting him," my mom insists. "Sister Jameela's family are also the ones who gifted two hundred Hydro Flasks to the Islamic Center a couple of weeks ago."

Anger starts to simmer less than an inch below my calm exterior. I'm not being heard.

She mentions marriage to me every week, but this is the first time I've been introduced to a guy's mother. My gut tells me to decline this first attempt at an arranged marriage. But it's true that another part of me is—well, kinda curious.

"Dear, I've heard a lot of good things about you, MashaALLAH," Sister Jameela says. "Your parents are humble, hard-working people and raised you to be the same. InshaALLAH you won't be one of those girls who would marry him for financial gain—my son likes nice girls."

By the blankness of her face, I'm not sure if she's complimenting or insulting me.

"I think you and Raheem would be good together. He's only four years older than you, not like the other engaged young ladies in this room. Most of their fiancés are closer to thirty." Sister Jameela leans across the table. "My son is ambitious and needs a wife who's not too career-driven to help him become the first Muslim Congressman from our state. You'd always be taken care of and wouldn't have to work."

Her condescension cuts deep. Does she think the diamond bracelet on her wrist lets her talk to me like I have no goals? I bet my mom didn't even tell Sister Jameela about me wanting to become a pastry chef.

Wait, what name did she say?

It can't be *my* Raheem, can it? (No, wait. We kissed, but he's not mine.)

No, no, I bet there's plenty of Muslim brothers in Albuquerque with that name—but my mouth is as dry as New Mexico's annual drought. *I'm sure it's not him.*

The deep pounding of the *daff* erupts from the speakers, so I'm saved from speaking. The newlyweds descend the stage and head toward the double doors, a trail of women clapping to the drumbeats behind them.

"Sharifa, I have to go." Sister Jameela gets up and takes a step away from the table. "But please call me and let me know your daughter's decision." She nods in my direction. "It was a pleasure talking to you, Fatima. *As-salaamu alaykum.*"

"*Wa alaykum as salaam,*" replies my mom. I can't form words right now.

Jameela leaves, heading toward the ballroom's closest exit.

I stare at the geometric design of the fancy carpet under my feet as my hands grip the edge of the table. Disbelief numbs me. "Ma . . . did she send you a picture of her son?"

"Yes." She picks her phone up off a gold napkin and swipes until she finds it. "Here. I'm glad you're at least interested enough to ask."

Ignoring her smug look, my fingers tremble as I clutch her phone and gape at the screen.

I know that strong, angular jaw. And those deep brown eyes and full lips are burned into my memory.

"Do you recognize him?"

I can't tell her the truth.

I hand my mom back her device and, while she's distracted,

I force out a couple whisps of air. "No, I don't think so." Why is this happening?

I *can't* admit I know the young man in the picture. We can *never* admit to becoming friends—or to sharing a private moment in my living room. My parents didn't send me to volunteer at a soup kitchen to hook up with some guy.

Ma would never understand.

"I–I'll be right back." My voice cracks. "Gotta find Zaynab and say goodbye."

I weave across the ballroom through groups of women, now back in their abayas and hijabs, to find our table. The dinner plates, fancy wineglasses, and carafes of unsweetened iced tea are gone. So is all Zaynab's stuff. I grab my purse and drag myself the short distance back to my mom.

Zaynab leaving without saying goodbye means she's still pissed.

Fighting with my best friend sucks—I need to make it up to her, need her to forgive me. I can't deal with this possible arranged marriage without her.

four

Saturday morning. Albuquerque's bright sunshine fills my bedroom.

Part of me welcomes it, but part of me wishes the night was longer. My confusion over what happened at the wedding won't go away.

Why didn't Raheem mention marriage to me before getting our parents involved?

Without warning, my mom barges in and pushes open the curtains. "Rise and shine. You missed *Fajr*."

I yank the comforter up to my chin. "Ma, I prayed up here." Sometimes going through the motions is all I can do, unsure if my prayers are even being answered. Life's just messed up right now.

"Are you sure?" She's standing by my only window, her arms folded across her chest.

Who asks their seventeen-year-old daughter that? My pissed-off glare bounces off of her.

Ten minutes later, half-awake, I tiptoe downstairs and find my parents waiting for me at the dining table.

"Good morning, my daughter. How are you this morning?" Dad's over-the-top chipper tone doesn't comfort me like usual. He's a gentle soul and I love that about him, but sometimes I wish he had a stronger spine. If Ma says I should get married, he'll agree.

"There's fresh fruit," my mom adds. "Whole-wheat English muffins and hard-boiled eggs, too." She rises from her chair. "Sit down and I'll get you some food."

The air in the room stills.

Oh Hell no.

My mom offering to wait on me confirms it: something is going on.

"Don't get up, Ma. I'll fix it. Good morning, Father." In need of an ally, I wink at him and head into the kitchen.

Hidden from view, I take a few deep breaths, letting the sweet scent of ripe cantaloupe fill my nose as I load a few slices on my plate. I know what my parents want to talk about, so I delay by adding a single egg, followed by an entire English muffin—and I smother it super slowly with sugar-free strawberry jam for good measure.

"Fatima?" My mom summons me from the other side of the wall, a hint of impatience in her voice. I wait a couple extra seconds, try to collect myself, and then head back out into the dining room. No words, just silence as I sit.

The two most important people in my life stare at me over the rims of their coffee mugs.

The intimidation level rises 1000 percent.

"Fatima, did you enjoy yourself last night?" asks my dad. "Your mom told me the women's side of the *Walimah* was nice." His steady gaze takes in every inch of my face.

You could hear yeast rise in the silence around the three of us.

"It was okay." I pop a piece of melon in my mouth. "They played some good music."

My dad arches his eyebrows. "What do you think of Brother Raheem?"

Goosebumps break out on my skin remembering our first encounter. It was perfection. Does what we did matter if we become husband and wife?

Unable to stop myself, I imagine Raheem's warm body pressed into mine for a slow song. *Stop that!*

Watching my mom's fingers tap the table, I'm sure her head will explode if I don't say something soon. But I finish half of my English muffin before answering.

"He's okay." Pushing my plate away, I clasp my hands together, not too tight, and wait for the interrogation to begin.

"*Hmmm.* Fatima, do you think he's someone you want to talk to?" My dad reaches over and squeezes my hand.

My attention fixes on the salt and pepper shakers in the middle of the table.

I want to be honest and say "Maybe," but nothing comes out.

I want to ease my hand out of my dad's grasp, but I don't move.

I want to be anywhere else.

Instead, my mom answers for me. Like usual. "Adam, why would she refuse?" she demands. "Raheem is a young man from a good family who's interested in her. It's a chance for our daughter to never want for anything—she wouldn't struggle like we have."

The small note of pleading in her voice surprises me.

"There's no reason Fatima can't at least meet him!" she insists to my father, like I'm not even here.

"Are you okay with this happening right now, Fatima?" Dad asks.

I have literally no clue why Raheem went the traditional route and had his mom approach mine. He hasn't answered my pre-dawn texts for a couple of days; to be honest, I wondered if Raheem was ghosting me, internship or no internship. My arms and legs tingle at the suggestion he might actually *want* me—but he really should've told me this was his plan.

Again, my mom answers my dad's question before I can even open my mouth. "InshaALLAH Fatima understands we'd never allow anyone to talk to her about marriage who wasn't a good Muslim brother." She taps her finger on the table between us. "The Harris family is well-respected, and the four-year age difference between the two of them is smaller than almost every other engaged couple at the masjid."

I'm not asking for any of this, though—it's just happening.

Although . . . if I *was* married . . . my life wouldn't be controlled by my parents. I'm not sure yet if the trade-off is worth it. Marriage has its own expectations.

My dad clears his throat. "Sharifa, it's still her decision."

Dad's reminder is heartfelt, but I know my mother won't accept anything less than total compliance. There's no point in me complaining about how unfair it is that parents control the whole process.

I give Dad's hand one last squeeze before releasing it. "Fine. I'll meet him." At least then I can ask Raheem what's *really* going on. Shifting my body, I face my other parent. "But don't expect miracles—his mom is a snob. You realize that, right?"

She says nothing. Dad lays a hand on her shoulder in some silent communication.

Turning back to me, he says, "After the first meeting, if you're not interested, I will let Raheem know." Concern crinkles the corners of his eyes. "InshaALLAH, we have a dinner to plan." At least his idea of a fancy dinner is full of comfort food: barbecue chicken, grilled corn, and potato salad, with banana pudding and pound cake for dessert.

Before the conversation can drag on, I beat it up the stairs in search of my phone. *Damn, still nothing from Raheem.* I shoot off a couple texts to Zaynab.

Will you be home in an hour? We NEED to talk 🙋

What's up is her only reply. Crap. She's still pissed.

Will you be there Zee? Please

I could cream the eggs and sugar for my favorite sour-cream pound cake in the time it takes her to answer me.

I'll be here.

Thirty minutes later, I'm clean and dressed. Nothing fancy: a pair of jeans and one of my dad's old button-down shirts. I'm wrapping a light blue hijab around my head when my mom sticks her head into my room without knocking.

"InshaALLAH we're having Sister Jameela and Raheem over for dinner tomorrow night." Her face is beaming.

"Already? You're not wasting any time." It's been less than an hour!

Ignoring my sarcasm, Mom tells me, "Your dad is going to get some *zabiha* meat while I take a shower."

I jump off my bed, carefully, so the hospital-perfect corners of the sheets stay intact. "Can he drop me off at Zaynab's?" I ask, flat, without a drop of emotion. My mom is like a dog hungry for a bone—if she detects a hint of nervousness, a hint of guilt, a hint of any strong feeling at all, she'll keep at me until the truth is out.

"Hurry. He's leaving soon."

I stuff my phone into my purse, race downstairs, and get ready to make peace with my girlie. Armed with four cranberry-orange muffins in a disposable pie tin, I'm standing by the front door in my only pair of Vans by the time my dad comes out of the master bedroom.

He laces up his boots and opens the door wide. "After you, madam."

"Thank you, kind sir." After a clumsy curtsy, I walk out of the house. Dad chuckles behind me.

On our way to Zaynab's Four Hills neighborhood, the questions begin again.

"So, be honest with me, Squiggles." My heart jumps a little. He hasn't called me that since I was eight. "Do you like what you've heard about this Muslim brother?"

I shrug. "Dad, are you sure he's interested? How long did you talk to him?"

The edges of his mouth flatten. "Fatima, Raheem told me himself he wants to find out if the two of you are compatible. He's an impressive young man, and him wanting to do things the halal way tells me a lot about his character. We had two conversations— each about an hour long. Late last night and early this morning."

Raheem has spoken to my dad for two whole *hours* and hasn't mentioned it to me . . . ?

"He lost his dad a couple of years ago, so family means a lot to him. And he's more than able to provide for you. Raheem assured me that if you two end up married, spending time together will be one of his top priorities."

Losing a parent has to be hard. It makes sense that he treasures his family now. So, okay, besides the mysterious hours-long conversations with my dad, this guy does sound pretty perfect.

"It's only the first meeting tomorrow, Fatima." Eyes on the road, Dad doesn't notice me picking at my cuticles as he continues. "It's normal to be nervous."

The first meeting.

He points at Hinkle Family Fun Center right outside my window. "Do you remember the last time we went there? It was your favorite place until you were twelve, and now someone wants you to consider them for marriage."

Five years ago is like another lifetime.

I can see the go-kart track, full of kids waiting for their turn. "Didn't I beat you in our last race?" I nudge him with my elbow.

He laughs. "You did—but I was the putt-putt champion."

We're both quiet the rest of the drive down Tramway Boulevard. The warm March breeze and view of the Sandia Mountains finally distract me from everything that's happened in the past twenty-four hours.

Dad takes the last left turn onto Zaynab's street and parks right in front of her house. I grasp the pie tin—her favorite muffins!—and get ready to grovel.

"Have fun," my dad tells me. "I'll text you when I'm done with all the shopping. *As-salaamu alaykum.*"

I give him a thumbs-up and get out of the car. "*Wa alaykum as salaam.*" My insides quiver as I walk up the driveway. Here's hoping the way to Zaynab's forgiveness is through her stomach.

Before I can knock, my bestie throws open the door and stands there, arms crossed over her chest. All she offers me is a curt "*Salaam*" before retreating into the house.

At least she left the door open. *Shit.* I hurry inside behind her.

We walk through into my favorite room, their massive kitchen. I leave my homemade muffins on the island and ease onto the barstool farthest away from Zaynab.

"I'm so sorry, Zee—everything with Raheem happened so fast. We just . . . clicked. Then it was hard to find a way to tell you, and, honestly, what's going on with him is a little scary, too. Will you forgive me?"

She drums her fingertips on the marble countertop, a hard stare fixed on my face. "I think I have a right to know if my very best friend since the fifth grade has a secret boyfriend. We're for life, Fatima. So tell me: How often do you two get together?"

"Oh my gosh, no! He isn't my boyfriend! I'm not sure *what* we are. He's been in northern New Mexico for an internship and we haven't seen each other since the day he drove me home which is when we kissed but he must be back *because my parents invited him over tomorrow.*"

Zaynab sits up super straight, her mouth open. "Slow down! I'm listening."

For a moment, the sound of the refrigerator's ice maker rumbles between us.

"You want honesty?" A short, high-pitched laugh escapes before I can stop it. "None of this feels real. Me, kissing someone as fine as him? I'm not that special."

"Says who?"

I don't want to argue, so I just continue. "There's more. Last night, my mom introduced me to Sister Jameela, whose son is interested in marriage—with me." I clear my throat. "It's Raheem."

Her eyes widen. "*Your* Raheem?"

"I'm not sure if he's *my*—yes, okay. Yes, my Raheem."

Zee waves off my words. "Wow, I . . . can't. Are you sure? What did the two of you do in his car? Wait"—she points to the muffins I brought her—"before you tell me, I need one of those."

"Fatima, is that you?" Sister Sarah, Zaynab's mom, appears from nowhere, rushes over, and wraps her arms around me. "Nobody told me you were coming over!" She glances at Zee, disapproval pasted on her face.

"Mother, chill out." My BFF rolls her eyes as she stands. "It was last minute. I didn't know you'd still be here."

Sarah, always smart, is wearing black suit pants and a bright yellow blouse with her shoulder-length braids pulled back into a ponytail. But it's her beautiful jewelry that really draws me in. I'd bet my favorite cream-cheese frosting recipe that her bangles and dangly earrings are all solid gold. They sparkle.

"You have to be at work this early on a Saturday?" I ask.

Sister Sarah fills her dark gray Hydro Flask with Evian. "Fatima, it's tax season and the entire staff is already there. Every CPA works crazy hours until April fifteenth." She laughs, shaking her head. "Actually, I'm planning an office brunch for the first Saturday after the deadline—you know, to thank everyone. I'd love to hire you to bake some cinnamon rolls and other goodies for it. What do you think?"

Yes! is my first instinct. Self-doubt follows a nanosecond later. "Um . . . I've never sold any of my desserts before. What if your staff doesn't like them?"

"Don't be ridiculous. I've eaten tons of your baking over the years, and I can't remember *anything* I didn't love." Sister Sarah strides over, claiming one of Zaynab's muffins as if to prove her point. "Plus, it's a great opportunity for you to practice filling an order. When you're a pastry chef and everyone's lining up for your desserts, I can brag I was your first paying customer."

"When do you need to know my answer?" My voice cracks a little.

She checks her phone. "If you could text me—or your friend here—by the end of next week, I'd appreciate it." Facing Zee, she says, "Daughter of mine, if Amber comes over and you two make nachos or quesadillas, please don't leave a pile of dirty dishes in the sink like last time. Goodbye, lovelies."

The second the front door closes, Zaynab blows out a huge breath. "Now you can tell me everything that's going on between you and your Muslim Prince Charming."

Excitement bubbles up inside of me when I think about him. We go and get comfortable on the couch, Zee grabbing a bag of Takis from the pantry first.

"Okay, so spill it. What happened in his car?"

"He drove me home."

"Ha ha," she deadpans.

I stare right at her. "I swear, it was just a ride."

"Nothing else?"

Even with my eyes open, I can picture Raheem's smooth skin, his muscular biceps stretching his shirt sleeves. "Nope . . . uh . . . nothing big."

Zaynab's not convinced. "Define 'big.'"

Titling my head away from her, I slide my damp palms down the front of my jeans. "He insisted on walking me to my door . . . but then he needed to pray Asr."

"And?"

"We went inside and . . . stuff kinda happened."

"What kind of 'stuff'?" She scoots forward until only one couch cushion separates us. "Fatima, *please* tell me you didn't sleep with him."

I cover my face with my hands. "*No!* We only . . . kissed a little."

Zaynab snaps her fingers at me. "Excuse me! Whatever you did, it was your first time, so it *is* a big deal. Since the two of you got all hot and heavy already, he's clearly interested. Why didn't he bring up marriage to you himself—why'd he make his mom do it? You've been texting, right?"

I shrug.

"Slightly sketchy. You like him enough to consider getting married in the next year or two? You ready for that?" My BFF takes a quick glance at my face. "There's a glimmer in your eyes every time I say his name."

My teeth skim my bottom lip. "Is it normal to be giddy one minute and nauseous the next?"

"Obviously."

And just like that, my attitude lightens. After clearing my throat, I ask, "Do you have anything other than Takis? I'm starving."

Minutes later, the island is covered with our impromptu feast. I annihilate slices of halal beef salami and sharp cheddar cheese cubes, while Zaynab works on two whole slices of mushroom quiche. "Is your mom going to be upset we ate all the little tomatoes off her veggie tray?"

She shakes her head. "As long as we don't touch her special hummus and leave her some quiche, she'll be fine."

Zee begins outlining her and Amber's graduation plans; half-listening, I try to focus. "We're having a small party here, about thirty people. You're coming, FYI. The University of New Mexico starts after Stanford, so her parents invited me to go with them all to California to drop her off."

My appetite disappears. They're traveling? "We've never been on a trip together."

"Your mom would never let you go anywhere without a parent."

Damn. She's 100 percent right.

Ever since she got a girlfriend, Zaynab and I don't hang out as much. "Sounds like you're going to have a blast," I admit, trying not to sound jealous.

Maybe Raheem is a good thing. At least I won't be a third wheel in *that* relationship.

Zee adds a handful of green grapes to her now-empty plate. "Girl, just be careful. Force him to explain why he didn't say anything to you about marriage before involving the parents. I mean, if it matters to you."

Caution and excitement war inside me, leaving me exhausted. Her advice is good.

"Don't worry—I will." I finish off the last two strawberries. "Just have to figure out a way to talk to him face-to-face, but in private. Without our parents listening."

Nothing's impossible, right?

five

"We need to talk."

My mom barges into my bedroom. Why she isn't grinning from ear to ear, I have no idea. Raheem will be here in less than thirty minutes.

Her eyes narrow as she straightens her shoulders. "You need to be on your best behavior tonight, Fatima. We don't want to scare away this young brother with your sarcasm. Try not to show him *that* side at dinner. Did you make a dessert to impress Raheem and his mom like I asked you?"

"Yep. A wedding cake. We can find out if he prefers Swiss meringue or American buttercream."

"That's the smart mouth we don't need."

"Should I just say nothing? You and Dad can talk for me."

She doesn't need to know I'm nervous. What if Raheem changes his mind after this one meal?

"Now you're just being silly."

"Ma, I still have to shower and get dressed." The bags under my eyes are huge, and I haven't even decided what to wear. "Let me do that. Or do you want me to keep our guests waiting while I get ready?"

Her perfect posture bends a little. "Be ready in fifteen minutes." She leaves.

Ten minutes in the shower has to be my new personal record. Dressing in a flowy white shirt and ankle-length black skirt, I briefly think I can almost pass as the hired help we've never had.

The notification ping from my phone forces me across the room.

Hi Gorgeous. Got back to Albuquerque this morning and read all your texts. Don't worry, I'll try to find some time for the two of us to talk tonight, to explain everything. Can't wait to see you again ☀

My hands shake as I pick up my *shayla*, wrapping it around my head twice and securing it with two straight pins. It's my favorite rectangular hijab. My chest tightens thinking about pretending Raheem and I are strangers. Can I do it? I slide on two coats of tangerine lip balm and head downstairs.

Ready or not, let's do this.

I walk into the living room and ease onto the edge of the couch.

My parents were only nineteen when they made huge, life-changing decisions. I'm still not sure I want to make the decision they did—marriage—but just once I'd love to freely decide something for myself, too . . . without any parental input.

When the doorbell rings at 6 p.m., everything in sight, including me, is spotless and has passed my mom's critical inspection. She motions for me to stand, so I do.

My dad opens the door and Raheem is front and center. My cheeks are on fire.

He steps in, followed by Sister Jameela. My gaze meets his,

and I can't turn away. His irises are the same warm brown I've been fantasizing about. I can't forget any of it.

"*As-salaamu alaykum*, Brother Adam, Sister Sharifa." Raheem's warm baritone gives me goosebumps. "Fatima, it's nice to meet you."

"*Wa alaykum as salaam*, Raheem," I say, hoping my voice doesn't tremble.

"You remember my mother, Jameela."

Oops. "*As-salaamu alaykum*, Sister Jameela."

My mom leads Sister Jameela past me, settling her at the dining table. My dad heads out the door to finish the grilling, and, strictly speaking, Raheem should follow him and help. But my first-ever potential husband lingers a breath away from me.

"Raheem, why don't you go outside and keep Brother Adam company?" His mom's question is more like a direct order.

Raheem clears his throat and flashes my mom his bright white smile. "Would it be okay if Fatima comes with me?"

Damn, Raheem's good.

He knows my parents expect him to adhere to every ancient rule of Muslim courtship. I mean, he just asked my mom if it's okay if we walk a half-a-dozen steps together—even though we're ending up where my dad will be able to see us.

My head twists toward the two moms. Mine answers without a hint of hesitation. "If she wants to go."

No one has to ask me twice!

Needing to escape the women's scrutiny—and wanting an explanation about this forced game of pretend—I follow Raheem out the door. We stand on the patio, my dad flipping burgers not fifteen feet away. We each claim a fanback outdoor chair right outside the door.

"Fatima, thanks for keeping our secret." His quiet words are almost carried away by the breeze, his eyebrows crinkling. "And thank you for waiting until I could explain. Please don't think my interest in marrying you isn't real."

A curl of warmth unfolds inside me, just from hearing these gentle words. It's a start. "So why didn't you mention it in any of your texts?"

Instead of answering me, Raheem stands. "I'll be right back," he says, joining my dad at the grill.

What even! I wish I could demand he sit down and explain himself, but I obviously can't raise my voice too much within earshot of my dad.

Still . . . he looks really good. And he's been good to me, too, mostly.

Within seconds, I start imagining kissing him instead of feeling mad. *Get a grip, Fatima.*

Does giving into my curiosity—and wanting to do it again—mean I'm going to Hell?

Watching Raheem charm Dad is like magic: the air is filled with my father's roaring laughter. It's a while before Raheem comes back and sits in the chair opposite me again. His knee starts bouncing.

Great. We're both on edge, apparently.

He squares his shoulders while his hands hug his thighs. "Fatima . . . I'm sorry I didn't say anything about my intentions. But doing it over the phone just wasn't right. It's better for us to discuss our future in person—like we are now." He flashes me a nervous smile. "Do you forgive me?"

The corners of my mouth inch up. That makes a certain kind

of sense, I have to admit. "I guess. So . . . you're interested in marriage? With me?"

"Fatima, I have to tell you a secret. Come closer."

This guy is crazy.

I glance over at my dad. He's piling a platter with hot dogs and barbecue chicken. I only dare to scoot my chair a few inches in Raheem's direction.

"I've always liked the girl I met at the Shared Table." He takes a deep breath. "Fatima, I'm attracted to you. Yes, we went a little too far—but doesn't going through our parents show you how serious I am?"

Believing Raheem is easy . . . but doubts nag at me anyway. "I'm not sure Sister Jameela is thrilled at the prospect of having me as her daughter-in-law. At the wedding, she came pretty close to calling me a gold digger."

His chair is now so close to me we're sharing his cologne. His shoulders hunch forward, and he gives a frustrated sigh.

"I'm sorry about that. My mom can be a little overprotective." He holds my gaze and offers a half smile. "I think that's something we have in common."

He knows he's right. "It might be," I say, a slight tease in my voice.

His smile widens a degree, then disappears. "The truth is, Fatima, several Muslim sisters have approached my mom about me marrying their daughters. They think more about my family's wealth than if we'd be compatible. You're not like that. You volunteer to help the needy—you even bake homemade desserts for them. I'm interested in girls like you—girls with more substance."

The longer Raheem holds my gaze, the more impossible it is not to be mesmerized. That gleam in his eye is my undoing.

"The meat's done!"

It takes a full fifteen seconds for my dad's words to register.

"Fatima, I need you to take one of these." He's walking toward us, a full platter of smoky goodness in each hand. Smudges of barbecue sauce decorate the front of his carpenter jeans.

Raheem rushes over to him first and claims one of the platters. "I've got it, Mr. Tate." He winks at me and disappears inside.

My dad hasn't moved, but his grin tells me what's going on in his brain.

"What?" I stand, smoothing my black skirt to keep my hands busy.

He shrugs. "I didn't say a word." But the approval in his eyes is unmistakable.

"You don't need to—got the message."

Inside, everyone follows the delicious aroma of the platters of grilled meat to the dining room table.

"MashaALLAH, Brother Adam, you're a master at the grill!" says Raheem, rubbing his hands together. Across from me, his plate is piled high with hamburgers, drumsticks, and a small mountain of potato salad.

My dad's smile covers most of his face. "My uncle taught me how to use charcoal when I was a teenager. No gas grilling for me!"

Mom sits on my right, hardly any food on her plate. "How's your chicken, Jameela?"

Across from her, Sister Jameela's posture is stiff. I've never seen someone use a knife and fork to eat a hamburger before—or wear all white to a barbecue dinner. She sets down her cutlery and dabs her mouth with a napkin before answering. "The barbecue sauce is very flavorful. Tangy, with just a touch of sweetness. Where did you buy it?"

I lift my chin. "Dad makes it from scratch."

"It tastes amazing," Raheem agrees. "I may have to come back and learn some of your secrets, Brother." He flashes me his winning smile. "Do you ever cook on the grill with your dad?"

My mom butts in before any words leave my mouth. "Fatima likes baking more than cooking. It's a useful hobby for her to have, but inshaALLAH she's headed to the University of New Mexico this fall to study nursing."

Her dismissal of my dreams cuts me to the bone.

Raheem raises an eyebrow at the pinched expression on my face.

"Yesterday, Zaynab's mom asked me to make some desserts for an office party," I shoot back, unable to keep a sharp edge from my voice. "She said she'd pay me."

Sister Jameela leans closer to the table. "Sarah Baker? The owner of that successful CPA practice downtown?" The softness in her voice is new. "How do you know her?"

"Her daughter and Fatima are best friends," Ma is quick to answer.

"Sister Sarah is *very* supportive of my baking," I tell Jameela. Glancing at my mom, I add, "And she's like a second mother to me."

Tension settles over the table. We quickly finish eating.

Clearing his throat, my dad asks, "Now, who wants some banana pudding?"

At the mention of her specialty, my mom is out of her chair. "Let me clear the table first." She glares at me, so I pop out of my seat and grab some dishes. I'll never hear the end of it if I don't.

Sister Jameela speaks up. "Brother Adam, thank you for offering, but I don't eat dessert." Turning toward me, she pauses. "Although . . . Fatima, did you make it?"

I can't tell if her interest is a good thing. "Yes. It's Mom's recipe, but I tweaked it. Everyone who's tasted it loves it."

Raheem's gaze lands on me. "Tell us your secret."

A simmering heat travels through my body. "I use evaporated milk instead of whole milk. The pudding turns out richer and smoother."

"Sounds delicious," he says. Catching the sparkle in his eyes, I'm positive he loves sweets as much as I do. If he does, he has to let me bake them. And sell them.

But his mom can't keep a frown off her face.

"Do you need any help?" Raheem holds out his plate to me, and when I take it, his fingers brush mine. The electric attraction between us is a powerful magnet.

"No—I'm good." I rush into the kitchen before I can trip over my own feet.

Dad carries in the platter of meat after us, setting it down on the counter. "So . . . Raheem would like to know if we're okay with you two texting each other."

"I'm fine with it," my mom is quick to say. "Fatima?"

Both of their faces shine with happiness.

I push out a forced sigh, trying not to sound too eager. "Fine, give him my number." This game of pretend is getting old.

Dad winks at me. "Will do. Can you put some banana pudding in a container? Sister Jameela apologizes, but they have to leave." He goes back to our guests.

Panic instantly sets in.

She doesn't like me! That's why she's leaving early. She'll try to convince Raheem to find someone better! Faster than a butane torch can burn sugar, I spoon the dessert into a plastic container and race to meet Raheem at the door, passing it to him.

"Tonight was amazing—especially the food." He holds up the half-filled container, smiling. "I'll text you later and let you know how much I like this."

Today we don't touch. It goes against the no-physical-contact-until-marriage tradition my parents believe in. We're right in front of our families, so . . . you know. It's not up to me.

Sister Jameela slips on her shoes, wearing a blank expression. "It was so nice to see you two again."

"I'm going to walk them to their car," Dad says, lacing up his Timbs.

We exchange the *salaams*, and the three of them are gone.

"Alhamdulilah, that went well. Raheem couldn't stop staring at you." Mom's picking up the last of the dirty dishes off the dining table. "I'll clean the kitchen. You've earned a rest."

Wow. She never lets me get out of cleaning. Hey, I'll take it.

Once I'm back behind my closed bedroom door, I settle onto my bed and open my laptop. Nothing in my inbox. I guess I won't be in that baking competition after all.

Although . . . my cursor slides toward my spam folder. A thin layer of sweat coats my forehead as I click it open.

"Oh . . . my . . . *gosh.*"

Congratulations!

Hi, I'm Pastry Chef Erica Newsome, and I would like to invite you, FATIMA TATE, to take part in our second Annual Teen Baking Championship. I and two other judges will be welcoming everyone to the Albuquerque Convention Center for three rounds of exciting competition!

Almost one hundred students from every corner of New Mexico applied, but you are one of only twenty people chosen.

This year's baking competition schedule is attached.

Thanks to our generous sponsor, Williams Sonoma, we'll be giving gift cards to those students who make it into the final round. Our grand-prize winner (and a parent) will also win a visit to the Culinary Institute of America in California, where they will spend time learning from professional pastry chefs during interterm.

We need to hear from each contestant by 9 a.m. on Monday. If, for any reason, you are not able to participate, please tell me as soon as possible. If you plan to compete, then you must inform us of your choice of recipe for the quick bread qualifying round.

This an amazing opportunity for teens, like you, who have expressed a real interest in the culinary arts. I can't wait to meet each of you and taste your wonderful desserts.

> *Sincerely,*
> *Pastry Chef Erica Newsome*
> *Head Pastry Instructor*
> *CNM Culinary Arts Program*

I'm off my bed, jumping up and down! Maybe my dream *isn't* so impossible!

Obviously, Zaynab is the first person I tell.

Zee, I made it into the baking competition!!

But the deadline is less than twelve hours from now, and I still have to choose a dessert to make. I search dessert cookbooks on the Albuquerque Public Library website and access five of them online.

A new text notification interrupts me scouring the third cookbook. I lunge for my phone and open the message.

Salaam Gorgeous. Great to see you tonight. Did you have a good time?

I actually squeal. **Wa alaykum as salaam. How was your dessert?**

Nothing. I've seen milk curdle in the time it takes for him to answer. He needs to understand waiting makes me crazy.

Promise me you'll make this at least once a month when we're husband and wife. It was amazing. My mom had a spoonful and she agreed it was delicious

My heart's pounding in my chest. **You made a good impression with my parents. But what about your mom? I don't think she likes me tbh**

Since I'm into you, my mom will come around . . . How do you feel about me?

My thumbs pause.

I like you . . . ig it'd be nice to see each other and not worry about keeping secrets from our families

Haha. Enthusiasm: weak, but I'm willing to work hard to get what I want. We'll talk soon. Goodnight Gorgeous. 💋

We're moving forward, but where we're going still isn't clear.

Not knowing what I want doesn't help.

six

My girl never lets me down when it counts.

Six days later—on Saturday morning at exactly 7:15 a.m.—Zaynab and I roll up to the convention center, me in her passenger seat. (It should be illegal for teenagers to be up this early, but whatever.) And she's not just my ride—she's my cover story for the competition.

A sea of teenagers in white chefs' coats and checkered chefs' pants floods the exhibition hall. Other than my white hijab, I fit right in. (Thanks to Zee's Amazon Prime account—bless her for letting me order my whites under her name.) The registration line isn't moving very fast, and my feet are already sore in my new non-skid work shoes.

Zaynab is busy checking out my competition. "Girl, you got this," she whispers.

When it's my turn to check in, the white lady sitting behind the table glares at my headscarf. "Name?"

"Fatima Tate."

She runs her finger down a printout. "I found you. Did you bring any supplies?"

"They're all right here." I hold up my caddy.

She writes on her list. "Okay, you're all set. Your sister can head into the ballroom and find a seat. You need to go to the Zia Room for orientation." She points to the left.

Zaynab steps closer to the registration table. "Sisters? Do we look alike to you?"

The lady examines her, then me. "No. I guess not."

Of course, Zee can't let it go. "She's not even original! It's not like we haven't heard that one before."

"Thanks," I mumble, pulling my bestie away from the table.

"Don't freak out," Zaynab says, reading my expression. "Hey, listen. You're going to kill it today." I wish I had as much confidence in my baking as she does.

"Don't forget to take pictures," I remind her, swallowing several times.

"I got you." Zaynab heads toward the ballroom's double doors.

I follow a group of teenagers dressed in pristine whites. I hope no one can tell mine were bought on clearance.

The second I step into the Zia Room, my brain tells me I'm not ready for this.

There are so many competitors. One of them is wearing a Sandia High School hat! That's a fancy public school. The students there can take *actual* baking classes.

Another competitor, her hair full of bleach-blond highlights, seems laser-focused on me. Disconcerting. I quickly take a seat in the second-to-last row and study the plain brown carpet under my feet.

"Okay, students, it's time to get started!" booms a tall woman from the front of the room.

It's Erica! I remember her . . . but she probably forgot me already.

"My name is Chef Erica, and I'm a certified executive pastry chef. This year, I'm one of the three judges who will be tasting and scoring the entries in each of the three rounds. Before we go over the rules, are there any preliminary questions?"

No one moves—until the girl who's been giving me the side-eye raises her hand.

"Chef Erica, if someone is wearing an extra piece of clothing—say, something on their head not listed in the rules—will they be disqualified?" She turns and stares right at me.

The room grows quiet.

Each student baker gawks in my direction, whispering. It takes every ounce of courage I have not to run out of the room. My hands have an iron grip on the sides of the chair.

The competition can't be over for me before it's even started. It just can't. I lied and deceived my parents to get here.

"What's your name, miss?" Chef Erica demands of the girl. My eyes dart to the pastry chef as my breakfast turns to lead in my stomach.

"I'm Alicia Hutchins, Chef." No one can ignore the confidence in her answer. She thinks everyone here agrees with her.

"Well, Alicia, your question is highly inappropriate." The chef takes a few steps toward my new nemesis. "I would suggest you focus on your own business. As head judge, I can tell you that every student here is dressed in accordance with the rules. Now, if you're done wasting my time, we can get started."

I'd hug Chef Erica if I could.

Cool as can be, Chef Erica reads off the same sheet we all got emailed last week. "For the preliminary round, you will complete a dessert of your own choosing from the first category: quick breads.

I want to ensure each of you understands you will have only two hours of baking time. Not a *minute* more." She scans our faces, her lips flat. "Desserts need to be on the display platter at your baking station no longer than fifteen minutes after the ovens are shut off."

A brave boy with wild black curls raises his hand. "I have a question, Chef."

The entire room falls silent a second time. Oh no. Not again. Is this also about me?

"And what is your name?" Chef Erica asks.

He peers down at the floor for a second before answering. "Brian Aguilar. From Las Cruces. If we have problems with our bakes and our quick bread isn't perfect, should we still have it judged?"

A silent sigh escapes my lips. Not about me. I still have a chance.

Chef Erica nods. "Great question. First I'd like to thank you, Brian, for driving over three hours from southern New Mexico to be here for today's competition. Second, to answer you, none of the judges expect perfection. We're excited to have twenty students here who are sincerely interested in professional baking, so yes, please share whatever you make. Relax and have fun!"

That's not even a possibility for me.

"We should be getting started in five minutes," she continues. "If you need a drink of water or a visit to the restroom, please take care of it now."

Not one student moves.

I blow out a stream of nervous energy as Chef Erica strolls over to me. "Good morning, Fatima! I hope you remember meeting me at the Shared Table."

How could I forget?! I jump up and nod furiously. "Hello, Chef."

She extends her hand and I grasp it.

"I want you to know no matter what Miss Hutchins said, I'm thrilled you're here and I expect great things from you. I've tasted your product, and I know you'll prepare us something amazing! Please don't hesitate to let me know if anyone else bothers you." Her expression goes from cheerful to serious. "We take bullying very seriously."

The edges of my mouth turn up. "Thank you, Chef."

She returns to the front of the room. "Please follow me into the competition area, contestants."

We walk into the main ballroom, and I gasp.

On one side there's a wall of ovens; on the other, ten baking stations. A large banner hangs from the ceiling welcoming everyone to this year's contest.

"Please find your assigned area, contestants," Chef Erica announces.

Too nervous to find Zaynab in the audience, I walk to station eighteen and put my caddy on one of the two stainless-steel workbenches. Everything has been provided and organized for my recipe (blueberry scones with orange glaze): on the counter, three stacked cutting boards and all the dry ingredients; in the mini fridge, eight ounces of heavy cream, a container of cubed butter, and half a dozen eggs.

"Hello, everyone. My name is Chef Erica Newsome, and I would like to welcome you to CNM's Second Annual Teen Baking Competition." She's speaking into a microphone. "This event brings together young people from across New Mexico who are

interested in studying pastry arts after high school. Let me introduce my fellow judges. First, we have . . ."

Tuning out her speech, I finally seek out Zaynab's familiar
face. *There she is.* Her confident smile is contagious and melts
away some of my self-doubt.

"Contestants, please try to keep your work areas tidy, as the
judges may walk around and observe your process. Remember,
spectators, no one other than the competing students and event
volunteers are allowed near the ovens. Okay, contestants: ready,
set, and bake!"

I block out the audience's clapping. Getting my batter right is
my first priority.

I open my tool caddy and grab my measuring spoons. As soon
as my cookie sheet is lined with parchment paper and my dry
ingredients are sifted together, I reach in and grab the contents
of the mini fridge. With my pastry blender, I combine my mixture
with cubed butter, tossing in the fresh blueberries after. Then I
mix the heavy cream, an egg, and some vanilla extract together in
a smaller bowl before adding it to the rest.

So far, no problems.

But the large digital clock on the wall tells me I've already used
twenty minutes.

With everything combined, I dump my mixture onto the
floured stainless-steel counter. My fingers quickly shape the dough
into a disk, which I then cover in plastic wrap and set in the fridge
to chill. My mother-taught housekeeping skills help me clean my
station in record time.

Gotta keep up this pace.

Once my oven is preheated, I take my dough out of the

refrigerator and set it on the largest cutting board, slicing it into eight wedges and placing them on the parchment-lined cookie sheet. After I brush each one with an egg wash, the whole tray goes into the oven.

I have eighteen minutes to make the orange glaze while the scones bake.

"The ovens will be turned off in forty minutes, students," Chef Erica warns. The baker closest to me mumbles, "Shit."

Not finishing on time *isn't* an option for me.

I whisk together powdered sugar, orange juice, and some more vanilla extract until the glaze is the right consistency. My internal clock tells me to check my oven, and bingo—the scones are ready. After pulling out the tray, I take my cake tester and check they're fully cooked (they are). I let them cool for as long as I can, and then I drizzle the orange glaze over the lot before moving them onto the display platter.

I sneak a peek at Zee. She gives me a thumbs-up.

Before my time is completely up, I stack all my dirty baking dishes and pack my personal tools back in my caddy. Neat as a pin.

A woman in a Teen Baking volunteer T-shirt approaches me, an official badge swinging from the lanyard around her neck. "Fatima Tate, your product is done and your station is in order. Congratulations! Please exit the stage and wait in the audience."

I find a seat beside Zaynab. Waiting while the judges decide which of us are advancing into the second round just . . . sucks.

Tapping my right foot again and again against the floor sorta helps.

"Don't worry, girl, you got this," Zee reassures me. "I ate at *least* five hundred scones from all your practice batches, so I know. The judges are crazy if they think someone else's baking tastes better."

"Zee, please be quiet." I scan the scowls of the people sitting behind us. "Someone will hear you."

"Like I care."

As Chef Erica walks to the front, the baking stations behind her, my pulse accelerates. *Thump. Thump. Thump.* I fasten a hand on Zaynab.

"I'd like to thank all the families and friends here to support these talented students." She gives the audience a gracious smile. "The judges and I agree: all the quick breads we tasted today were impressive, especially as none of them were made by professional bakers."

If she doesn't hurry up and tell us who's advancing, my grip on Zaynab's forearm might cut off her circulation.

"To all the students—even if you're not selected for the next round, you should be so proud of yourselves for entering."

I should've told Raheem about this. It would've been nice to have two people here who believe in me. I could be cutting off his circulation too. (Plus, he's a good-looking distraction.)

"Our first semifinalist is number three: Alicia Hutchins."

Fantastic. The girl who asked if my hijab is against the rules. I can't bring myself to clap.

Next, Chef Erica announces numbers five, seven, eight, ten, twelve, thirteen, and fifteen and the names of teens I can't remember. I'm sweating. And then—

"Our second-to-last semifinalist is number eighteen: Fatima Tate."

Zee grabs me in a huge hug and shrieks, *"That's right!"*

"Zee, you're so loud!" A single happy tear falls down my cheek. "I didn't hear the name of the last baker—and no one else did either!"

"I don't care! I want everyone to know how proud I am!"

I'm advancing. I'm a semifinalist. I'm a baker someone believed in. This is one of the best moments of my life. Tomorrow my face will ache from all this smiling, but it's worth it.

This could be the first step in my culinary career. My parents would be so proud . . . at least my dad would be. Not for the first time, I wonder if winning here might be enough to convince them that I *can* be a pastry chef.

Maybe. If I hadn't lied to them. Now they can never find out.

Zee leans back in her chair and—like she's a mind reader—asks, "When are you going to tell your parents? You know how your mom is. Will you *really* be able to disappear for the next two Saturdays without her finding out about this?"

Hell if I know.

"Fatima? That's your name, right?" The guy from Las Cruces with the beautiful curls is standing right in front of me. "I'm Brian. I want to apologize for Alicia. We're not friends, but we were both in the competition last year—and she's still an asshole."

Zaynab busts out with a "DAMN!"

"A Muslim girl in our senior class beat her out for valedictorian and she's reaaaally sour about it. So it's not personal, exactly."

I give Zee a quick side-eye. "Hi, Brian. Yes, I'm Fatima. And this super-loud person beside me is my best friend, Zee."

They exchange hellos.

"What was it like last year?" I dare to ask.

Brian glances around. "The same, except I had way less baking experience. Alicia and I didn't get past the first round. Are you going to the bread class?"

People stream past our little group. My hands grip my thighs. "Um, what bread class?"

"Last year, they had a special class for students who made it into the second round." He points toward the judges. "You actually got to meet some of the instructors in the culinary program, and they taught the kids to make focaccia and sourdough bread. One of the guys from my school made it into the final round using what he learned there."

A realization hits me. "You made it into the next round, too, right? Congratulations to both of us."

"You just didn't hear my name over Zee's yelling." His one-sided grin is kinda cute. "I've gotta go but check your email in the next couple days. Maybe we can be partners in the class!"

His enthusiasm is genuine and brings out my smile in return. "If I get an invitation to the class and can make it, I'll definitely be your partner."

"Awesome! See you soon, Fatima."

"Bye, Brian."

We wave to each other, then he walks away.

Zee pops out of her chair and drags me out of mine. "We should celebrate!"

"Totally!" I agree.

Yes, I'm happy I made it into the second round, so happy . . . but the sudden ache in my chest reminds me I forged my mom's signature to get here.

Is it *haram* to follow your dreams?

Second Annual New Mexico
Teen Baking Championship Schedule

First Round: Quick Breads, third Saturday in April
Second Round (Semifinals): Pies, third Saturday in May
Final Round: Decorated Two-Layer Cakes, second Saturday in June

All three rounds of competition will be held at the Albuquerque Convention Center. Each student must wear a white chef coat with black-and-white checkered chef pants. In addition, there is a list of baking tools each participant needs to bring to any round they are competing in. For safety reasons, jewelry and open-toed shoes are prohibited.

The judges do not allow participants to have a smartphone with them in any of the three rounds. Thank you for understanding.

seven

Forty-eight hours later, it's noon on Monday—and my butt's already sore. Endless sitting in front of a computer is *not* a real high school experience. But this is charter school.

I pass the local public high school every day. It would've been easy to commute to. But my mom convinced my dad this type of education would expose me to less of the teenage behaviors forbidden in our faith. (She got that all wrong.)

Thankfully, graduation is soon—and morning classes for today are done. I stand and file out behind all the other students, seniors like me, who were also in main lab.

Lunchtime. We don't have an official cafeteria, just a room with a row of microwaves, three vending machines, and a sprinkling of tables. A swarm rushes to grab seats. I don't bother, because I get to leave now—most of us don't; I carefully organized my classes for half-day sessions—but I usually grab a snack first.

"*As-salaamu alaykum*, Fatima."

I pause mid-stride by a wrought iron table. I know that voice. Crap! It's Imani the Gossip. She's dressed in her normal plain black abaya and oversized white hijab.

And she waves me over to sit with her.

No way out now.

As I get closer, her eyes rake over my thrift-store outfit: a men's button-down shirt and dark gray joggers. Her mouth curls into a sneer. She shouldn't care: my clothes are loose enough to hide my shape, and my hair's covered—Islamically appropriate in my book. Not all of us want to wear black abayas every day of our lives.

"*Wa alaykum as salaam*, Imani." I hesitate at the chair across from her. "I'm surprised you're here. Don't you only attend evening sessions?"

"My parents said I could go to a bridal shower after Maghrib prayer and miss Thursday's classes. So I'm making up that time today."

All of today? She'll be here for seven hours, sitting in a windowless room and working through her online classes in silence. Even with a thirty-minute lunch break, that *blows*.

Imani pats the table. "Why don't you sit down? We haven't seen each other since the wedding. How's your senior year?"

Without a ready excuse, I park myself across from her. "Hate it here, as always."

Imani ignores that. Instead, she asks, a little *too* casually, "Are you still volunteering at the Shared Table?"

My Spidey-Senses go on high alert. "I stopped to concentrate on finishing my classes." The lie rolls off my tongue. Other than my family and his, no one knows about Raheem's courtship. I want to keep it that way.

A basketball rolls toward us, and a tall guy with a clean fade wearing one of the school's varsity sweatshirts comes over and picks it up.

"Hi."

What?

I'm in shock this hot dude even spoke to us. We don't have cliques here, exactly, since the school is computer-based, but some people are *definitely* more popular (and have more TikTok followers . . .) than others. I've seen this guy: He's on the school team, obviously, and he's always spinning or dribbling between classes.

"H . . . hi," is all I manage to say.

"What do *you* want?" Imani points to the three girls giggling behind him, gawking at us. "Go back to your table—your fan club misses you."

He steps away, grabbing the basketball. Then he's gone.

When I don't close my mouth fast enough, Imani raises her eyebrows.

"What?" she says. "That guy needs to know we're not like these other girls who care if he says hello. My parents would lose it if they found out I was friends with boys at school."

When did a simple hello become a problem?

What would she think if she knew I kissed Raheem?

"Why do they have *varsity sports* at an online school anyway?" Imani groans. "They should use that money on upgrading the computers!"

Okay, kind of true, but time to get away from this girl and her judgments. I stand. "I've got to get home. Can't be late—my mom expects a text as soon as I walk in the door." My second lie today. Pointing to the lunchbox on the table in front of her, I remind her, "You should eat something before lunch ends."

"Thanks, I will. MashaALLAH, you should hurry, then." She grins. "We haven't hung out in forever! My grandmother in Lebanon sent us a couple extra abayas from her trip to Kuwait. If you want one, let me know."

"Thanks." I haven't worn one of those since freshman year. "I'll think about it."

"InshaALLAH, we'll see each other at *Jumaah* prayer this Friday. You can tell me then."

"Sure. *Salaam.*" I rush away from the table before it slips out that I spend Fridays doing my homework and almost never go to community prayer.

I catch the bus. Raheem texts me on my way home. **I know how we can spend more time together. Do you like surprises? See you soon** ☺

I suppress an uncharacteristic giggle. He's thinking about me. Is that a crime?

When I get home, my mom is humming. She can't keep her pearly whites hidden. Weird. Maybe the apocalypse is coming?

She ambushes me as soon as we sit down to dinner. "Fatima, are you busy after school tomorrow?"

I push my plate toward the middle of the table, my appetite deserting me. "Don't think so. Why?"

"InshaALLAH, your first personal training session with Raheem is on Sunday!" Sharifa Tate is almost *giddy*. That's something I didn't think I'd ever see.

I pinch my lips together. "It is?" Is this Raheem's surprise . . . or another decision my parents made for me?

"Before you find a reason to complain, he asked your dad—and I think it's a great idea." My mom tilts her head to the side. "Tomorrow we'll go to Target and buy you some new workout clothes."

"Save your money, Ma. I don't need a cute outfit to sweat in."

She inches to the edge of her chair. "Well, *I* for one want you to look nice."

As soon as possible, I excuse myself. Rising panic pushes me up the stairs.

Closing myself in my room, her words stick at the front of my brain: *your first personal training session.* My skin tingles at the idea of spending time with him alone . . . but then it hits me: My parents will *never* let me be with Raheem unchaperoned. If I can't find someone to go with me, my mom will be there, front and center.

Oh Hell no.

I snatch the phone off my desk, plop onto my bed, and text my guardian angel.

Zeeeeeee. Do you want to work out with me on Sunday? 😄

Sunday morning, I'm sitting by the registration desk, deep into the solitaire game on my phone and waiting for my teenage chaperone.

"Hey! Sorry we're late." Zaynab appears inches away from me.

"Who's we?" I glance up.

A familiar redhead is beside her. Amber! "Hi, Fatima," she says. "Really great to see you again." Zee's hand goes to the small of Amber's back; even the glances they exchange are super cute.

"It's nice to see you, too." I didn't expect my bestie to bring her girlfriend, but I try not to show my surprise. (After all, *I* was the one asking Zaynab to be the third wheel today. It's fair.)

We head into the ladies' locker room where I change into plain gray sweatpants and a long-sleeve shirt. Stuffing my street clothes in my duffle, I shove the entire bag into an empty locker.

Zaynab touches my arm. "Are you still making desserts for my mom's employee breakfast next Saturday? You didn't forget, right?"

"InshaALLAH, I'll make cranberry-orange muffins and cinnamon rolls on Friday. But don't *you* forget! You have to be at my house by 7 a.m. sharp on Saturday to drop me off for the competition's bread class—then you can take my desserts to your mom's office. I told my parents I'd be with you."

"Sounds like a plan." She turns to Amber, who obviously knows the whole story. "You ready?"

I don't even wait for her answer. "Let's go. Raheem's probably wondering where we are." I lead them out of the locker room and into the workout area.

My new personal trainer is leaning against the wall.

He stands up straight when our eyes meet, his branded shirt stretched tight across his broad chest. "Hello, Fatima."

I gulp down my nervousness.

"Hi," I manage. I told him to expect Zee, but he doesn't comment on Amber—just rolls with it.

"So, let's have you ladies do a quick ten minutes on the stationary bike and then the elliptical. Afterward I'll show you how to use some of the other machines. Okay?"

He flashes me a bright smile. Me melting into the floor is a real possibility here.

I finish my warmup under Raheem's watchful eye. Sneaking glances at Zaynab and Amber working out side by side and giggling, a tinge of jealousy hits me. Their chemistry is seriously undeniable, and they look even more like best friends than Zee and I do.

"Something wrong, Fatima?" he asks, following my eyes.

I step onto the elliptical, and he sets the pace and incline of my workout. "No. No problems here."

"Wonderful. Now I need you to focus more on keeping a steady pace—and less on distractions around you." His head tilts toward my best friend and her girlfriend. Zaynab is pushing it hard on the treadmill. "Start with a set of fifteen."

After a short time on the elliptical, I'm out of breath. It's been a minute since I've worked out, and the armpits of my shirt are drenched in sweat—even the back of my neck under my sports hijab is damp.

My gaze drifts up and down Raheem's unquestionably perfect body without his permission. My face grows hot, and I pause my leg reps after only five.

Zaynab walks by and glances at us. To my surprise, she frowns at Raheem.

Raheem sees me staring in Zaynab's direction again. "Everything okay? For real."

"Yes," I say. I wish he'd get closer—his mouth inches from mine . . . But he keeps a respectable distance.

"Then time to get back to your workout, Gorgeous."

Raheem helps me for the next thirty minutes on different exercise machines. After that, he has me do three grueling sets of sit-ups, push-ups, and planks, which burn. When I'm all done, I guzzle two cups from the gym's water dispenser, then wander over to Zee, who's on the seated overhead press. "Hey sis. How much longer are you and Amber staying?"

"Amber's already in the shower. After I get cleaned up, we're gonna hit the IMAX," Zaynab says. "You wanna come?"

My eyebrows scrunch. "Wait, I can't. You're supposed to take me home. Can you drop me off on the way?"

Before she can answer, Raheem appears beside me. "Fatima, I'll drive you. My next client isn't for an hour, and nothing's more important to me than your safety." He gives Zaynab a cool glance. "I'd hate to leave you stranded somewhere."

Zee shoots him a serious death glare in return. "Aren't you cute? Not today, Romeo. We got you, Fatima."

Wow. I can tell that one of these two people is going to be pissed when I choose the other. "Zee . . . since you hate missing the previews, it's okay. I'll go with him."

"Whatever." She turns and charges into the women's locker room.

I stare between her retreating form and my potential future husband.

"I don't think she approves." Leaning into my personal space, Raheem asks, "Be honest: Is there a problem between the two of you?"

"No." I lift a shoulder. "Never."

He leaves it alone. For now.

"One thing: my parents think she's bringing me home," I tell Raheem.

"It's important we spend a little time together, Fatima. Alone. We'll just have to be on our best behavior today." He leans forward, not breaking eye contact with me. "Give me a few minutes. I'll meet you in the lobby."

The glimmer in his eyes makes it hard for me to breathe. Or disagree.

I rush into the locker room, where Zaynab and Amber are waiting for me.

84

"It's too bad you can't hang out, Fatima," Amber says, and I can tell she means it. "Zee told me you have plans. Maybe next time we can do something together, just the three of us!"

"Just be careful, Fatima." Zee grabs their stuff. "I've been watching him today. I don't know—the more I see, the less I like. Someone *that* perfect usually isn't. I'll text you."

Amber waves, and they're out the door.

I rinse my face with tepid water from the sink and pat it dry with a paper towel. Grabbing my purse and duffle bag, I head out.

Raheem really is beautiful: his prominent cheek bones are on full display when I join him at the front desk. "Okay, let's get you home." He holds the front door open and I step into the blistering sunshine.

Is being around him my new normal? Is this a done deal?

No. Don't stress. Enjoy it.

When we reach his sedan, Raheem gets the passenger-side door for me. "Thanks," I murmur. Part of me is still convinced this isn't real.

We head north without saying a word to each other.

Eventually, he breaks the silence. "Fatima, I don't want to get between best friends, but seriously, what's going on with you and Zaynab? She was very abrupt with us. You and I, we're getting to know each other and, inshaALLAH, on the path to getting married. If you need someone to talk to about her, I'm here to listen."

About her? That sounds a little wrong. But I really could use a listening ear.

"No. I mean—not really." I pause. "It's small things. We haven't hung out a lot lately. Busy seniors, last semester. And now that she's dating Amber, there's not a lot of time left for me . . . I know it's selfish to be jealous of all the time they spend together, but . . . sometimes I am."

Raheem nods like he gets it. "You miss her."

His understanding gives me comfort. "I'm the worst best friend. She *deserves* to be happy. And now, whatever this is—between you and me—I'm just thinking, when will we actually see each other? What if I lose her?"

"That would give us plenty of time to get to know each other." He slows to a stop at the next red light. "No, don't worry, Gorgeous. The two of you will find a way. So—baked anything new lately?"

"Always." I'm glad for the change of topic. That was a little too heavy. "I tried this new fudge recipe."

Raheem smiles. "I'd love to try it." The energy between us is almost visible. As he changes lanes, he asks, "What about the competition? Have you convinced them to let you apply yet?"

"Not exactly," I hedge.

"Maybe if I talk to your parents, I can help them understand how committed you are to the culinary arts. What if I offered to pay for your degree? Then they wouldn't push you to study nursing."

He doesn't mention that the offer is conditional on us becoming husband and wife.

"Maybe." Changing the subject again, I say, "Aren't you graduating with a double major in English and political science? What made you choose those fields?"

He nods, his smile fading. "We were talking about you."

I laugh. "Caught me."

Raheem laughs, too. "Okay, no more talk about parents or jobs or school. Did you enjoy today's workout?"

I shrug. "It was okay. I'm not that into pumping iron." Not sure how he'll take my honesty.

He pauses, then says, "No problem. What's something you haven't done for fun in a long time and want to do again?"

A surprising question, but an easy one. "My dad and I hiked one of the Sandia Heights trails once. But we haven't been back."

He parks at the condo. "So why don't *we* go? Last summer, I hiked up there a lot."

I release my seat belt right after Raheem does, excitement bubbling inside me even as I avoid his gaze. "You *know* my parents would never approve. We'd need a chaperone."

He runs his fingers along the back of my hand. "Fatima, what if I talk to your dad? InshaALLAH he'll say yes and we'll go together."

"That . . . would be amazing."

With our deepening bond, I wish he'd plant a feather-light kiss on my lips. No such luck.

Coming around to the passenger side, Raheem helps me out of the car. "Fatima, is it okay if I don't walk you to your front door?"

I take a single step toward home. "Um—yes." My fingers clutch the sides of my shirt.

Raheem shifts an inch closer. "I don't want you to think all of this is just about physical attraction. We should like each other, too."

A breath catches in my throat. "Do you mean everything you say, or are you just trying to impress me with your self-control?"

"Why? Are you impressed?" Raheem's face cracks into a full grin, but there's an anxiousness to it. "Thank you for letting me bring you home. Have a good day, Gorgeous."

Could Raheem be as nervous about this process as me?

eight

If I were braver, I'd tell my mom I forged her name. Instead, I'm standing in our kitchen surrounded by pie dough, practicing for the next round of a competition I'm not even supposed to be in.

I form two twelve-ounce disks of dough and wrap each one in plastic, then set them in the fridge. Next, my hands move fast peeling, coring, and slicing two pounds of Granny Smith apples. After that, I melt some butter in a large cast iron skillet, adding in a cup of sugar and a teaspoon of cinnamon. When that's all combined, I dump the mound of apple slices into the mixture.

The front door opens and closes, but I'm in the baking zone. I don't stop.

"*As-salaamu alaykum.*" My mom's voice calls, interrupting my concentration. "Fatima, where are you?"

One last stir and I set aside the pie filling and turn off the burner. "*Wa alaykum as salaam.*"

She pokes her head into the kitchen. "Are you making apple crisp? Whatever it is, it smells tempting."

Her compliment brings a temporary smile to my face. "Since I'm making muffins and cinnamon rolls for Zee's mom, I decided to whip up some apple pies for us. Dad can even take one to the dealership." A little guilt-baking. "Do you need me?"

Please, please say no.

My mom is still in her scrubs. She drops today's mail on the dining table. "No. My next stop is the shower. InshaALLAH, by the time I'm done, the pies will be in the oven and I'll heat up some leftovers for dinner." Seconds later, she disappears behind the master bedroom's door.

While the apple mixture cools, I take the dough disks out of the fridge and shape them into their pie tins. Thirty minutes later, I slide my two apple pies into the oven.

After washing all the dirty baking dishes, I rifle through the pile of mail. The electric bill—with a big red PAST DUE NOTICE warning on it—catches my attention. I shove it under the grocery store ads before noticing a business-sized envelope with my name on it.

The return address is UNM Admissions office.

CONGRATULATIONS is printed across the back seal. *No. No. No.*

I grab it and run upstairs. I stash it beneath my pillow and panic-text Zee.

Help. My UNM acceptance letter came today. What am I going to do?

Instead of answering, Zaynab calls. I answer immediately.

"We've talked about this before!" she reminds me. "You need to curse or scream or whatever it takes for them to listen to you! *Screw* following her plan. You can't go to nursing school just to shut your mother up."

I climb onto my bed, temples throbbing. "Doesn't your mom have expectations of *you*? Well, *mine* expects me to go to college, get a 'marketable' skill, and get married to a respectable Muslim brother. You know that. Nothing's happened to change how they want my life to go."

"I'm not buying it. You've got choices."

I lean against my headboard. "You mean getting married? I'm not actually even sure yet if he'd support culinary school. Anyway, now you're telling me to marry a guy to get away from my parents? Are you serious?"

"Fatima, that's *not* what I'm saying." Her voice gets louder and louder. "*You* can't be serious right now. I said you have choices. And if you're really not sure what he thinks of you becoming a pastry chef, ask him!"

My head still hurts. "Can you come over?"

"No, I gotta go." Zaynab goes quiet a little too long. "Hey, me and Amber are going to get food from Potato Corner in Coronado Center. Do you want to go with us?"

I almost say yes, but I know it's not possible: my mom would never allow me to hang out this late on a school night. "I want to, but I have homework to finish. Tell Amber I said hi."

"Will do. Peace."

With our conversation over, I lay down on my bed and stare at the popcorn ceiling for answers. (Of course none are forthcoming.)

"Fatima, your pies are ready!" My mom's loud voice echoes from downstairs.

"Okay, Ma!"

I pull the UNM letter out from its hiding place, walk over to my window, and hold it up to the fading sunshine. Part of me wants to get this over with: rip open the envelope, show the contents to my parents, pretend to be happy.

But how can I when I know nursing will never be my choice?

"Did you hear me?" My mom's catlike skills are *real*, because she made it all the way up the stairs and into my bedroom without me hearing a thing. "What's that?"

"It's a letter. It's nothing."

She stretches out her hand. "Let me see that, please."

I exhale, then put the envelope in her hand. The scent of cinnamon and apples wafts up to my nose. "Ma, I need to go downstairs—the pies." My gaze shifts between her face and my acceptance letter.

"I'll be right behind you."

Damn. I should've hid the envelope until she went to sleep.

I rush to the kitchen, grab a potholder, and set both half-sheet pans on their own trivets. The pies are a shade darker than golden brown, but I'm still pleased; it was good practice. I hope this recipe will be good enough to impress the competition's judges.

Mom hovers near me.

"*As-salaamu alaykum.* Where are my girls?" My dad calls as he walks through the front door. "Something smells delicious."

"*Wa alaykum as salaam.* We're both in the kitchen." My mom calls out. "There's something we all need to sit down and talk about."

The three of us end up at the dining table.

"Fatima has some good news, Adam."

My fleeting hope she'd let me lead the conversation dies.

But, weirdly, my dad's focus is glued to his phone.

"Adam, you're not listening. What's wrong?"

"Sorry, Sharifa. I don't want to bring you bad news, but the dealership was vandalized last night. Whoever it was, they damaged a few of the customers' cars in the service department, then spray-painted a bunch of new inventory in the lot."

"Was anyone hurt?" she asks, alarmed. "Do you think APD will arrest whoever did it?"

He shakes his head. "Thank ALLAH it was after hours and no one was hurt. They didn't arrest anyone yet, Sharifa, but there's a good chance they will since we got a decent picture on last night's security video."

"Dad, do you think you're in danger there?" I blurt. Nothing can ever happen to him. I'd be *devastated*.

My parents share a silent conversation before he answers me. "Fatima, inshaALLAH I'm safe. Don't worry about me. The vehicle damage is extensive and will cost a lot of money to repair, but insurance should cover almost all of it."

His reassurance doesn't give me any comfort. My stomach is still in knots.

Mom taps her finger on the table. "Fatima, don't forget your *good* news."

Pointing over my shoulder, I tell him, "I made two pies. They're cooling on the kitchen counter."

"MashaALLAH. Good, because I'm starving!" he exclaims. It takes so little to make my dad happy.

My other parent clears her throat. "That's not the good news I mean. Our daughter received her UNM acceptance today." She waves the envelope in the air, then drops it in front of me. "Since we're all here, I'd love to hear what it says." A vein in her neck is bulging and she's glaring at me.

"Ma, please calm down." I pick up the envelope and tear it open. "'*Dear Fatima, we are proud to accept your application to the University of New Mexico,*'" I read aloud, "'*and invite you to begin your college career with us this August* . . . blah blah blah.'"

"Let me see the letter," says my dad in a strong but soft tone.

Handing it over, I watch his eyes take in every word. He drops the letter, his keys, and his wallet on the table, then comes around and wraps me in a bear hug. "We're so proud of you, sweetie." He studies both of our sour faces. "Is there a problem here?"

My mom is the first to talk. Like always.

"Adam, your daughter is still holding on to the idea of becoming a pastry chef. She wants to go to culinary school. But she has an opportunity to get a four-year degree! Between the state lottery scholarship and living at home, she can graduate with no debt at all."

"But Ma—"

She puts a hand up. "Fatima, if you don't want to study nursing, then think about nutrition—or even social work. Getting your bachelor's in a marketable skill is more secure than spending your life working in a hot kitchen somewhere."

With every word out of her mouth, a small part of my dreams disappear.

"Ma, why can't I decide for *myself*?" Keeping my hand pressed flat, I fight the urge to ball up my fist and slam it on the table. "You've been a nurse for a long time, and you love it, I get it, but it's just not for me. I can't even stand the sight of blood—it's disgusting."

Mom taps her index finger against the wood over and over. "Then check out *other* programs," she insists. "You'll have two years to take classes you're interested in before you have to choose a major."

We've had this argument more than once. How can I make her finally hear me?

"But I already know what I'm interested in!" My fingers curl, my nails clawing into the table. "If I applied to the CIA campus in California—or CNM's culinary arts program!—I could earn an associate's degree in baking and pastry arts. You're making it sound like anyone with a regular high school diploma can open their own bakery. They can't. This is competitive work!"

Why is everything a battle?

My mom swivels around to my dad. "Adam, why haven't you said anything? Our daughter won't listen to me; maybe she'll listen to you."

Dad is silent for a moment.

"Fatima, you know I'll support any direction you want to go after high school," he begins, and my heart swells. "But your mom has a point." It deflates just as fast. "Getting a bachelor's degree without having to pay for tuition and fees is a wonderful opportunity," he continues. "You shouldn't pass it up too quickly. Look, the University of New Mexico is considering you for a second scholarship, in addition to the state lottery one. Are you sure UNM doesn't have a culinary program?"

My fingers tug on the cuffs of my long-sleeve shirt. "I asked the UNM rep at the college fair last semester. The closest thing they have is hotel and restaurant management, and I'm not interested in that. Both of you know this."

From where he sits at the head of the table, my dad reaches over and wraps his hand around mine. "Please take a few days to think about it. Maybe talk it over with Raheem and get his opinion."

What *I* want is never good enough.

Now it's my mom's turn again. "Great idea, Adam. She should discuss this with him. Fatima, does Raheem think it's a good idea for you to study to become a pastry chef—or to get a degree in a more stable career?" She sits back in her chair, daring me to say something else.

The two of us stare across at each other, neither one willing to give in. My mom clenches her jaw.

"Sharifa, can you order some food from Dion's? Let me take a shower, then I'll go pick it up." He winks at me. "We'll celebrate Fatima's college acceptance with Albuquerque's best pizza and salad."

He gets up and heads into the master bedroom, my mom right behind him.

My foot bounces up and down under my chair, a tsunami of negative thoughts flooding my brain. I'm here complaining about my parents pushing me to go to study for a steady job when my dad could lose his. He started as a mechanic when I was in middle school, and now he's the head service manager for the entire dealership. What if corporate finds a problem within the dealership and holds him responsible for the damage to the cars on the lot?

My dad's suggestion pops back in my head. *Maybe talk it over with Raheem.*

Sinking down, I remember every second of the last time we were together. The swamp cooler is on but does nothing to cool my elevated body temperature—something that happens every time I think about being the wife of Raheem Harris.

I yank open the refrigerator door and grab the ingredients for cranberry-orange muffins. After they're done, I'll start the cinnamon rolls for my first paid baking job. These desserts better be the best thing I've ever made.

I should tell Raheem about my acceptance in the competition. He can't support my culinary dreams if I'm not honest with him.

And he did offer to pay for culinary school. Maybe if we get married, I won't be a burden to my parents and whatever I earn can help them.

Can it really be that easy?

My mind comes back to the batter I'm in the middle of making. When I'm surrounded by flour, sugar, and butter, I can pretend my screwed-up life is fixable.

The answers to all my problems might be right in front of me.

nine

It's 7:27 a.m. Saturday morning. I'm standing outside of a CNM baking lab sipping my homemade chai, trying not to fall asleep. The email invitation said we could just wear an apron—no need for white chef coats. I've got mine, Brian has his, and so do the other seven students who're already here.

"It's too early for her foolishness," Brian mutters. I follow his gaze and take in Alicia wearing a full chef uniform.

She grins a little too wide as she joins us. "Hi everyone! Thanks for waiting for me to go inside."

A laugh leaves my lips. Alicia cuts her eyes at me, but before anything else ridiculous comes out of her mouth, my new baking buddy comes to my defense. "Don't flatter yourself. They just haven't unlocked the classroom yet." Brian winks at me, and Alicia scowls and turns away. "She'll behave now."

An older bald-headed chef opens the door and brings the doorstop down with his foot. "Welcome, students! Come in, find a partner, and pick a workstation."

The large rectangular workspaces each have two six-quart stand mixers, two cookie sheets, and small bowls of prepared ingredients. Brian and I snag one right across from a long, stainless-steel table.

"Hello. My name is Chef Steve, and I'm one of the beginning baking instructors here at CNM," Chef Steve tells us, making his way from one side of the room to the other. His manner is brusque but confident. "After working in fine dining establishments in New Mexico for close to thirty years, I switched careers and came to teach where my journey began. Does anyone have any questions?"

A girl raises her hand. "I do. Chef Steve, does someone who wants to become a chef need to have some natural talent? What you learn in classes can only take you so far, right?"

Chef Steve adjusts his toque, then rubs his fingers along his chin.

"I'll answer that question for you, dear." Chef Erica strides inside and stops in front of her. "I've met a lot of people in my many years in this industry who believe that natural ability is everything. Even when I was in Paris, studying pastry at the Cordon Bleu, some of my classmates judged those they viewed as less talented. But listen to me: a strong work ethic and a true love of what you do are the only qualities a pastry chef must have to be successful."

Chef Steve clears his throat, not once but twice. "Everyone remember Chef Erica Newsome? She's the chief judge of the competition and head executive pastry chef here at CNM."

"Good morning, semifinalists. I'm so pleased each of you are here today. Right now we're going to get started on your focaccia. Each team is making two trays, one of which I will donate to a local soup kitchen." She stops long enough to hold my gaze.

Right in front of me, Alicia turns and shoots me a quick side-eye.

"Please read the printed instructions on your workstation. I'll be demonstrating the recipe for you. Chef Steve is available if anyone needs help at their tables." Chef Erica takes her bowl out of the mixer in front of her and removes the plastic wrap cover. "Your flour is already measured out for you."

"Have you ever made focaccia before?" I whisper to Brian.

He shakes his head. "This is my first time making *any* kind of bread. I don't have the patience for it. What about you?"

"The closest I've gotten to baking bread is watching bread week on *Great British Bake Off*."

He laughs. But we manage to follow the instructions and use the dough hook to mix everything on a low speed for about five minutes—the starter, water, olive oil, salt, combined flour, and dry yeast.

"All right, students. Now that you've combined all the ingredients in the first part of the recipe, take your bowl off the stand," instructs Chef Steve. "Sprinkle some flour onto your work surface and dump your dough onto it. Knead for five minutes. Coat your bowl with a layer of olive oil and put the dough back in. Then bring it over here and cover it with a sheet of plastic wrap. While it rests, Chef Erica will show you a foolproof chocolate chip cookie recipe." As an afterthought, he reminds us, "Don't forget to wash your hands."

As Erica stirs the cookie batter, she speaks. "The focaccia dough should proof for a minimum of forty-five minutes, up to an hour. Then we'll get these cookies baked!"

Brian and I are the first ones to finish, and I'm eager to watch the executive pastry chef do her magic. The grin on my face might be permanent.

Erica hands Chef Steve her bowl of cookie batter, which he puts in the fridge.

"Did you see that?" I nudge Brian with my elbow. "I've never refrigerated my cookie batter before. Have you?"

I can't remember being this pumped in a class ever. *This* is what I want to be learning. I can be amazing at this—I just know it. Nursing will never be for me because I don't love it this much.

Brian's eyes study everything with the same eagerness as mine. "A pastry chef I follow on YouTube did it in one of her videos. I tried it and it works." He points to Chef Erica's station. "Let's hurry so we can get a good view of the next part."

Fifteen minutes later, it's back to bread dough. After we're done with that, Chef Erica asks us to portion out the batter. She's not playing favorites, we're just the students closest to her.

Chef Steve hands both of us an ice cream scoop. My partner fills his scoop with batter, running it along the inside of the bowl then dropping the correct amount onto the cookie sheet. After a couple of tries, I get the hang of it, and we finish the first tray.

"Okay, let's have another pair do the second full sheet pan."

While Chef Erica answers questions from the other cookie-scooping team, Chef Steve directs everyone else back to their work-stations. "I've placed a parchment-lined sheet pan for each of you beside your mixers. First, turn your dough out onto the pan and brush it with olive oil. Next, shape it into a rectangle so it reaches all the corners. Try your best to keep the dough the same thickness."

Chef Steve's instructions are more abrupt than Chef Erica's but I don't care.

Getting it right is more important. I'm going to have to practice this focaccia recipe a million times.

We have a thirty-minute break before the final proof, so I take the opportunity to snoop around the lab. I linger by the commercial ovens, wander past the huge refrigerators, and end up beside a wall of storage. Each wire shelf has plastic storage bins filled with cookie cutters, pastry bags, offset spatulas, and every other baking tool anyone could ever want.

The number of different recipes I could make in a place like this is *limitless*.

"Do you like our little setup here, Fatima?" Chef Erica is on my left, her black-soled work shoes helping her sneak up on me.

"It's amazing." I focus back on her. "It's literally a dream come true!—Sorry, I'm a little excited."

"I know the feeling," she agrees, nodding. "It's nice to meet young people who love baking as much as I do. Have you considered applying to the CIA even if you don't win the baking competition?"

Licking my lips, I say, "I've thought about it a little."

Understatement of the century.

Chef Erica's eyes narrow. "I don't say this to everyone, Fatima, but I've tasted a few of your desserts, and CIA admissions is always searching for students with your obvious talent."

My eyes tear up at her compliment, but the corners of my mouth drop into a frown. "I got my acceptance letter from UNM this week." I can't hold back a small sigh. "My parents want me to major in nursing or social work—they think stability is important. Recession-proof, too."

Chef Erica folds her arms across her chest. "I'm not a parent, but I understand their hesitation," she says, her voice calm and steady. Adults never talk to me like this—like I'm an equal. "But between you and me, everyone has to eat—and people will always want the desserts pastry chefs create. *That's* our job security."

Checking the wall clock, Erica tells me, "Fatima, if you decide to follow your heart and go into the culinary arts, we also have a fantastic program here at CNM."

"I'd love to study here," I admit, breathless.

"Think about it. You could live at home. We're going to give each of you a couple of brochures, and my email is at the bottom of them. I'd be happy to answer any questions about our program or discuss what other culinary schools have to offer."

Her encouragement is everything I've wanted but never had from my parents. No matter what happens, I'll always have this moment.

Chef Steve approaches us. "Chef, everyone's back at their work-stations."

"Thank you for letting me know, Steve." She urges me to walk in front of her. "Time to finish up."

I walk over to my area and slide in beside Brian. "What?" He's staring at me.

My question is rewarded with one of his sly grins. "Fatima, you're my new hero. The whole time you and Chef Erica were back there, Alicia couldn't take her eyes off the two of you. I think she even cursed you under her breath. What were you chatting about?"

"Nothing much." I shrug. "She asked me if I was thinking of applying to the culinary program here. And what the Hell is that girl's problem with me?"

"Jealousy. Not a good look." Brian uncovers his proofed dough. "Chef Steve told us how to finish our focaccia. Do what I do and tell me the whole conversation."

I talk while we each brush the tops of our doughs with olive oil, use our fingertips to press indentations into them, then scatter halved Kalamata olives and grape tomatoes over the unbaked focaccia. When Brian writes his name on a strip of masking tape and sticks it to the side of his sheet pan; I do the same thing to mine.

Forty-five minutes later, Chef Erica stands in front of the room.

"I'd like to personally thank each of you for spending today with us. Every student here is capable of becoming an incredible professional chef. Please take home your focaccia and share it with your families. We'll see you back at the convention center in two weeks for the semifinal round of the baking competition."

She leaves the room before any of us can thank her.

I grab my bread and follow my partner out of the baking lab, then out of the building. Brian heads over to a red Honda Accord and presses his key fob to unlock the doors.

"Do you need a ride somewhere?"

"Thanks, but my best friend is on her way."

"Right. Cool."

The sudden silence between us is weird.

Brian's eyes scan the area without landing on anything specific. "Can I ask you a question, Fatima?" There's a hint of hesitation in his voice.

I hug my dirty apron tighter against me. "Sure."

"Is it true you can't date?" He gives me an uneasy smile.

Wow. Not expecting that. Maybe Brian will think the sweat on my forehead is from the super-bright sunshine beating down on us.

With a cough, he says, "I, *um* . . . I asked one of the Muslim guys in my class and he said it's, like, a rule or something."

Is he asking me out? Novice here.

"It is true," I force out. "Muslims aren't supposed to date—but some do it anyway." I paste on my best fake smile to hide my nervous energy. "I've never had a boyfriend, but I'm talking to a parent-approved guy right now."

Brian runs his hand through his curls. "If you two can't date, what's there to talk about?"

"We're getting to know each other."

"Sounds like dating."

"No," I explain. "We're trying to find out if we're compatible for marriage." Brian's a nice guy and I don't want to lie to him.

His mouth drops open. "Whoa. Congrats, I guess." The lack of enthusiasm in his voice says it all.

"Thanks." Shit, this is weird.

Mercifully, Brian opens the driver-side door. "I'll see you at the next round."

"See you then. Bye."

He gets in his car, waving as he drives away.

I have no idea what just happened. What if he *had* asked me out? I would've bet money someone outside my faith being interested would never happen.

Zaynab arrives three minutes later. "Hey! How was class?"

I jump into her Mini Cooper, latch my seat belt, and hand her a chunk of focaccia. "It was great, but Brian kinda freaked me out."

Zee has a strange twinkle in her eye. "Las Cruces guy?"

"He's funny and just as into baking as I am. We're both bread newbies . . . but being partners with him was fun."

"So . . ." She raises her eyebrows. "Did you tell Brian about Raheem?"

"I kinda had to." I take a minute to think what to say. "Brian asked me if Muslims were allowed to date."

"No way! What did you say?" Zaynab pulls out of the parking lot, heading north.

My memory runs through every detail of our brief conversation. "I told him the truth about Raheem and that there's a possibility we'll end up married."

Brian *is* kinda cute, in his torn jeans and scuffed red Vans. But no one, not even my best friend, needs to know that.

Determined to change the topic, I say, "Zee, we've got to find a way for me to attend a baking program this fall. After today, I *have* to be a pastry chef. Actually, before I say anything else, how did your mom's office thing go? Did they like my desserts?"

Between bites of focaccia, she gives me the update. "First, you owe me big-time. I had to sit at my mother's office for hours with a fake grin pasted across my face and make pleasant small talk with her staff."

"Zee, tell me already."

She weaves in and out of traffic on I-25. "Your stuff was a hit. The office manager wouldn't shut up about your cinnamon rolls. 'They're so flaky and buttery! The perfect amount of sweetness!' She even said they're better than the ones at the Frontier restaurant on Central Ave."

The praise boosts my confidence. "Wait, do you disagree? Some best friend you are!"

"Girl, please. I stashed three cinnamon rolls in my bag just so those people wouldn't eat them all." Her smirk tells me she's serious.

"You didn't! Is there anything left?"

"Nope." She veers onto Montgomery Boulevard. "We're stopping here."

She pulls into the parking lot of my favorite specialty baking store.

"I'm giving you thirty minutes to look and obsess over every kitchen gadget they have." Zaynab opens her car door. "Then we can hit up that boba shop by your place."

Today's blue sky just got bluer!

"But you hate shopping? Remember the Black Friday we stayed in Cost Plus World Market for three hours and you almost murdered me with a bottle of truffle oil?"

It's not my fault they have the best selection of international chocolate.

"Exactly." She points to her Apple watch. "This is me being supportive of your culinary dreams."

We get out of the Mini Cooper. "Thank you, thank you, thank you."

"Let's get this over with."

Squealing, I follow her inside.

An hour later, armed with my favorite matcha milk tea, we're almost to my house.

"Now that *that's* over, tell me about your day. How was the bread class?"

"I'm not sure where to start—every minute was amazing. We met this guy named Chef Steve who went to school right here at CNM and worked in the industry forever until he started teaching. And the main judge from the competition was there, Chef Erica—her credentials are *ridiculous.* She studied at the Cordon Bleu in France!"

"What about Miss Hijab Hater? Was she there?"

Not even the mention of my nemesis can dim my happiness. "Alicia was there, trying to show off in her chef whites when everyone else just wore an apron."

"Ew. Well, don't worry about Alicia. She's irrelevant."

"Right. But Zee, guess what? Chef Erica talked to me one-on-one and encouraged me to apply to culinary school!—And yes, okay, forget Alicia, but Brian told me Miss Thing couldn't take her eyes off us the whole time. He thinks she's jealous."

Zaynab stops at a red light. My stomach growls as the smoky aroma of grilled meat from the Taco Cabana restaurant on the corner hits me.

"So what happens when Raheem comes to the next round and notices you being all friendly with Brian?"

My cheeks are suddenly burning hot, and the slight spring breeze doesn't give me any relief. I need to tell her the truth. "It's not an issue, because . . . because Raheem doesn't know I made it into the competition."

Zaynab pulls into the condo lot, shuts off the ignition, and faces me. "What do you mean he doesn't know? Why not?"

A confrontation with her is the last thing I want. Time to come clean. "I mean, he knows about the competition . . . but nothing . . . else."

My BFF opens her mouth then closes it a second later. She recovers fast. "So you didn't tell him you're in it. Or that you've already competed and made it into the semifinals. Fatima, you told me the final round is going to make the city news. When you're one of the last five bakers still in it, how are you going to keep that a secret?"

I have zero answers.

"And what about Sharifa and Adam? They're going to find out. Then what?"

My stomach cramps. "We don't know if I'll even *be* one of those five, so I haven't worked it all out yet. Please take the rest of the focaccia home. It's not like I can tell my parents where it came from."

"You need to figure this shit out."

Knowing her, Zee probably wants to shake some common sense into me, but instead she grabs my cupcake container from the back seat. "Here you go."

I drop it into my lap and give Zaynab a hug.

"Thanks for today. I couldn't have done it without you." Then my body is moving while my brain is standing still. I step out of her car. She waves.

After her small green car rounds the corner, I make my way to our courtyard and take a seat in the white plastic chair right outside the front door. I clutch the cupcake carrier to my chest.

I've made a mess of something super important to me.

But baking is *it* for me, and my parents don't get that.

Raheem says he supports what I want to do—so I'm not even sure why I haven't been honest with him. My future with him could be amazing: a life I've only dreamed of.

But that scares the Hell out of me, too. So does how much he's starting to matter to my plans.

ten

I walk into the gym's lobby ready for my second personal training session with Raheem, determined to tell him the truth about everything. (My parents think Zee is here with us, but she and Amber had other plans.)

He's already there, a huge grin on his face. The familiar scent of his earthy cologne welcomes me.

"Hi." My breath shallows as I approach him. For some reason, he's wearing cargo pants and a deep red T-shirt. "Where are your workout clothes?"

Raheem's normally chill energy changes into something unfamiliar. He steps close enough that I can tell he likes minty toothpaste. "I got someone to take my clients for today." He clears his throat. "Fatima, will you go somewhere with me? We shouldn't be alone . . . but there's a place I want to take you." His forehead is dotted with sweat.

This unsteady voice and pleading look are new. Is he *nervous?*

I want to be alone with him, too, even if I refuse to admit it. Even if I shouldn't want to.

My cheeks warm. "Yes. I'll go with you."

We get in his car and head north. Neither of us speak, and the atmosphere is tense.

He navigates the winding road for a couple of miles before we pull up to a small information center with a sign that reads Elena Gallegos Open Space.

"Welcome, folks!" An older woman with patches of gray in her hair steps out of the building and greets us. "Do you know what trail you'll be hiking today?"

Hiking? I can think of plenty of worse things we could be doing right now!

"We'll be taking the Pino trail." Raheem gives her a ten-dollar bill. "This should cover the fee."

"It's only two dollars, so let me get your change," she says, her ponytail swaying in the brisk breeze.

He shakes his head. "Consider it a donation."

"Thank you, young man. My name is Esther and if you need anything, please let me know."

I lean back in my seat. Is he trying to impress me?

He parks a little farther into the lot. "Surprised?"

"Yes." I open the passenger-side door and step into the fresh air. "But you bringing me here means a lot. You remembered what I said."

There are only three other parked cars. We'll get a few private hours together to learn more about each other.

Raheem opens his trunk, takes out a large shoebox, and hands it to me. "Here, try these on."

I lift the lid and gasp. Inside is a pair of navy blue Salomon hiking boots. "How did you know I wear a size eight?" I pick one up.

"That was easy. I looked in one of your shoes the first time I was at your house."

That's kinda creepy, but okay. All's fair in love and war, they say. I tuck my doubts in the back of my brain.

Raheem slips on a black and red North Face jacket, then hands me a matching navy blue one. "Put this on and change your shoes so we can get started."

"Thank you for these, but you don't need to spend a ton of money on me."

He grabs a black leather backpack out of the trunk and slams it shut, a deep laugh escaping him. "I planned this surprise, and you need hiking boots to enjoy it. They cost less than two hundred dollars and are my gift to you. We're here because it's something you've been wanting to do."

I've never had a pair of shoes or piece of clothing that cost that much money. He takes my purse and sneakers and stores them under the passenger seat.

"If you're trying to impress me, it's working." I point to his shoulder. "What's in the backpack?"

"Water. A couple granola bars. And a first aid kit—safety first." He winks.

"Wow, you planned this *out*." I swat a single fly away from my nose.

"You'll learn I don't do anything halfway." His words come out strangely sharp—but then his face softens. "Are you excited?"

He's just nervous. He arranged all this for me and wants me to like it. *Of course* I like it.

"How do you expect me to answer when you're this close, smelling so . . ." I force my mouth shut just in time.

"Good? Is that what you wanted to say?" A smile explodes onto his face; he picks up and kisses the back of my hand.

"I was going to say you smell clean," I mumble, stuffing my hands into the jacket I'm borrowing.

"I'm not proud—any compliment you give me, I'll take. The trail is this way."

He leads me to a well-worn path. A small lizard scurries past me as I struggle to keep up with his longer strides.

"Wait, did you read this sign?" I walk up to it and point. "Have you ever seen a rattlesnake up here?" My eyes scour the nearby ground.

"Don't worry: as long as we stay on the trail, we should be fine," he tells me, amused. "If we don't bother them, they shouldn't bother us."

Is that how that works?

He keeps walking, and so do I.

The dry earth crunches underneath my new boots. The vibrant green shrub and bright April sky help me to forget we're here without parental permission. Cacti are everywhere; I linger near the ones with delicate pink flowers blooming. I feel an unfamiliar sense of freedom.

Raheem's brisk pace forces me to speed walk. My lungs are on fire by the time we stop—and that was only the first mile.

I plop down on a bench carved into a huge boulder—its smoothness reminds me of a marble countertop. "When every muscle in my body aches tomorrow, I'll try to remember this view." Most of the city of Albuquerque is visible from this altitude, spread out like a multicolored checkerboard below us. The still silence is only interrupted by the flutters of butterfly wings.

"Here, take a couple of sips." He hands me a Hydro Flask. "So, you like your surprise?"

I shade my eyes from the sun. "I love it. But . . ."

His grin drops. "But what?"

I swallow. "I need to tell you something. It's hard. I don't want you to be mad at me."

"Whatever it is, you can tell me."

Everything about his thoughtfulness today convinces me: he *wants* to make me happy.

"You remember the competition I told you about?" I gulp down my fear. "Well . . . I never told you, but I forged my mom's signature on the permission slip and . . . I got in."

There. Now my conscience is clear. But what if Raheem is so disgusted that he rats me out to my parents?

Too late now.

"Is there anything else?" He hasn't taken his eyes off me.

"I made it into the semifinal round."

Raheem sits beside me. There's a long silence, and then: "Gorgeous, thanks for telling me."

"You're not upset?"

He lifts my chin and I'm lost in his gaze. "InshaALLAH, soon we'll have no secrets between us."

A wave of relief hits me. "I guess you already know I got my UNM acceptance letter, too," I whisper.

Raheem nods. "Our moms talked. But are *you* happy about it?"

His reply is everything—he gets it.

"How can I be happy? My mom is still pushing for me to study nursing." I bite the inside of my mouth. "Can I ask you something?"

Raheem's staring at me. "Sure."

"If we were married . . . and I worked as a nurse . . . would you be okay with me changing careers? How much control do you expect in my decisions?"

He rubs his chin. "Right now, try to be respectful of your parents—they're still responsible for you."

"I've heard the dutiful daughter speech before. Thanks." *Yeah, thanks for nothing.* I swivel my body away from him.

He puts a hand on my shoulder. "Fatima, *control* isn't the right word. Couples need to discuss things. In the future, if you and I were married, your parents wouldn't be party to any of our decisions. Once you're a pastry chef, you can work wherever my legal career takes us."

"Yes? Me being a pastry chef—that's truly okay with you?" Picturing us together is getting easier and easier. "That sounds amazing."

"As your husband, you'd be my responsibility." Lowering his voice, he tells me, "And I take care of what belongs to me."

Raheem stands, takes both my hands in his, and eases me to my feet. His mouth leaves a whisper of a kiss on my cheek. "We have one more mile to go before we head back down—and your beauty can't distract me."

The second mile has more rocks, so Raheem helps me where it's more challenging for a beginner. I manage to trip over a dead branch *and* almost step on an anthill. Very graceful.

"Here, eat this." He hands me a peanut butter granola bar.

I grab it, rip it open, and sink my teeth into chewy goodness. "Thanks. How often do you come up here, anyway? You seem super comfortable."

He takes a long swig of water. "Not too much. Between my job and my classes, I don't have a ton of free time."

The strong sunshine fuels my courage. "Was it your idea to approach my family, or does your mom just want you to get married

ASAP?" I bite down on my bottom lip, not sure if my question is too direct.

Raheem reaches out his hand to me. "Let's talk while we head back down the trail."

Shouldn't that question be a no-brainer?

I grab his hand as we start our trek back the way we came. Adrenaline from navigating the tough trail mixes with the sparks from our physical connection. Gnats buzz around us, and a road-runner stares at us from the farthest edge of the brush. Unless the rattle of a Western diamondback interrupts us, nothing can spoil this time together.

We pause, stopping to look toward the horizon. Raheem opens up. "I want to find a wife now because there's a list of things I want to achieve. I need a partner who can help me. And it's tough staying on the *Siratul Mustaqeem* all alone."

The straight path is hard for me, too.

He keeps sharing. "If I'm being honest, my mom's a strong woman, but it's been hard for her since my dad died."

Thinking about my own parents and how they're always together, I know Raheem is right. "Do you miss him?"

He stares into my eyes. "My dad wasn't perfect, but I loved him."

We continue back down the trail. I stumble again, this time over a rock, but Raheem's grip steadies me. Catching my breath, I press, "So it's all about what your wife can do for you?"

"Of course not." His forehead wrinkles. "We can help each other. Whatever you study in college, I'd pay for it one hundred percent. And after your graduation, if you didn't want to get a job, that's fine with me." Raheem stops and faces me. "InshaALLAH no wife of mine will work in a career she hates. I'll take care of us."

My hand rests in Raheem's like it belongs there. His promises make everything sound so easy—a future where my greatest dreams are possible.

We're silent the rest of the way down. As we near the parking lot, Raheem asks, "So are you ready for *my* questions?"

Questions?

"I guess so," I answer, my nerves lighting up.

"You've never asked to see where I live." He turns his face to meet my eyes. "Why? Aren't you curious?"

The question catches me off-guard. "Don't you still live at home?"

Raheem chuckles. "Yes, I do, but it sounds worse than it is. If I moved out, Mom would be all by herself. *Really* by herself. The house is five thousand square feet, with five bedrooms and seven bathrooms."

I hold back a laugh. "You studying real estate in your spare time?" He's describing it so casually, like everyone in New Mexico lives in a huge house like that.

The sides of Raheem's mouth inch up, but I spot a hint of defensiveness in his eyes.

"You don't have to impress me with your family's money," I reassure him.

"I know. I like that about you, Fatima. A lot."

Swallowing a huge breath, I tap my fingers against my thigh. Time to change the subject. "When you're married, are you still planning on living with your mother?"

"No way. My wife and I will start our married life in our own space. I'm not sure if it'll be a house or an apartment yet. Do you have a preference?"

Part of me can't believe he's asking my opinion. "No, not really."

He clears his throat. "But if you *had* to choose?"

Are these the kind of decisions I'll be making soon if I become his wife?

"Okay, okay," I say, blowing out a breath. "An apartment is fine, since it would be just the two of us . . . but I'd die for a baker's kitchen with marble countertops, two convection ovens, and a massive walk-in pantry."

"Sounds like you'd prefer a house."

Imagining myself married and living in a beautiful house is crazy. *Isn't it?*

"Let's get you back to the gym," he says.

We both stroll to the parking lot hand in hand. When we reach it, Raheem wraps his arms around me, and I melt into him. "Thanks for trusting me enough to come here today."

Our lips meet . . . but the kiss is over before I want it to be.

He opens the passenger door for me. "We can keep your boots in my trunk—for our next hike."

It's great Raheem wants to spend more time getting to know each other. What I need—what I really need—is time, the time to decide if this guy should become a permanent part of my future.

Can I trust myself to make the right decision?

Maybe. Maybe not.

eleven

"Fatima, are you ready yet?" My mom hovers in my doorway as I step out of my closet. "Our guests should be here any minute."

Her nervous energy hits me from a couple feet away. Raheem and Sister Jameela are on their way over, but you'd think my mother was expecting Michelle Obama.

Examining me from head to toe and from every possible angle, she says, "MashaALLAH, working out at the gym agrees with you."

"Thanks," I whisper. I'm dressed up: a caramel peasant blouse and my favorite black wide-leg pants. My weight is the same, but she'll never believe it. The only thing that's changed about me lately is that I'm regularly staying up for late-night texting with Raheem—we've started talking again. He listens to me and doesn't act like my opinions aren't worth much. Maybe my heart is lighter?

I wrap then pin my hijab on my head. After one last check in the bathroom mirror, I'm ready and follow my mom downstairs.

I survey the kitchen with a grin. Each of my three homemade desserts sits on a wooden trivet, the sweet scents of apples, brown sugar, and cinnamon perfuming the air around us. I like there to be options.

As my mom takes the pot roast out of the oven, the aroma of

slow-cooked beef overwhelms the smell of sugar. "The food smells great, Ma."

She stops slicing grape tomatoes in half and glances in my direction, her eyebrows raised. "Why have you been so agreeable lately? Anything you want to tell me?"

"Nope." I push away the lingering guilt of sneaking around with Raheem. I'm too excited to see him again.

She pauses before going back to the tomatoes. "You get prettier every day. I'm sure at least *one* of our guests will be pleased."

Saved by the doorbell! Just as I leave the kitchen, my dad strides past me. "I've got it."

Raheem walks in, followed by his mother. I feel my cheeks' color rising.

When we were together on Sunday, he was dressed for hiking. Now he's wearing black dress pants and a burgundy button-down shirt. One glance at the tenderness in his eyes and my heart jumps.

"*As-salaamu alaykum*, Sister Jameela," my mom and I say together, and she eases past me to greet my potential mother-in-law.

Jameela's judgmental gaze lands on my outfit. I'm lucky Marshalls had a caramel-colored pashmina to match. Her pursed lips show us all she doesn't want to be here.

"*Wa alaykum as salaam*," she replies. "I hope we're not late." Her words reek of fake sincerity.

With his warmest smile, my dad reassures her. "Don't worry. You two are right on time."

I exhale, counting to ten in my head. How would I do it if I were forced to deal with Jameela all the time? She's way worse than my mother.

The rest of us exchange salaams.

"What do we have here, Fatima?" Raheem heads straight toward the desserts on display in our open dining room. "Choices? I'd love a slice of pie and some apple cobbler after we eat dinner."

We each fill our own plates from the porcelain dinner platters on the table. Raheem and I were across from each other last time, but for some reason my dad directs him to sit beside me. That's different. What does it mean?

The aroma of garlic and rosemary from my mom's pot roast smells amazing, but my nervousness at being only a few inches from Raheem kills my appetite. He doesn't say much during the meal, but every time I sneak and check him out, he's beat me to it.

The fading sunshine creates a kinda romantic vibe . . . if only our parents weren't here.

But the atmosphere is weird, too. Loaded.

Sister Jameela strikes up the first real conversation. "Brother Adam," she starts. "I saw a news report concerning some vandalism at the dealership where you work. Did the police ever catch the criminals?"

Where the Hell did that question come from?

"Not yet, Sister Jameela. APD is still investigating and reviewing the security videos." My dad's scowl deepens. "Several of the customers' vehicles had a lot of damage, but Alhamdulilah, insurance covered it all."

"I'm relieved. Please know, if it keeps happening, we'll always have a position for you. We own the only two Lexus dealerships in this state."

"MashaALLAH, that is a very generous offer, Jameela." My mom is her biggest fan.

Even I'm impressed. But is she offering because she cares, or for some other reason?

"Is anyone hungry for apple pie or cobbler?" My dad's redirection saves my sanity. "I can make coffee and heat up water for tea."

I scoot my chair back and reach for my plate.

My mom's gaze zeroes in on me. "I'll take care of the dirty dishes. You can stay there."

The quick glances between my parents as they clear the table give me goosebumps.

When they're done, they return to the dining room without making a sound, my dad positioning himself beside my chair while Raheem stands. My eyes dart around the room. Everyone is looking at me. Each cell in my body tells me something's happening—

—and then Raheem drops onto one knee.

My mouth opens, but shock keeps me from saying anything.

"Your parents told me I didn't have to make a grand gesture, but I wanted to show everyone how serious I am about you."

Sister Jameela comes around the dining room table and hands him a small black box.

"Fatima Noor Tate," he asks, "will you marry me?"

Another surprise move?

Opening and closing my mouth like three times in a row might make him take back his proposal . . . but a million questions pop up in my head.

Breathing through it, I swivel around in my chair toward my parents. I can't miss the joy on my dad's face, and the triumph on my mom's. Turning back to Raheem, I study him. His strained neck muscles, his eyes turned toward the dull beige carpet. I try to understand why he would've done this now.

Isn't it too soon?

So many doubts creep along the edges of my mind. But taking this step would make everyone happy—including me, I think.

Shouldn't this be an easy decision?

"My parents were right," I begin, voice shaky. "You didn't need to get down on one knee." Raheem snaps his gaze up to mine.

"Yes, Raheem," I tell him, with everyone watching. "I'll marry you."

As he slides the engagement ring on my finger, my skin tingles. The diamond is bright yellow, sparkling in the light. It's too beautiful.

Since it's against Islamic tradition to hug or kiss before the *Walimah*, Raheem winks at me, then stands.

My dad embraces him.

Sister Jameela even squeezes my shoulder. "*Mabrook*, Fatima. I've never seen my son so happy. InshaALLAH, the two of you will have a blessed marriage." Wow, at least it's positive.

"Your ring is stunning," my mom says. "Let me get a better look." My hand trembles as I hold it up for her to inspect.

Is it really mine?

"MashaALLAH, it's a gorgeous diamond, Jameela," says my mother, gushing. "Raheem has great taste in jewelry."

"Raheem always knows what he likes," replies my future mother-in-law. What does she mean by that? I don't know if it's a dig, but I ignore it.

"We need to hurry and pray *Maghrib* before the sun sets." My mom's suggestion gets everyone moving.

I lay out two prayer rugs for the guys and then three for the two moms and me, right behind them.

Raheem whispers to my dad, "I've got a ton to be thankful for tonight."

Knowing him, my dad is on his way to becoming my fiancé's biggest fan.

The focus I should have for prayer evaporates. On a normal day, it's a struggle for me to get in all five of my *salahs*. Today it's even harder.

When we're finished, I fold up all five rugs and put them away. We return to our seats around the dining table, and Dad hands out dessert while my mom takes care of the drinks. Everyone, except Sister Jameela, digs into their pie; mine remains untouched.

My new fiancé touches my arm. "Why aren't you eating, Fatima?"

The real truth underneath it all is this:

I don't really believe in fairy tales coming true. What happens next? I boarded this train, but I have no idea where it's heading.

"Fatima, Raheem asked you a question," my mom reminds me.

I face him. "Sorry. I'm still a little surprised."

I can't ignore the flutter in my chest when he glances down at my left hand and announces, in front of our parents, "This is the beginning of my promises to you."

twelve

The next morning, I'm a tangle of nerves as my dad drops me off to meet Zaynab for breakfast. She's not Raheem's biggest fan, but obviously I can't go through all the engagement stuff without my best friend.

Right away, I spot Zaynab at the back of the café. She's impossible to miss, the only brown face in the place. I hurry past a wall of windows and plunk myself opposite her.

"Salaam."

She half smiles at me. "How are things? Ready for the semifinal round?"

I adjust the engagement ring on my left hand, careful to keep it hidden under the table.

"Practice is slow," I reply. "And there's finals. My parents made me promise I'd stay home for the next three days and study just so they'd let me come to breakfast with you." I roll my eyes. At least when I'm married, they can't dictate every minute of my day.

Scanning a neighboring table, my eyes zero in on a plate of French toast coated in powdered sugar. "Did you order anything yet?" I'm stalling, but I really don't know how to tell Zee I accepted Raheem's proposal.

Zaynab shakes her head. "I'm tempted to get another cup of

coffee. Amber bugs me about drinking too much, but she's not here, so . . ."

I know all about her caffeine addiction. "How much coffee have you already had?"

She lifts up her hands in surrender. "Only one cup of instant before leaving my house—I swear. I'll be good. Anyway, what do you want?"

"A breakfast burrito and a lemonade. I'll go order."

"Put your money away. You paid last time."

She's out of the booth before I can stop her. I twist the yellow diamond back and forth under the tabletop, taking deep breaths.

Before I've figured out what to say, Zaynab is back with our drinks. She puts my lemonade on the table in front of me, then slides into the booth holding a tall glass of OJ. "Sooo," she says. "Your text said you had something important to tell me."

Zee stares at me, hard. This might turn into an interrogation. All we're missing is a blinding spotlight.

I pick up my lemonade with my ringless hand and take a sip of it for courage. "It's more something to show you."

After one last peek at my left hand, I take a big breath and lay my hand—and my cards—on the table. The yellow diamond glimmers.

"A rock like that can only mean one thing," Zaynab says. My smile shrinks as a frown grows on her face. "Are you happy about it?"

I am, aren't I?

Nodding, I say, "My parents and his mom knew, but it was a total surprise to me. Happened last night."

"Right." My best friend forces a smile, but it isn't genuine. Her reaction leaves a bitter taste in my mouth. This is so wrong. It's not supposed to go this way.

In a weak voice, I ask, "Do you think I'm making a mistake?"

Zee sighs. "Raheem isn't my favorite." She inches her body forward. "As long as you said yes because that's what *you* want and you're not bowing to parental pressure—then I'm proud of you."

But she doesn't sound happy, and there's a flicker of worry in her eyes. It's no surprise she's concerned I'm caving to my parents. I've done it my entire life.

"I *do* want to marry Raheem. He's handsome and kind and he cares about my opinions. But sometimes—" His offer to pay for culinary school and support me becoming a pastry chef shouldn't be a huge reason I'm accepting his proposal, but who am I kidding? It was. And I'm too embarrassed to admit that to her.

I swallow hard. "Sometimes I think we're rushing things," I tell Zee instead. It's the truth, if just a partial one.

Her face softens. "Fatima, there's something I wanted to tell you, too."

A guy in a light blue polo interrupts us. "Sorry for the wait. Which one of you lovely ladies had the omelet?"

My heartbeat thumps inside my chest. What does Zee need to tell me?

"Right here," she tells the waiter, and he sets the omelet in front of her.

"So that means the breakfast burrito *smothered* with green chile is yours," he says to me, smiling. "Is there anything else I can get either one of you?"

"We're good." Zee's curt answer doesn't faze our server.

"Thank you," I squeak out. One of us should be polite.

He grins at me and walks away.

"Zee?" I prompt her, tapping the table between us.

My best friend meets my gaze, and an unfamiliar emotion stares back at me: guilt.

"This is much harder to say now because of the diamond on your finger, but you deserve to know." Zaynab pushes her plate away without taking a single bite. "Yesterday, Raheem was outside the Gymboree Play and Music on Holly Avenue. You know . . . the place with the baby classes and shit? For new parents?"

"So?"

"He wasn't alone." She rubs the back of her neck. "Raheem was with a woman and a baby."

"That doesn't mean anything!" I shoot back, horrified. My instinct is to defend him, but I don't know why. My stomach tightens. "Maybe it was a classmate or—or a family friend."

"Nope," Zee says, shaking her head. "I went inside and asked at the front desk. The three of them went to the weekly Mommy and Me class—it's every Wednesday afternoon, and it *wasn't* their first time."

Some inner doubts wake up. "Did he see you, 007?" Panic grows inside me, and I don't know what to think. "Why were you spying on him?"

Zaynab's nostrils flare. "I was coming out of Menchie's with a frozen yogurt, and I just kind of spotted him. Fatima, I wasn't spying on him, but I saw him. I did. And you needed to know. Best friends protect each other."

My eyes sting. She's always looked out for me, but I just can't accept what she's saying. "I know you don't like Raheem, but what exactly are you accusing him of? Why couldn't it just be his relative or something? It might not have even *been* him."

Zee takes her first bite of omelet, but her chewing is a crawl. "I saw his face and recognized his Lexus." Frosty anger threads through her words. "It's not that I don't like him. It's that no one's that perfect. And he's not."

A tiny part of me knows she's right. Without thinking, I cut into my burrito, but the first cheesy bite doesn't bring me its usual joy.

We eat for a few minutes in total silence. But Zaynab's not finished with me.

"Fatima, just ask him," she starts up. "It's a simple question: 'Why do you go to a Mommy and Me class every week with a woman and a child?'" Frustration changes her voice. "You say you want to be with Raheem for forever, but you didn't even tell him when you entered the baking competition. Why?"

Ouch. A direct hit.

"I wanted to make it past the first round. What if the judges hated my scones? Looking like an idiot in front of him—I couldn't risk it."

"Lame excuses. You know something's not right with him."

"You don't get it, Miss National Merit Scholar! You've already impressed Amber—in fact, you impress everyone." My BFF's self-confidence is always front and center. "I'm not special like you."

Zee snaps her fingers in my face. "That's bullshit! You're the most amazing baker I know, and you're compassionate and funny and a million other special things. You deserve to be with a guy who knows just how amazing you really are. Does Raheem?"

She hasn't heard any of our private conversations. "He wants to marry me."

"That's not the same thing."

It irks me when she's right. I fidget with my new diamond. "Okay," I agree. "I'll ask him."

I've never broken a promise to Zee, but I'm afraid this might be the first time.

Hours later, I'm burrowed in my comforter watching my favorite baking shows on Netflix when I hear the front door open. It must be Dad. We're discussing my *mahr* tonight.

Muslim brides, even today's modern ones, are entitled to a dowry. We don't have a wedding date yet, but I guess Raheem is thinking ahead—my dad thinks it's a great idea, since it's an Islamic tradition for the groom to give the bride agreed-upon marriage gifts.

I think the whole dowry thing is ancient and ridiculous.

But, since we're not skipping this part, I could ask for driving lessons and a car. More freedom would be awesome. But is that too much? Yes, Raheem's family is wealthy—he's twenty-one and drives an $80,000 car. But that doesn't mean I should ask for something so expensive.

A knock at the door interrupts my thoughts. "Fatima, can I come in?"

"The door is not locked, Dad."

He's wearing his usual after-work outfit: loose-fitting carpenter jeans and a basic navy-blue T-shirt. "Hey. Had a good day?" He finds a spot and sits on the edge of my bed.

I close my laptop and face him. "Fine." It's not like I can be honest with him. I can't even think about what Zee told me, so I don't: I just box it up inside my head.

My dad reaches over and squeezes my hand. "It's okay if you're nervous. Now, did you think about your dowry?"

Somehow, he knows about the tightness in my stomach. I reach over, picking my list of *wants* off my desk and holding it out to him.

I follow his eyes as he reads every word.

a. *A two-week vacation in France within the first two years of marriage.*

b. *Within five years of buying our first home, I'd like a professional bakers' kitchen with appliances and finishes of my choosing.*

c. *Any earnings I make during the marriage belong to me and I decide what to do with them.*

d. *Full tuition and fees for the culinary arts/baking program of my choosing.*

When my dad is finished reading, his wrinkled brow worries me. "Sweetie, you know in Islam, any money a wife earns is hers to keep. Why did you include that?"

Just to be sure. I can't admit this to him, but I want to help him and Mom out financially. They're too proud. But I see the past-due notices come in; I know my mom has less than five sets of scrubs; I know even takeout is an extravagance for us. Ma buys me new clothes to impress my future mother-in-law while I worry about their credit card debt. Last year, I wanted to get a part-time job to help, but both my parents told me to focus on getting an education.

"You have your whole life to work," my mom reminded me.

Biting down on my bottom lip, all I say is, "I want it spelled out so Raheem knows it's important to me." Lies, lies, and more lies.

I'll ask for *ALLAH's* forgiveness later.

Dad tilts his head to the side. "Okay. Are you sure there isn't anything else? You could ask for money or jewelry."

"Raheem already gave me this beautiful engagement ring." I hold out my left hand. "I'm good."

My dad rubs the back of his neck. "Fatima, I'm glad you've found someone who will be able to provide opportunities for you that I couldn't."

Wait a minute. "That's not fair. That's not what I—"

He holds up a hand. "All parents want better for their kids, and inshaALLAH the two of you will have more security than me and your mom did. It's what I've always wanted for my only child."

I lucked out in the dad department.

Straightening his shoulders, my dad says, "We need to discuss something else."

"Sure. What's up?"

"Are you okay with everything happening so fast?" he asks, his face now more serious.

I hesitate. Can I be honest?

"Raheem's great . . . but sometimes I'm not sure. What's the rush? We've only known each other for a few months."

"Fatima, I've seen the way he looks at you. You're important to him," Dad assures me. Then he clears his throat. "Raheem's connection to you is getting stronger, and the more time you two spend together, the more chances something inappropriate could happen."

Shit. I should've figured out *this* conversation was what he was getting at.

We're taught in Islam that physical attraction is natural, but love comes after you're husband and wife. If those feelings come before and the couple does something *haram*, I'm not sure a happy ending is possible.

No way I can tell my dad some of the stuff he's concerned about has already happened.

"Dad, this isn't a subject I want to talk to you about, ever." Can I hide under my comforter until he gets the hint and changes the subject?

"It's my responsibility to make sure you're not pressured into something you don't want," he says in a somber tone I've never heard before. "On the other hand, I don't want you to be too scared to grow up."

I squirm under his scrutiny.

"About the marriage itself. No matter how long you wait, you're going to be nervous. I don't want simple nervousness to push you into making the wrong decision."

"It won't." I really hope that's the truth.

Dad stands and opens his arms. I scramble off my bed and hug the man whose quiet strength is more than I deserve.

"Your mom and I both love you so much. Raheem's an impressive brother, but he has to deserve you."

Maybe. The problem is, I'm convinced it's the opposite.

thirteen

I wake up Wednesday morning after the sun has risen.

Jumping out of bed, I take less than five minutes in the bathroom, then rush to make up my predawn prayer. (Up here, at least, avoiding my mom's disappointed glare for missing *Fajr* is possible.) After I'm done and my prayer rug is folded, I grab my phone and hurry downstairs to find something to eat.

My dad is front and center at the dining room table reading today's *Albuquerque Journal*. From the sounds coming from the kitchen, my mom is also awake.

"*Salaam*, Fatima. How are you this wonderful morning?" The paper is between us, but I can hear his joy. "Excited to be graduating today?"

Kinda. "Just glad finals are over."

Being here with my parents, it hits me that very soon this might not be my home anymore. Other than the Islamic calligraphy on the wall and our comfy couch, there's not a bunch of stuff I'd miss. All my baking tools would go with me wherever Raheem and I end up.

But it's the three of us, together—the Tate family—that make this place special to me. Am I ready to become a Harris?

"Fatima, are you okay?" my dad asks.

"Oh . . . yeah. Everything's fine."

"Good. Your mom and I have a gift for you." He hands me a plain white envelope. "Don't be shy, open it."

My mom joins us, studying every move I make.

I lift the flap, take out the single piece of paper and unfold it. My eyes bulge.

Thank you for your payment in full for Fatima Tate's Driver's Education Class. Her thirty hours of classroom instruction will start the first Monday in June.

"No way!" I run straight into his arms. "Dad, this is amazing!"

"In less than a month you could have your instructional permit," Mom says. She's laughing. "How did we get this old, Adam?"

"You're still beautiful to me, Sharifa." The tenderness in his voice is exactly what I'd hope to hear from Raheem after thirty years of marriage.

My parents' special graduation breakfast starts in an hour. I wanted Zaynab to come, but my mom insisted on only inviting Raheem and his mom. Why she went to the trouble of hanging streamers and decorating downstairs with sparkly CONGRATULA-TIONS, GRADUATE! banners for just the five of us, I'll never get. But it's kinda sweet, and it'll be nice to celebrate today.

Hunger leads me into the kitchen, but I stop short at the entrance.

Sharifa Tate, my workout-obsessed health nut of a mom, has a layout of all my favorite breakfast foods on every counter.

I rub my eyes. Twice. The scene stays the same.

The sweet aromas of cinnamon French toast and crabmeat quiche with aged Swiss cheese tickle my nose.

How did they afford all this? It *must* be a prank.

"Why are you so quiet?" my mom asks. "Don't you like your surprise?"

My mouth's already watering when I spot a full plate of halal turkey bacon and a carafe of fresh-squeezed orange juice.

"Ma, I don't know what to say." I glide over to her and throw my arms around her. "You don't like it when I eat this stuff. 'It will make you gain weight' are your exact words."

She steps out of our hug and moves a stray hair behind my ear.

"My only child is graduating high school and she's also found herself a wonderful young man." If I didn't know my mother, I'd swear those were tears in her eyes. "Don't you think that's reason enough to indulge?"

"I guess." Last night, I overheard my parents talking about a low-balance alert from their bank. They shouldn't have spent the extra money on this breakfast.

My dad closes his newspaper as I leave the kitchen. "Okay, Squiggles," he says. "Go get dressed and inshaALLAH when you're done, our guests will be here and we'll be able to eat." He rubs his belly in exaggerated circles.

"Love you, Dad." This goofy man is everything to me.

"Fatima, someone's here to see you!"

I emerge, clean and dressed. The moment my gaze meets Raheem's, my heart pounds in my chest.

We haven't talked since our engagement, just exchanged a few random texts. I told him I was busy studying for finals. (If I'm honest with myself, I needed a little space.)

"*As-salaamu alaykum*, Brother Adam and Sister Sharifa." Turning to me, he gives me his full attention, like I'm the only person on earth. "Sunshine," he says in the husky voice I've missed. "You're so beautiful today."

Tingles erupt on every inch of me.

Mom stands between the living and dining room, a sly grin teasing her face. She and my dad return Raheem's *salaam* in unison.

"*Wa alaykum as salaam*, Raheem." I grip the sides of my olive-green maxi dress. "Thank you. You do, too." It slips out like we're here alone.

"My fiancée thinks I'm beautiful. It's my lucky day."

Trying to hide my embarrassment, I focus on the early-morning sunshine cascading through the window.

"Raheem, where's your mom?" My dad is the first to ask.

"She had another meeting and couldn't make it. But she asked me to give Fatima this." He grips a slim rectangular box. "An early graduation gift."

Jameela Harris is giving me gifts now? I can't help but arch one eyebrow.

Ignoring this, Raheem turns toward my mom. "Sister Sharifa, something smells delicious. I'm glad to be here and glad that I could contribute in a small way."

Contribute? What's he talking about?

"I made some of Fatima's favorites. You two can sit on the couch while my husband finishes setting the table." My mom half-skips past my dad into the kitchen.

My fiancé sits on the couch and pats his hand on the space to his left.

I manage to sit and face him but keep a cushion between us.

"There's about to be a ton of changes for both of us, but I came here this morning to show you how committed I am to starting our lives together the right way."

His strong jaw and creamy brown skin pull me into a cage fight between my sense and my sensibilities. (See, I learned something in English class.)

I'm not sure what he means. Glancing over my shoulder, I catch my dad's gaze on us. I wonder, briefly, which one of us my fiancé is trying to impress.

Raheem hands me the rectangular box he brought with him. "I'd love for you to accept this," he says, loud enough for my parents to hear. "It was my grandmother's."

The significance of this present hits me like a sledgehammer. Holding it in shaky hands, I lift the lid. Inside, a gold necklace with a heart locket greets me.

"It's beautiful," I whisper. My fingertips trace the outline of the charm. "I'd be honored to wear it."

"Breakfast is ready," Mom announces as she strides back into the room. "You opened your gift, Fatima! What is it?" She rests her hand on my shoulder, sounding more eager than me.

I hold the box up to her. Her loud gasp rings in my ears. "It's gorgeous. Do you like it?"

Is she blind? The words don't leave my mouth. I can't remember the last time Dad bought her any fancy jewelry.

"Sister Jameela gave it to me," I tell her. "It belonged to Raheem's grandmother." My chin quivers at how special this gift actually is. Daring a peek at my fiancé, I remember to say, "Please thank your mother for me."

The breakfast goes by in a blur as my dad and Raheem talk about his upcoming first year of law school. This is happening.

We're a real couple.

Like he can read my mind, my fiancé catches my eye and puffs out his chest.

"As long as both your parents agree, Fatima, would you like to have dinner with me? It would be a nice ending to your special day."

Both of them nod their heads. Raheem is like the Pied Piper of parents, I swear.

I giggle like a middle schooler. Embarrassing. "Sure! Where do you want to eat?"

"It's your big day. We'll go anywhere you'd like." It's the perfect thing to say. My dad's grinning.

My mom gets up from the table. "Adam, can you help me clear the table? These two might want a few minutes to talk."

Then we're alone.

Raheem clears his throat. "Are you okay? I can tell something's up."

Wow, he can read me. My gaze drifts around the empty dining room, then returns to him. "I'm fine, it's just weird. My parents have never let me go anywhere alone with a guy."

Raheem laughs. "Have you ever been engaged before?"

"Of course not!"

He laughs louder at my fake frown.

After a quick glance toward the kitchen, his hand cups my

shoulder. "Don't worry, Gorgeous. It means most of your important firsts will be with me."

Heat works its way up my spine at his insinuations. Or maybe it's just my dirty mind.

My remaining doubts melt away like semisweet chocolate chips left in a hot car. I recognize my future . . . and he's close enough to touch.

Then Raheem pushes his chair back and stands.

"Sunshine, I have a client in an hour. I'll be thinking about you until we see each other after the graduation later." Anyone would forget their own name staring at the twinkle in his eyes.

My parents rejoin us as I get up from the table.

He shakes his head. "I've been here enough times. You don't need to walk me to the front door." Raheem turns in my dad's direction. "Please email me Fatima's final dowry list."

He nods. "InshaALLAH, I will send it to you tomorrow."

I take a few brave steps forward. "Thanks again for the necklace, Raheem. It's so beautiful."

"Something beautiful for my beauty," he says, his deep voice waking up something low in my body. "See everyone this afternoon. *Salaam.*"

The moment the door closes behind him, my mom is all over me.

"Fatima, Sister Jameela giving you a necklace that belonged to her mother means she's accepted you. MashaALLAH, it's such a blessing!" She clasps her hands. "Why aren't you smiling?"

"Ma, I'm happy." I grab the black jewelry box and hold it against me.

She walks back and forth across the living room carpet. "I don't understand. A quality young man wants to marry you and will support any career you choose but you're still too quiet. What will make you happy? What *more* do you want?"

A moment to absorb all the changes happening.

A minute to process them.

A day to be happy in the moment.

Instead I'm glued to my spot on the carpet as her criticisms sink in.

"Why don't you go upstairs and come up with a couple of restaurant ideas? Your mom and I will take care of the kitchen." My dad's suggestion ends the one-sided conversation. I accept the escape route he's offering me.

By two o'clock in the afternoon, almost everyone important to me is inside one of the smaller auditoriums in the convention center. It's packed with our charter high school's small graduating class: 200 seniors in red robes and black caps.

I did it.

For a moment my sadness takes over, because Zaynab's fancy private-school graduation is in thirty minutes and there's no way we could attend each other's. InshaALLAH, she'll be with me this Saturday at the baking competition's semifinal round, though.

And even if she's not here physically, Zaynab still floods my phone with text messages.

Congrats Girl. You did it!

Followed by, **You're going to KILL IT this weekend** 🔥 🧁

I text her back. **No, congrats to US!!!** 🌿 🌿 🤍

When I make it to my cheering section, Raheem presents me with a dozen long-stemmed red roses. "Congratulations, Sunshine."

Even my future mother-in-law is smiling. "MashaALLAH, Fatima, I'm so proud of you. My mother's necklace suits you. Welcome to the Harris family."

My dad snaps a picture of this Kodak moment.

I run my finger over the heart locket, my eyes filling with happy tears. It's a day closer to living out my dreams.

fourteen

The next morning, my phone is blowing up with texts from Zee.

I need your help. Mom told me to ask if you could bake for her staff mtg this Friday. With graduation, I forgot. She's pissed I screwed up! Can you stay over tonight & make the desserts here? She'll pay you. Text me ASAP!

After calming her down, I'm up and dressed by the time my parents wander into the living room for *Fajr* prayer.

"Wait a minute. Who are you? My daughter never beats her parents getting up before sunrise," my dad teases.

"Why are you awake and so alert this morning?" My mom's the more direct one.

"Sarah Baker needs some desserts for a staff meeting tomorrow and Zee forgot to tell me. She wants me to make everything over there, but I'm more familiar with our kitchen. I'll just bake here and bring the goodies to her house." No need to mention it's great practice before the semifinal round. "Zee asked me to sleep over tonight—is that okay?" I cross my fingers behind my back.

My parents exchange glances.

"I don't mind. Be sure to take your house keys because tomorrow I'm working a twelve-hour shift at the hospital." She turns to my dad. "Adam?"

He finishes laying out the prayer rugs. "My schedule's normal for the rest of the week until Saturday. The dealership has a required safety training in the afternoon."

I can't stop smiling at my luck. It's last minute but it's another paying baking job. My first few days after high school are great.

Now's the time to take a risk.

"Don't forget I'm hanging out with Zee all day Saturday, too. We might go see a movie at Century Rio." It's not a lie. I *am* hanging out with Zaynab—she and Amber are driving me to the convention center for the competition.

"I remember," Mom adds.

We complete our prayers. My mom goes back to bed while my dad gets ready, then leaves for work.

I head into the kitchen. I'm making a double batch of both cranberry-orange muffins and milk chocolate fudge for Sarah Baker's staff meeting. Once all the ingredients for both desserts are spread out on the counter, I soak four cups of dried cranberries in water.

With my oven preheating, I sift together salt, flour, sugar, and baking powder into our largest mixing bowl. Then I combine the eggs, orange juice, and canola oil in a glass measuring cup. Using a dinner fork, I form a well in the dry ingredients and pour the wet ingredients in. After the batter is just mixed, I fold in the drained cranberries and fill each of the twenty-four muffin cups.

By the time my mom joins me in the kitchen, twenty-four goodies are cooling on two large wire racks. "*Salaam*, Fatima. Oh, they smell delicious." She picks up a muffin and sinks her teeth into it. "MashaALLAH, these are delicious! Sarah is fortunate her daughter's best friend loves to bake."

"Ma, I'm the lucky one. I'm being paid for this."

"What else are you making?"

"Milk chocolate fudge with toasted pecans."

"I love your fudge."

"When do you eat fudge?" I stash the muffins in two round pie takers, then put them in the fridge.

My mom's gaze stays on me while I'm working. "Sometimes I nibble on a fourth of a square."

I roll my eyes and start chopping pecans. Once that's done, I pour sweetened condensed milk and chocolate chips into a copper pot on low heat and stir. After the mixture combines and becomes silky smooth, I take the pot off the burner, stir in the nuts, and, the last step, pour it into two eight-by-eight parchment paper–lined baking dishes. I smooth out the edges and put the fudge in the fridge to set.

"Fatima, Jameela texted me a minute ago. She wants to stop by in an hour to tell us some important news."

"Important news? Did she say she needed me here for this conversation?" I'm three seconds away from washing all my baking dishes. "Zaynab's picking me up soon."

Ma puts her breakfast plate in the sink. "Find out from your friend what time she'll be here. Then take a shower and put on a nice dress for the woman who will, inshaALLAH, be your mother-in-law one day. And before you ask, I have no idea what Jameela is going to say."

I take the stairs two at a time. Zee says she can't pick me up for at least an hour anyway when I text her, so I'll be here when our guest arrives.

The next forty-five minutes fly by. Dressed and ready with my face clean and moisturized, I rejoin my mom in the living room. I'm wearing black wide-leg pants and a white button-down that skims me mid-thigh. At the last minute, I remember to put on the gold necklace that belonged to Raheem's grandmother, too.

"Please fix your hair." Sharifa Tate misses nothing.

I bring it into a ponytail and secure it with a huge white scrunchie. "Done."

The doorbell tells me my time is up. No need to worry, right? She likes me now.

My mom opens the door with a casual smile. No one outside my family has a clue the amount of stress-induced cleaning this place goes through every time we have visitors. "*As-salaamu alaykum*, please come in."

Sister Jameela looks fierce in her navy-blue suit, her white and cream hijab tucked inside a cream blouse. She comes inside and steps out of her black heels. "*Wa alaykum as salaam.*" When she does notice me, it's like I'm an afterthought. "I'm glad you're here as well, Fatima."

"Nice to see you, too," I say, and I kinda mean it. She's not my *favorite* person, but we need to find a way to connect—after all, her son and I are engaged. "Is Raheem okay?" My fingers play with the engagement ring on my left hand.

"Yes, he's fine. Let's sit in the dining room. I have a few things to show both of you." She lifts up the leather briefcase in her hand and leads the way.

Wow, our guest is bossy.

My mom is the last one to sit down. "Jameela, would you like something to drink?"

Sister Jameela shakes her head. "No, thank you." This woman

is used to everyone waiting on her—even the force of nature that is Sharifa Tate is expected to accommodate her. *Damn*. This will be my fate, too.

"The day my son bought your yellow diamond, I decided to host your engagement party." She pulls an iPad from her briefcase. "I've already booked the hotel space, arranged for the menu, and found the perfect dress for Fatima."

"I think a party is a great idea," my mom says, her bubbly tone bizarre to me. "How can we help?"

Whoa, whoa. Wait.

I'm dizzy trying to digest Sister Jameela's *surprise*. Of course my mom loves the idea.

Raheem's mom has a gleam in her eye. "I'm glad you're okay with my planning it, Sharifa." She points to flower arrangements and table settings in her pictures folder. "I will need your guest list soon. I'll be in Denver this weekend, but my party planner must send out any last-minute invitations by Monday at the latest."

I don't believe what I'm hearing. "You've done all this already? Without telling me?" My mom glares at me, but I can't stop. "What's the date? I might be busy then. Is my presence even necessary?" Anger seeps through my pores.

"Fatima, that's enough!" my mom's sharp tone silences me. "Let her explain."

"Thank you, Sharifa." Sister Jameela's smug smile turns my stomach. "Two weeks from Saturday, the event will be held at the Sheraton Uptown. It's a wonderful opportunity for my son to network with some of my business associates and the local community leaders. Everyone I've spoken to is excited to meet Raheem's fiancée."

Being on display isn't my idea of a party. "How much is all this going to cost?" I demand.

Sister Jameela locks eyes with me. "I don't want your family to worry about anything. Since this was my idea, I insist on paying for the entire thing."

This woman is a total elitist and doesn't care who knows it.

Just because my parents can't afford a fancy party doesn't mean she shouldn't ask us first or include any of us in the planning. What is this, *The Crown*?

I sit there silent as stone. Both moms go over every single detail of my engagement party. Neither one of them asks for my opinion or brings me into the conversation.

Knowing I might lose it, I mumble, "Be right back." I race upstairs before either of them can object.

I text Zee an SOS: **HELP!!!! Come save me!! Explain later**

I shove a change of clothes and a toothbrush into a small duffel bag; anything else I need, I'll borrow. I race downstairs, my feet touching carpet the instant the doorbell rings. I yank open the front door to see my prayers have been answered.

"Hey, I'm *so* ready to go. Let me get your mom's desserts and we can leave."

"Well, hello to you, too," Zee teases.

She steps inside and freezes in the entryway. The two moms zoom in on her. "*As-salaamu alaykum*, Zaynab. How's your mother?" my mom probes, nosy as ever.

While she answers my mom's questions, I hurry into the kitchen, grab the fudge and muffins from the fridge, and rush back to the front door. "Ma, we've got to go. I'll text you my very short list for the party. Nice to see you again, Sister Jameela."

We're out the door and halfway to Zee's car before either of us speaks. "Why is Raheem's mom at your house?"

It's so screwed up, part of me doesn't want to tell her.

"She decided the day Raheem proposed to throw us an engagement party. Everything's already planned: the hotel, the food, the flowers—all of it's done. The invitations were mailed before she even told me about it—me, her son's fiancée!" An ugly truth fractures my heart. "To her, I think I'm just a prop to help launch his political career."

"Whoa. Damn." We're in the car and pulling out of the complex before she asks, "So where's my invitation?"

I'm too upset to laugh.

I fish my phone out of my purse and shoot my mom a list of three names. "Expect an invitation for you and your mom. I put Amber down for one, too. Things still good between the two of you?"

Zee doesn't complain about things. It takes a million questions for me to get the really personal stuff out of her. We just do *not* go there when it comes to her relationship.

"We're good," is all she says.

I need more. "What does that mean?"

Zaynab glares at me. "It means Amber and I haven't had any major arguments and the last time we were together she had a smile on her face."

"That wasn't so hard." I hesitate. "Has she ever said you're bossy?"

Her eyes narrow. "Why would she?"

She's forcing me to say what we both know is true. "Because you're super fearless and opinionated, and your girlfriend is bubbly and happy." I'm pushing it, but I continue. "Do you think . . .

sometimes . . . Amber goes along with things because you want them?"

"Where's all this coming from?" Zaynab is too smart not to know why I'm asking. "Is this about *my* relationship—or *yours?*"

"Never mind, Zee."

By the time she parks in her driveway, we've agreed we're binge-watching *Criminal Minds* and ordering Vietnamese food. After stashing the desserts in the fridge, I sink into the chestnut-colored leather couch in the family room while Zee handles dinner via her phone; once our order is placed, she joins me. "So . . . when's your fancy party?"

"Two weeks from this Saturday." I pull up my phone's calendar and count. "How is it okay to give the bride-to-be less than three weeks' notice for her own engagement party?"

She shrugs. "The Harris family is über-wealthy, so maybe they do shit like this all the time. Did you ask his mother what's on the menu? What if the hotel food is nasty? Or bland?"

A worse thought pops into my head. "Zee, what about the desserts? I'll freak out if she ordered some dry, tasteless cake!" I open my messages. "I'm texting my mom. Make *du'a* she can convince Sister Jameela to take me to the bakery and let *me* choose."

"Do I have to wear something bougie to this party of yours?" Zaynab reaches for the remote and signs into Netflix. "When are you going shopping?"

"Ugh . . . I don't have to. My future mother-in-law already bought me a dress." My anger surges back. "Why would she think I'd be *okay* with every decision being made for me?"

Zee nods. She always has my back. "That lady is way too controlling. Doesn't she want the two of you to get along after

149

the wedding? Why's she poisoning the well?" She scrolls through *Criminal Minds* and clicks on the current season. "How does Raheem deal with her?"

"No idea." Their master/servant relationship turns my stomach—I'm beginning to think that my fiancé lets his mom control too many parts of his life. In our faith, respect is due to every mom, but Sister Jameela is too much.

Speaking of. Time to confess about my talk with him.

I let out a steadying breath. "So . . . I told my fiancé about making it into the semifinal round."

Without taking her gaze off the screen, Zaynab says, "I'm proud of you. Next you can bring up the woman and baby he was with at the strip mall. Let's find out if your Muslim Prince Charming is remotely worthy of you."

The saliva in my mouth dries up. I'm not sure I have it in me to confront him.

I'm sure it was nothing, anyway. She's probably wrong. I bet it wasn't even him. It couldn't have been him.

We're at the end of our third episode when Zaynab's mom gets home, our takeout containers littering the coffee table in front us, the episode's credits rolling.

"*As-salaamu alaykum*, lovelies. It smells like lemongrass and ginger in this kitchen, and I'm starving. Did you remember to order something for me, Zee?"

"It's in the fridge."

Sarah Baker isn't in her regular business clothes; instead she's sporting a white tee and black jeans. She pulls out her labeled dinner. "Thank you for writing my name on this, Fatima. Are those my desserts I see in here?"

"*Wa alaykum as salaam.*" I nod even though her back is facing me. "Yes."

"Mother, how do you know *I* didn't put your name on your food?" Zaynab's voice is tinged with fake hurt.

Ms. Baker turns and glances between the two of us. "I know and love you, daughter, and that's not your handwriting." Her gaze finds me. "Fatima, thank you for your baking. I'll leave a business check on the kitchen counter for you before I go to the office tomorrow."

Zaynab's phone rings. "It's Amber. I'll be back." She rushes down the hallway toward her bedroom.

Sarah, armed with a plate of sweet and sour catfish, claims the couch cushion her daughter left. "So how are you, Fatima? I'm glad Mr. Harris didn't skimp on your engagement ring. It's exquisite."

Afternoon light illuminates my yellow diamond as I stretch my hand out toward her. "It's kinda hard to believe it's mine. I'm just trying to remember it's real."

She puts her plate down. "Make sure you get what you need from this marriage. Don't be swayed by a physical attraction to Raheem—or by his family's wealth. If the two you don't connect as people, with similar values and visions for the future, no amount of money will fix that."

It's always been easy to be honest with my best friend's mom.

"But I'll have to change myself to fit in with them, won't I?" I hug one of the burnt orange throw pillows.

Sarah grasps my hands in hers. "Fatima, we all change and grow, but we shouldn't change ourselves for other people. Please stay the kind and genuine young lady I've watched you become.

Do that and no matter what obstacles you face, you'll come out of it the same wonderful person you are now."

Her positivity is sweet as a gentle wave, but it's nothing compared to my raging river of self-doubt.

"But what if the way I am right now"—I point at my beat-up Adidas and jeans—"isn't enough?" I think again of Sister Jameela's engagement party plans: the expense, the glitter, the huge flower budget, the high-class guest list. I'm nothing like that.

Her frown is immediate.

"If anyone tells you that or makes you feel that way, *you're* not the problem. Tell me the truth: Has Raheem ever said anything of the kind?"

I shift. "No, nothing. We're just . . . so different. Our lives."

A loud phone alarm ends our conversation. She jumps up. "I'm so sorry, but I have an important business call to take. If you want to talk again, Fatima, I'm always here for you."

She leaves me alone with my thoughts.

"What if I'm not special enough for him?" The thin whisper I hear is mine.

No one answers.

fifteen

I'm trying to stop myself from freaking out.

Breathe, Fatima. Breathe.

The semifinal round of the baking competition is today. Being back here, I'm convinced I should've practiced more. My limbs tremble.

Amber pats my arm. "Fatima, don't be nervous. Zee always tells me you make the best apple pie in town. Show the judges that!"

"You got this," my ride-or-die chimes in. "Pretend you're baking for my mom's office or your parents."

The two of them walk toward the ballroom hand in hand, and I head in the opposite direction—to the drab, stuffy conference room where us contestants wait to compete.

Here we go again.

Brian waves me over and I sit beside him in the back. That helps. (I see Alicia has selected a seat up front—figures.)

Chef Erica smiles at us. "Okay, students. Congratulations on making it to this round. The ten of you impressed the judges with your quick breads, and that's why we can't wait to taste today's apple pies." Scanning the room, she asks, "Are there any questions?"

No hands go up.

Brian leans close and whispers, "Are you okay?"

I nod, even though my gaze keeps landing on the exit sign. "I'm scared I'll burn the crust I've made a million times."

"As long as we do better than Alicia, it's a win in my book."

I cough back a laugh.

"Time to follow me, students," Chef Erica announces. Her calmness ramps up my nervousness.

We walk after her. I'm the last one to enter the ballroom.

My best friend and I must have a strong connection, because somehow Zee and Amber are sitting in the chairs closest to my baking station. Amber waves and gives me a thumbs-up.

I repeat, "It's just an apple pie," to myself while checking all the ingredients are in my assigned mini fridge.

Chef Erica introduces herself to the audience and explains the rules for the semifinal round, but I tune out both her and the spectators' applause. Her last words are the only words I hear.

Ready, set, bake.

Time to get to work!

First, I follow the dough recipe I've practiced; then, when my two disks of dough are stashed in the fridge, I do the filling. The apples are peeled and sliced, mixed with sugar, lemon juice, cinnamon, a sprinkle of flour, and a dash of salt—then, the whole bowl is set aside. After preheating my assigned oven, it takes me twenty minutes to roll out both disks, line the pie plate with the first, put in the apple mixture, and top it with the second. I trim and crimp the edges of the upper layer of dough, then brush the pie with a light egg wash. Cutting five vent holes in the top crust is the last step.

I peek at the audience.

Big. Mistake.

My fiancé is sitting in the same row as Zaynab.

Even with two empty seats between them, they're talking, and they no longer notice me at all. I'd pay a million dollars to hear their conversation.

This can't be good.

Focus, Fatima!

I set my pie in the preheated oven, then make sure every inch of my baking station is spotless. The deep aroma of cinnamon and sugar brings me good memories of baking successes in my house. Finally, I take my pie out and set it on the counter to cool.

"Are you almost finished with your dessert, Miss Tate?" The volunteer assigned to me is standing right next to my station. "There's only a few minutes left."

His words fan the anxious flame inside me.

Fishing a pair of oven mitts out of my tool caddy, I move my apple pie from the cookie sheet onto the display platter.

"I'm done!"

And with not a second to spare, because Chef Erica announces, "All students should have their pies on the platters at the edges of their stations. A volunteer will now escort our student bakers back to the Zia Room to wait while the judges taste each entry."

Making homemade caramel is less nerve-racking than sitting here.

I pick up one of the CNM baking program pamphlets scattered around the conference room to distract myself—but Brian falls into the chair beside me. "Hey, Fatima, how do you think your pie came out?"

A burst of nervous laughter escapes. "*No* clue. On the outside, it was the right golden brown, but you can't really tell until you cut into it." I flatten my lips. "What about you?"

He runs his hand through his thick, perfect curls. "My crust cooked too long, but I hope that means not a lot of liquid oozes out when they cut into the pie." Brian scoots his chair around to face me. "I bet you practiced every day."

His teasing gives me a reason to grin. "Think we're ready for the *Bake Off* tent yet?"

He laughs so loud, the other semifinalists sneer at us.

"I'd be better off if they wanted a drip cake. Having to decorate with fondant or buttercream and make it look professional—that's way over my head." Brian's face freezes and he taps my shoulder. "Someone's trying to get your attention."

"Fatima!" Raheem is standing in the doorway.

I almost trip over my own feet rising and rushing to him. "You shouldn't be here." My chef coat is suddenly limp with sweat. *He's the last person I want to see me like this.*

He ignores me and picks up my left hand. "Where's your ring?"

"I'm sorry. It's against the rules to wear jewelry."

"Didn't realize you were a stickler for the rules." Raheem holds my gaze, hard, and I don't know what to say. We both know I'm not.

"I, um . . ."

My fiancé rubs my shoulders. "Fine. Well . . . don't be nervous, Sunshine. I'll be here when they announce you made it into the final round. I believe in you." Raheem points in Brian's direction. "Who's your friend?"

Uh-oh. *Is that a hint of jealousy in his voice?* I'm not sure if I'm flattered or annoyed.

"Just another contestant," I reassure him. "How long have you been here? Were you watching the whole time?"

My little distraction works. Raheem refocuses on me. "Since the beginning. That guy with the stupid TikTok hair keeps staring over here. Maybe you should explain to him about us, so I don't have to."

Whoa. There's a slight growl under his words. My distraction failed. Even though I shouldn't, I squeeze Raheem's hand and I lie. "I will. Okay?"

"Just remember you're *mine*," he whispers. With a wink at me, he leaves.

Releasing a long breath, I tiptoe back and sit down beside Brian again.

He's staring at me. "Are you okay, Fatima? Who was that?"

Putting on yet another fake smile, I say, "That's Raheem, my fiancé."

"He's pretty intense." Brian messes his curls again. "He knows we're just friends, right?"

"Yeah, I told him."

"Is he okay with you having guy friends?" He's staring at the floor. "Can you even be friends with me in your religion?"

For a minute, I have no clue how to answer him.

"Don't worry. Raheem is just protective of me," I insist. "It's true I've never had a guy friend before. But we're baking buddies and there's nothing wrong with that!"

Hopefully my words reassure at least one of us.

Before the conversation can continue, Chef Erica comes back into the room. "I need all students to follow me back into the ballroom for the judges' announcement."

Brian smiles at me as we line up. We enter the ballroom single file, taking our reserved seats to wait for the verdict. A wave of nausea hits me; I don't dare move again, or I'll puke.

"Before I announce the five finalists, the other judges and I want to let you know how hard it was for us to choose between the apple pies. They were all so well made—each baker should be proud." Ericka points at our row of panicked faces. "If I call your name, please come stand to my right."

As if on cue, my palms dampen and I rub them down my lap. My heart pounds in my chest, and I glue my eyes to the wall of ovens.

"Our first baker to make it into the final round is Fatima Tate." My body goes motionless.

Did she say my name?

Raheem is out of his seat, clapping. Both Zaynab and Amber are yelling my name. I get up and take one shaky step after another until I reach Chef Erica. I hear nothing, but as my breathing slows, two other finalists join me.

". . . The next student also competed last year. Alicia Hutchins is our fourth finalist."

Alicia prances up to join us at the front of the room. I ignore her and cross my fingers, hoping Brian's name is called next.

The room quiets. Chef Erica clears her throat. "The last student to make it into the final round is Brian Aguilar."

The audience and I erupt in cheers as Brian stands and joins us. When he walks by me, we high-five each other.

"These five students will be back in two weeks for the final round of our Teen Baking Competition. Thank you all again for coming!"

Before I can run to *her*, Zaynab runs to *me*, wrapping me in a giant hug. "Girl, I knew you could do it!" she shrieks.

Zee doesn't get emotional often, so this moment means a lot to me. "Thanks for always believing in me," I whisper, squeezing her.

We walk back to Amber, whose cheesy grin is on display for all to see. "Fatima, I'm so happy for you! Zee says you never believe how good your desserts are—now you can't deny it!"

Zaynab embraces her girlfriend and laughs. "You're a total sap."

"Is it my turn to congratulate the finalist?" Raheem slips in next to me. "You did amazing, Sunshine—like I knew you would." He lifts my hand and kisses my bare ring finger.

Amber giggles, but Zaynab rolls her eyes.

Still, today can't get any better. *This* is the Raheem I agreed to marry. His earlier outburst—that had to be a blip.

"Are you hungry?" His hand skims my lower back and stays there. "Let me take you out to eat."

"Well . . ." Oh no. This is awkward. "I'd love to, but . . . Zaynab and I planned to—"

It's Amber who saves me. "We think you two should go out. This is the first time you have something big to celebrate as a couple. Right, Zee?" Zee's face is blank.

But getting to have dinner with my fiancé, alone, twice in a week? Can't lie. Works for me.

"Zaynab, your girl here is very kind. How about the three of you go out to dinner tomorrow night? I'll even pay." Raheem squeezes my hand. "You like Sadie's?"

"Great suggestion!" chirps Amber, hugging her girlfriend's arm. "Now, the two of you go have some fun!"

Amber should work for the UN. "You're the best," I tell her.

Even Zee's stone face cracks into a smile. "She is. And before you ask, yes—if your mom calls, I'll text you."

Raheem extends his hand to me. I glance back at Zee as I take it, unable to shake the feeling I'm looking between my future and my past.

Raheem pulls his car into the parking lot of the Melting Pot. I raise an eyebrow at him.

"You mentioned wanting to come here a few days ago. Making you happy is my job."

I squeeze his hand as we walk to restaurant entrance. He lifts our joined hands, staring at my engagement ring, which is back on my finger. "It belongs there," he says.

A guy with wavy black hair opens the front door. "Mr. Harris, please come in. We have your favorite table ready for you and your guest."

"She's more than my guest. Fatima is my fiancée."

"Congratulations!" He shakes Raheem's hand, then faces me, covering his heart. "Nice to meet you, Fatima. I'm Michael, the manager. Welcome."

Some Muslims have issues shaking hands with members of the opposite sex, but I'm not one of them. I guess he's trying to be respectful.

The manager shows us to a table with a reserved sign on it and leaves.

"Do you own this place?" I whisper to Raheem when we're alone.

Raheem spends the next thirty seconds scrolling through his

phone, a scowl creasing his brow. "No, *I* don't own it, but Mom and I both own stock in the real estate group that does."

"What's wrong?" I ask, crossing and uncrossing my arms over my chest.

He lays his phone on the table. "Nothing. Just preoccupied."

"About what?"

Instead of answering the question, Raheem changes the subject. "So . . . you and Brian are friends for real, huh?" His tone sharpens. "You were happy when the judges called his name."

"No, we're just—we're friendly. I don't know his life story or anything." I fiddle with my yellow diamond. "He stood up for me when another baker asked if my hijab went against the uniform rules."

His clenched jaw relaxes. "InshaALLAH, the next time I see him, remind me to thank him for looking out for my wife-to-be."

I force a smile. It doesn't sound like thanking Brian is what he's talking about.

Michael returns with our menus. Raheem doesn't ask me what I want before ordering half of the items listed. I scan the dining room while he does: we're the only customers in the restaurant.

The tension between us thickens until Raheem reaches out, intertwining our fingers. "Let's enjoy our time together, Gorgeous."

When the food arrives, every dish is so tasty—from the bread we dip in cheese fondue to the grilled lobster tails—that I want to lick my fingers clean. When it's time for dessert, Raheem holds a chocolate-dipped strawberry close to my mouth. "Let me feed you, Sunshine."

I scan the empty tables around us. "Um . . . okay." I've only seen this kind of thing in movies—I didn't think it happened in real life. I open my lips, and the sweet chocolate mixes with the tart strawberry. Heavenly.

"Sunshine, you've got something right there."

"Where?"

Before I can grab my napkin, Raheem runs his thumb under my bottom lip. "It was a drop of chocolate," he says. "Gone now."

His eyes focus on my mouth for so long, breathing becomes difficult. He closes the distance between us and joins his lips to mine. Our kiss deepens and every inch of my body is aflame.

I'm lost, pulled into a sea of growing desire.

Seconds before I self-combust, he pulls away. "Fatima," his deep voice grabs me, "will you go somewhere else with me?"

Tingles shoot up and down my arms. At this precise moment, I'd follow him to Mars. Without any hesitation, I nod.

A teeth-baring smile breaks out on his face.

In a blur, Raheem pays the bill and escorts me back to his car. We head north.

"Where are we going?" I ask.

He leans toward me, and I breathe in his sweet chocolate breath. "Patience."

I nibble on my bottom lip.

Twenty minutes later, Raheem stops in front of a spectacular Spanish-style house with a red-tile roof and a large, rounded arch entryway.

"We're here, Gorgeous."

"Where's here?"

"Home."

My heartbeat thuds in my ears so loud, I can't hear my own thoughts.

Raheem dashes out of the car, opens the passenger-side door, and leads me toward his front door.

"Is your mom here?" I ask.

"She's in Colorado," he replies, turning the key in the lock. "Shopping for our engagement party."

Should I be here? Am I really following Raheem into his house—alone?

He steps inside. I linger on the threshold.

"Come on. I promise I don't bite." He winks. "You trust me, don't you?"

We're getting married. Of course I trust him. It's expected, isn't it?

"He wasn't alone . . . Raheem was with a woman and a baby."

No. What Zee saw—it just can't be true. I decide to believe it's not. "Do I need to take my shoes off?" I ask.

Raheem shakes his head. "Not necessary. You know, we have a bedroom just for prayer. It's filled with Islamic books and Turkish rugs. No furniture at all."

The entrance hall is beautiful. There's a path of multicolored flower mosaic tiles lined by larger ceramic ones—the different shades of blue and orange are so beautiful, I don't want to walk on them. A wrought iron banister encloses the spiral staircase to my right. The walls are a soft cream, and a row of dark wood beams frame the super-high ceiling.

"This house is *amazing.*"

Raheem chuckles and grabs my hand. "Wait until you see the kitchen."

We walk into my dream space. Marble countertops; gleaming appliances; generous lighting; a huge sink; four barstools at a rectangular island, all made of a dark wood I don't recognize.

He points to the countertops. "Isn't marble the best stone for people who love to bake?"

"You know it is." I skirt around him and run my fingers over the off-white surface speckled with turquoise. "Your mom must be a great cook to have a kitchen like this."

My fiancé drifts over to me, a slight smile building on his face. "No. Jameela Harris doesn't spend a lot of time in here, but our housekeeper loves to cook." He slides a hand around my waist. "Can you imagine yourself baking cookies and cakes in a space like this next Ramadan? Once we're husband and wife, I'll give you the kitchen of your dreams." He turns me and cups my cheek. "Can I kiss you?"

Several flimsy layers of armor drop off me.

"*Y-e-s.*"

Our lips meet and our bodies press together. I missed being in his arms.

"Sunshine, can I tell you a secret?" He locks his gaze on mine. My voice doesn't work, so I nod. "I pledge to give us a great life. Fatima Tate, I love you."

I never thought someone would say those words to me.

"When I caught that . . . *Brian guy* eyeballing us, I knew it was time to tell you how much you mean to me." He takes a single step back. "We're bound to each other."

An idea pops into my head. It's more than words: it's showing Raheem my true feelings.

After a couple of seconds of thought, I'm okay with what I want to do. My fingers tremble as I reach up, remove my straight pins, and unwrap my hijab.

"Allow me." He reaches behind me and pulls my hair loose from my ponytail. His eyes drink me in. "Come with me, beautiful."

Raheem guides me down a long hallway. There's a door. I pause in front of it.

"We don't have to go in my bedroom if you don't want to." His rich baritone caresses my ear.

But my heart has already decided. I open the door, step over the threshold, and perch on the edge of his huge bed.

Raheem yanks his shirt over his head. My eyes are stuck on his smooth brown skin.

"You can touch me if you want to."

His invitation is *everything*.

And I really want to.

He takes hold of my hands, kisses each palm, presses them onto his powerful chest. His warm, smooth pecs are the best things I've ever touched. Our skin-to-skin contact awakens an intense need throughout my entire body.

"Let me help you with this, my love." Raheem slides off my jean jacket and reaches for the bottom of my white tee, easing it up and off.

My clothes land on his bedroom floor. My arms go up to cover my bra, but Raheem whispers in my ear, "Don't hide yourself from me. I want to see all of you." Awkwardly, I unhook it.

He presses me down, and I lay back onto his bed, underneath him. Unfamiliar heat floods me as I bathe in his scent, his fingertips tracing along my ribs.

Raheem kisses his way down my neck to my shoulder. "Fatima . . . do you want me to stop?"

Our eyes lock. We're already engaged and committed to each other. Does it matter if we sleep together now?

I pull Raheem to me. "Don't stop," I breathe.

sixteen

A watched soufflé doesn't rise.

Zee's only answered one of the last four of my texts. It isn't like her, but I know I can't obsess—I just have to wait. At least I'm going to see her tonight.

I change my outfit four times waiting for her to pick me up. Even though we were together yesterday, it feels like a lifetime ago. I'm not the same person anymore.

"Knock, knock." My mom appears in my doorway, and I freeze. Can she tell there's something different about me? Like . . . via mom radar?

Am I giving off no-longer-a-virgin vibes?

She points to the random clothes piled on my bed. "Is this a special occasion?"

"No—nothing special. Zee and I have been craving Sadie's, that's all." I yank a two-piece, light brown *Amira*-style hijab out of my dresser and slide it on. It matches my dark brown tissue tee and white jeans perfectly.

"Hmm." I can see her desire to clean growing as her eyes scan the room. "I'm trying to understand your sudden need to eat out all the time."

I shove my phone and wallet in my purse. "Ma, you're still in your scrubs. Why don't you just take a shower and relax? Do you want me to bring you some food?"

For the longest minute of my life, she stares into my soul. Offering to bring her takeout might have been too much.

"No . . . your dad went to Sprouts to get me sushi." She yawns. "InshaALLAH, text me by ten if you're not on your way."

By the time Zaynab pulls up, I'm already sitting on the curb outside the condo complex. Didn't make sense to give my mom further opportunities to ask probing questions.

"Hi!" I say as I jump in. "Thanks for the ride, as always."

Zee stiffens. "No problem."

Her reaction's off. "Are you okay?"

No answer. *Great start.* "Weren't you and Amber supposed to pick me up?"

Faster than it takes to burn brown butter, her expression changes from blank to pissed off. "Do you *see* her here?"

Oh shit. "Zee, what happened?"

"Nothing." She's facing me now, eyes filled with anger. "So what did Raheem and you do last night? I hope it was something *amazing*, since you blew me off."

A deep pit cracks open in my stomach. There's an issue with Amber, I can see that—but *I* upset her, too. Have I been self-absorbed lately?

Ding, ding, ding! We have a winner!

Zaynab slams on the brakes as we reach the restaurant. "Let's get this over with," she snaps, exiting the car before I'm out of my seat belt. Fighting back tears, I follow her inside. Amber waves at us from a corner booth.

"Yesterday was amazing, Fatima! Congrats again!" Amber is

all smiles as we slide in. "Did you and Raheem have a good time last night?" The curiosity in her voice is hard to miss.

"Yes." I fiddle with my engagement ring. "The Melting Pot. Delicious." My matter-of-fact answer is flat, emotionless.

"The perfect place for a romantic dinner!" Amber giggles. Embarrassment flares beneath my tissue tee as I remember the after-dinner activities. "My parents go there every year for their anniversary. Zee, you and I should go!"

Zaynab palms the table. "Maybe! After our parents stop fighting!"

The smile drops off Amber's face. Scanning the room, I notice we've caught the attention of two guys at a table near us.

"Keep your voice down," I warn Zee.

"You trying to shush me? I'll yell louder so everyone hears."

Ouch. Consider me told off. My focus shifts to the yellow tortilla chips and chunky salsa in the middle of the table.

"So because of *their* shit, I can't suggest a nice date to *my* girl-friend without her getting bitchy?" Amber snaps. She's never cursed around me before. Curling my shoulders forward, I do my best to disappear.

Zaynab glares at me. "Since you're here, Fatima, you're in this conversation. Amber's mom is pissed that we're having our joint graduation party at my house, and it's become this whole big stressful *thing*. She's rich, right? She actually asked me if our backyard was 'roomy' enough for 'an event.' Like this is a black-tie gala we're hosting!"

"My mom didn't mean it like that," Amber says, her voice soft.

Being shoved into the middle of a spat is the worst. "Do you two need a minute alone?" I ask, moving to the edge of my seat. I want to tell Zee about last night, but obviously it's not the moment.

"Fatima, please stay," Amber says. "You heard her side. Will you listen to mine, too?"

"Where's the waitress?" Zaynab complains. She sees the woman and snaps her fingers.

Grabbing a tortilla chip from the center of the table, I dip it in salsa and squeak out, "I'm listening, Amber."

She waits until I finish crunching. "My mom's new hobby is party planning. When I told her Zee and I wanted a double party, she got excited. I never told her she could host it! She wrote down theme ideas, and the next day, the entire thing was just . . . well, planned. So when she couldn't do it the way she envisioned it, she was super disappointed. She didn't mean to be insulting!"

"Aha." I spot a glimmer of hope. "So the bad energy between you and Miss Moody is because both of *your moms* want to host the same party? That's it?"

Amber runs her fingers through her shoulder-length red hair. "Yes."

A flash of light in the darkness. "This isn't even about you guys, then. And it sounds like a big misunderstanding. I don't think you should let it screw up your night."

"Exactly what I've been trying to tell her." Amber stares at her girlfriend. "I just need help getting it through her thick skull," she says, a smile building on her face.

"That's what best friends are for—all part of the package." Nudging Zaynab with my foot under the table, I ask, "Don't you have something to say?"

When her frown disappears, I know the storm has passed. "Okay, *maybe* my reaction was too much," Zee confesses, a drop of regret in her tone. "But to be fair to me, you know how much I hate drama. Watching them have it out, like, passive-aggressively . . . I cannot deal."

Watching them work this out, my mind wanders to Raheem. As a couple, we have no real back and forth, no discussion, I realize. We don't work through things the way Zee and Amber can. Most of the time he thinks he's right—and I end up agreeing with him.

Maybe it's the wealth difference. He's used to special treatment.

By the time the waitress brings our food, Amber and Zaynab are good again. My plate of gooey cheese enchiladas is smothered with green chile—exactly how I like—and the reconciled couple across from me is sharing a platter of chile rellenos and a chalupa. The last thing on the table is a wicker basket filled with sopapillas, golden brown and ready for a drizzle of honey.

"Amber, wait a sec—I haven't mixed it all together yet." Zaynab can't stop her girlfriend from stealing a spoonful of refried beans and stuffing it in her mouth.

A dollop of melted cheese stays on top of Amber's lip. Zaynab picks the food off and pops it in her own mouth.

Amber scrunches up her face. "You're so nasty. Why do I put up with her, Fatima?" She leans over and plants a kiss on Zaynab's cheek.

The scene in front of me brings me back to last night—Raheem rubbing chocolate from my mouth, everything. I take another bite of enchilada, the spice hitting my mouth in the best way.

"Aren't the two of you cozy?"

Imani appears beside our booth like a magician. She folds her arms across her chest, disapproval written on her face. I haven't seen her since graduation, and honestly, I was kinda hoping never to run into her again. Luck isn't on my side.

Tonight, her attention is locked onto my friends.

"Sarah Baker's daughter is deep into the *haram*. Your mother must be so proud," Imani accuses. Zee's hands clench the edge of the table. "I'm surprised you don't have a beer in your hand, Zaynab. Why not partake in more forbidden stuff?"

Amber whispers in Zaynab's ear, but Zee's hand is already balled up in a fist.

Miss Teenage Judgment Police scowls at me. "*As-salaamu alaykum*, Fatima. I'm surprised you're with these two. Do your parents know where you are and who you're with?"

Amber pleads with me. "Fatima, don't respond to her ignorance."

But I know Zaynab and there's only a few more seconds before she beats this girl down.

"Don't worry—I'll handle this." Scooting closer to the intruder, I reach up and snap my fingers at her eye level. "Imani, no one asked you to come over and interrupt our dinner. You're rude, obnoxious, and will never have what this couple does. Love is love, and who the Hell are you to say what's *haram*?"

My chest rises and falls. I've never been this mad. Maybe it'll be me beating her ass.

"Someone who lives for gossip and spreading half-truths about every teenager in our community has no room to say anything to anyone EVER."

Imani's face falls for a split second—but she recovers just as fast. "It isn't my fault your friend is astray and needs me to show her the right way to practice her faith." She strikes back. "Not everyone's *deen* is so weak."

Zaynab speaks up before I can. "You want to judge me? Does my best friend know your parents pushed the idea of you and Raheem getting married? They believed if they got the two of you together, your whole family would be set for life. How does it feel knowing Sister Jameela Harris didn't think you were good enough for the guy Fatima is now engaged to?"

I gasp—but I still lift up my left hand, so she gets an eyeful of my yellow diamond.

"*As-salaamu alaykum*, ladies. How's the food tonight?"

Raheem's arrival startles all of us.

Staring into his deep brown eyes has my mouth dry. *Why is he here?* Surreptitiously, he checks me out like he wants a repeat of last night. My body tingles as his familiar cologne brings it all back.

"*Wa alaykum as salaam.*" My shyness is returning.

"*Wa alaykum as salaam*, Brother," Imani greets him. "Your fiancée should choose better friends." She pivots, then storms off.

I move over and Raheem sits down beside me. Even here, even when I'm angry, the physical closeness is almost overwhelming to me. "What did I walk into?"

"A member of the teenage morality squad has a problem with my girlfriend showing me affection in public." Zaynab bangs her fist on the table. "Screw her!"

"Muslims in our community should mind their own business." My fiancé's tone is detached, but his words are accurate. "Don't you agree, Fatima?"

"Of course Imani should mind her business." Turning to Amber, I ask, "Are you okay?"

She's clinging to Zee's arm. "Maybe." Her smile is missing its usual spark. "Is that how most of the Muslim community would talk to us?"

"We're a new generation," Raheem reassures her. "That sounds like her parents' opinion. Many attitudes aren't so rigid. You'll find other Muslims who aren't offended by your relationship."

Zaynab whispers some magical words in her girlfriend's ear, and now they're both smiling. "Listen, if you two are good, we're heading out."

"You are?" I ask, my voice cracking. Both of their plates are more than half-full.

Raheem flags down a random waiter. "Can we get two to-go boxes and a menu please?"

After a few goodbyes, they leave with their boxes, pretty obviously to do more making-up and hashing-out in private. My fiancé seats himself across from me.

He takes my hand and interlaces our fingers on the table, stroking my thumb with his. Is it bad how much I like to touch him? Maybe this is just a sign I'm falling in love.

"Did you three have fun before I showed up?" he asks.

"Yeah, Amber's awesome. I'm glad they found each other. She smooths out Zee's hard edges, if you know what I mean." Swallowing down my nervousness, I ask, "Why are you here?"

"After last night, I wanted to check on you." Raheem's expression darkens, and he clears his throat. "Since we're alone, this is a good time for us to talk."

I raise an eyebrow at this sharp matter-of-factness.

"I'm not the kind of guy who wants to control who your friends are, but Zaynab throwing her life choices around in public concerns me."

Our eyes meet, and his are without anger. Something colder stares back at me.

I yank my hand out of his grasp. "What are you talking about?"

"Sunshine, don't misunderstand me. After law school, I'll work a few years, then run for city council," he explains without any emotion. "To have a chance of winning, I have to lock down the Muslim vote, and most of them wouldn't approve of a lesbian relationship in my circle. Appearances are important. You get that, right?"

The way he explains it sounds so logical. But it's not. He's a hypocrite—and, I realize, kind of a bigot.

Who *is* this guy sitting in front of me? The guy I shared my body with?

My gaze drifts to the window. A single streetlight battles the growing darkness.

Anger builds inside me. From a well I never tap.

"Do you think my having a best friend who's a lesbian would *hurt your political career*?" I scrutinize him.

Raheem's eyes go moon round.

"Are you a Black Republican or something?" I sneer. I can't stop shaking my head. "I can't believe you would say this to me. Clearly we don't know each other at all."

"Fatima, please don't misunderstand me. Zaynab is great, but I am thinking about the future I want to create for us. Trust me, and you'll see how amazing our lives will be."

A morsel of bitter laughter parts my lips. "How can I trust you?"

Raheem holds my gaze. "You did last night." I shiver: the words are frosty.

The waitress picks this moment to appear. "One veggie burrito."

He waves her away. "I need that and my fiancée's enchiladas to go now."

The woman's smile doesn't break. "Of course, let me get this out of the way, and I'll be back with your food packed in take-out boxes." She takes our plates and leaves. Working in the service industry must suck.

She returns with our food in separate to-go containers. I give Raheem the silent treatment as he drops a wad of twenties on the table. As I rise, he takes my hand again—and transfers a small jar onto my palm.

"Here, this was supposed to be a surprise." Now he's pouting. "I guess it's ruined now."

"What's this?" I lift it up, examining the label. "Wow. I've seen pastry chefs on YouTube use edible gold leaf before, but I've never tried it." My face softens a little. "Well. Thank you."

"Maybe you could decorate your final-round two-layer cake with it." Raheem presses his lips. "Assuming you even want me there."

He gets up and I trail behind him out to his car in silence.

I hate this tension between us, but I'm afraid to poke the bear and start another fight. Plus, I'm *not* the one in the wrong.

We're halfway to my house before Raheem speaks again. "Fatima, we're engaged." Impatience stains his words. "I want to spend the rest of my life with you—didn't I prove that last night? It's my responsibility to protect you."

Listening to him hurts my stomach. "Protect me from *Zaynab?* We've been best friends forever. She knew me first."

We stop at a yellow light. Glaring at him doesn't change anything—he's facing straight ahead.

"I'll always know you in ways she never will. I'm not ultra conservative, Sunshine, but there are some things done in the dark that should stay there . . . Don't you agree?"

Each word coming out of his mouth is tainted—almost threatening. And his arguments are total crap.

"You didn't say any of this when she covered for us last night," I throw back at him.

We pull into my complex and Raheem shuts off the car. "I like Zaynab, and I'm glad she's been a nice friend for you, but as your future husband, we need to agree *I'm* the person you go to first." His thumb traces the outline of my lips. "Is there really room in your life for both of us?"

Usually, his touch would be my undoing. But not tonight. I feel nothing in this moment.

Stop being such a coward.

I'm this close to demanding he tell me about the woman from the Mommy and Me class . . . but without proof, I chicken out.

But if Zaynab is brave enough to be her authentic self, despite our community's judgments, I *can't* shrink away from the truth about Raheem.

It might be time to find out what the Hell is going on there.

I let him lead me to my front door, but I'm still seething in silence.

Raheem whispers promises in my ear, things that usually make me blush. His breath caresses my cheek as he lowers his lips to mine. "Fatima, please don't worry. InshaALLAH, once we're married, we'll be too busy to think about minor stuff like this. I'll be in law school—and you'll be in culinary school."

He backs up a few steps then raises my hand and kisses my engagement ring.

Does he expect me to trade my friendship with Zaynab for the price of culinary school education and a privileged life? Is that what I'm doing?

"*Salaam*, Sunshine." Raheem winks before walking out of the courtyard.

I'm frozen on this spot. An avalanche of tears wells up in my eyes.

Raheem says he loves me. BUT. It's a huge BUT. More than one.

He doesn't trust me being friendly with Brian. He's questioning my relationship with my closest friend. He's holding my culinary education hostage, willing to provide it only if I do what he wants. I have no clue if his love is real, or if he's using the words and promises to control me. We're not even husband and wife yet.

What if this is just the start?

In the quiet of the courtyard, I let my tears fall.

seventeen

It's Tuesday morning, less than a week to go before my engagement party, and I'm in the tasting room of my favorite local bakery with both my mom and Sister Jameela to order a last-minute cake.

At least my future mother-in-law chose the best place. The scent of powdered sugar hugs me.

My fiancé's mother insisted we find a second cake, because "not everyone likes the German chocolate one" already on the menu. With her making all the decisions, I'm an outsider in the whole thing.

My mind keeps wandering back to my night with Raheem. It deepened our connection—at least I thought it did. It did on my end. But he really messed up at the restaurant, and he's been texting me less and less.

Could he be embarrassed we had sex?

Or maybe it was a test—and I failed it. Is it my fault we committed a sin?

"Fatima, try a piece of the Meyer lemon layer." The woman beside me *resembles* my mom, but her eagerness for me to eat a forkful of cake almost convinces me she's an imposter. "It's heaven in a bite!" she gushes.

I'm busy looking at the desserts instead of sampling them. My face is so close to the display case, my cheek grows cold. "You really want me to try all these flavors?" Reluctantly, I join Mom and Sister Jameela at their testing table and scan the menu in front of me. "A vanilla sponge with raspberry filling would be fine with me. No tasting required."

My mom nods. "I'm glad you know what you want." She gives me a knowing look. "You're right not to taste test. You don't want the dress Jameela bought you to be too tight."

I'm not in the mood. I fiddle with the hem of my hijab.

Sister Jameela eases her fork into the corner of the red velvet slice. "This one would be my choice."

"But it's my choice today, right?" I press.

Neither of them replies to the question.

Our consultant joins us in the tasting room. She's wearing a gray business suit and her hair is pulled back into a perfect gymnast bun. "Well, ladies, have you made a decision?"

I flip through their cake pictures without making a sound. It's obvious she's not asking me.

"We already have the German chocolate, so for the second cake I'd like to order a three-tier vanilla cake with a raspberry filling, covered in buttercream. Let's also add twelve dozen red velvet cupcakes with this luscious cream cheese frosting." Sister Jameela rattles off her order with an authoritarian air. "Can you have those additions ready for this Saturday?"

The tight smile on the consultant's face evaporates, then returns. "Normally, we'd need at least a month, this being the busy graduation season. But you're a very special customer, Mrs. Harris." Her smile stretches almost to the breaking point. "I'll make sure all the desserts are perfect and delivered on time to the engagement party."

Everyone's forgotten the bride-to-be even exists.

I clear my throat. "Is there any way I can come back and watch as they decorate the desserts for our event?" My mom's mouth drops open but that doesn't shut me up. I'd kill for an hour in a real working kitchen. Any help I can get before the final round of the competition would be great. "I'd love to find out which pastry bag tips the bakers use to create their frosting designs."

"Ah . . ." Our consultant is speechless for at least thirty seconds. "Let me ask." She speed walks out of the room.

"Jameela, please excuse my daughter," my mom apologizes for me. "Baking is her hobby and she's obsessed with it."

"No need to say anything, Sharifa." Sister Jameela turns her attention to me from across the table. "Fatima, I'm sure my son could find a local pastry chef to give you decorating lessons once the two of you are settled after the wedding."

The consultant rejoins us. "I spoke to the store manager, and for liability reasons, we're not allowed to have non-employees in our kitchen. I'm so sorry, Mrs. Harris." She's speaking to my future mother-in-law. Typical.

Is this a glimpse of my future?

Sister Jameela nods. "Thank you so much for asking. I'll meet you at the cash register." She gets up, turning to us. "As soon as the arrangements are finalized, I'll take you both home."

When they're gone and we're alone, my mom starts in on me. "Fatima, you put that woman in a terrible position. Yes, they're filling a rush order for Sister Jameela, but that doesn't mean they can break the rules for you!" She rubs her temples. "What were you thinking?"

I tap my fingers against the tabletop. "Are we done? I just thought it was worth a shot. I have a training session with Raheem in less than two hours, so we'd better go."

Her eyes gleam. "Well . . . it's good you're exercising on a regular basis. This summer is the beginning of so many great things for you."

I hope she's right.

My mom pulls into the gym's parking lot. "Have a great session. I'm on my way to Walmart. Do you need anything? Face wash or Tampax?"

My breathing hitches as I do some mental math. "No, I'm good. Thanks." Armed with my duffel bag, I head into the gym's lobby.

Oh no. I've always hated non-baking math, but I can count.

The bodybuilder at the registration desk checks the computer screen after I swipe my membership card. "Are you Fatima Tate?"

"Yes." Soon, I might hate myself.

"Raheem Harris, your trainer, is running forty-five minutes late with his clients. Would you like his next appointment in an hour or to reschedule on a different day?"

"I'll be back in an hour." My feet take me outside, and after a quick text to my mom, I lean up against the side of the building clutching my phone.

I double-check to confirm my suspicions. According to my calendar app, my period is a week late.

This can't be happening. My life will be over before it starts.

I'd pay big money to get that stabbing pelvic pain that always comes on the first day of my cycle. The paper-thin hold I have on my emotions dissolves, and I cry waves of tears into my hands until nothing more comes out.

I know what I have to do. My new destination is up ahead, marked with a bull's-eye.

The grass under my feet is halfway brown. A small lizard scurries away from me, probably sensing the trouble I'm in. I am doing the one thing you *never* want to do as an unmarried Muslim seventeen-year-old.

I don't let my eyes wander or meet anyone's gaze, but with each step I take toward Target, my shame grows. A positive pregnancy test will put an *end* to my dreams of culinary school. I fight the urge to run home, curl into a ball, and refuse to leave my bed.

Why the Hell didn't Raheem and I wait?

It's not like we didn't know there's a chance of pregnancy every time you have sex, even if it's your first time, even if it's only once. (My seventh-grade health teacher made sure I would never forget that information.)

One moment of weakness could bring shame on my family forever.

Steeling myself, I enter Target and grip a red plastic basket. A lump grows in my throat as I turn left into the personal care aisle—and almost crash into a store employee.

For a second, his face contorts, but then his *customer-is-always-right* mask goes back on. "Hi! Can I help you find anything?" He's a twenty-something guy wearing the regulation red polo and tan khakis, and he even gives me a half-smile.

Does he know why I'm here? Can he tell I'm not a virgin?

Get a grip. I doubt he lurks around this aisle to count how many teenage girls have to choose between Clearblue Easy and First Response. He's not Imani.

Wouldn't she love to see me now?

"No, I'm good." The pregnancy tests sit on a shelf right behind his head, so I turn and grab a box of Always. I drop it, with a thud, into my basket.

He means well, but he needs to find another customer to help.

One, two, three, four steps and he's around the corner.

I'm alone. After a couple of minutes staring at my options, I glance up and down the aisle one last time, then shove the two-test pack under the box of pads already in the basket. Super sneaky.

Time to go. My fingers won't stop trembling.

To distract myself, I wander through the baking section and stuff a roll of parchment paper in my basket. As I reach one of the self-checkout lanes, another helpful store employee approaches me.

"Did you find everything you were looking for today?"

Avoiding direct eye contact, I manage a weak smile. "Yes. Thanks." The moment she leaves to help the next customer, I pay for my items, double-bag them, and hurry out the automatic doors.

Don't lose it.

I'm trudging back down the hill to the gym. As soon as I reach it, I rush for the locker room.

How would I tell my parents they're going to be grandparents before the wedding day?

What if Raheem changes his mind and I end up a single parent at eighteen?

Stepping into a bathroom stall, I rip open my duffel bag, stuffing my Target purchases under my workout towel and sports hijab and leaving the bag close to bursting. After changing into my exercise clothes, I leave the stall, put the bag in an empty locker, and lock it away.

Should I tell him about the pregnancy tests?

I'm unsteady on my feet walking into the workout room.

And then I see it. I stop in the middle of the warm-up space, my mouth gaping open. The scene in front of me turns my stomach even more then the stench of dirty socks mixed with Axe.

Across the room, Raheem is standing beside a very beautiful woman. I'll never fill out an outfit as well as she does, no matter how many times I come to the gym and sweat.

She backs out of one of the arm press machines, letting her fingers trail across his bicep and staring at him like he's her personal eye candy. They're too far away for me to hear their conversation, but she must have cracked a joke, because my fiancé laughs. As she puts a hand on his chest, my body sways.

The world around me spins a little.

And instead of pulling away, *he tucks a stray hair behind her ear.*

"Excuse me. Are you finished using the warm-up area?" some random guy asks.

I shuffle forward, off the mats. "S . . . sorry."

At the sound of my voice, Raheem swivels in my direction. His eyes widen, knowing he's caught. "Fatima—wait!"

Run.

Not caring we're in public, I turn and bolt back into the women's locker room and hide in a bathroom stall.

Everything hurts—my pride, my self-esteem. Everything is ruined.

I can't even cry a single tear. I'm too numb.

Eventually, after who knows how long, my feet find their way out of the stall, and I splash lukewarm water on my face. Then I get my duffel bag out of the locker and text Zaynab. My fingers aren't working, really, so it takes a couple of tries to get the words right. **Help. Gym.**

Her reply is immediate. **Be right there. Wait for me outside.**

I speed past the registration desk toward the front door. My fiancé's standing in the lobby, waiting for me, but with my shoulders pushed back I walk past him. The sandalwood scent of his cologne strengthens—I know he's following right behind me.

"Fatima, why are you leaving without letting me explain?" Raheem tugs on my sleeve, but I yank my arm out of his grasp and keep moving. The dry heat of the June afternoon is no match for my anger.

He steps in front of me, blocking my path. "You owe it to me to at least listen," Raheem insists, his voice almost . . . menacing?

For a brief moment, his hard expression frightens me.

But I won't be stopped. "Leave. Me. Alone. I don't owe you a damn thing!" Pointing behind me in the direction of the gym, I tell him, "Go back to your *client*!"

He takes a step backward. "Sunshine, I can't let you leave without knowing where you're going. Your parents think I'm driving you home."

I wipe at the sweat beading on my forehead. "Zaynab's on her way."

"No. Let me finish up with my client, then I'll drop you off. We don't have to talk at all. I can wait until you're not angry anymore." The forced smile on his face doesn't fool me.

"Nope. Not going *anywhere* with you," I spit back at him.

Raheem inches closer—close enough to invade my personal space—and whispers, "Running to Zaynab isn't the answer. Do you really think she's the best person to give you advice about your relationship with your soon-to-be husband?"

My body stiffens. "Who cares what you think? Did you even mean it when you said you loved me?"

I push past him, booking it to the edge of the parking lot. My legs are wobbling, so I ease myself down onto the curb. Rocking back and forth helps, but my heart is still breaking.

Congratulations—if the tests are positive, that's the father of your first child.

The screech of tires and the slam of a car door force me back to reality.

"Fatima, are you okay? Did Raheem put his hands on you?" Zaynab's kneeling beside me.

I answer with my last ounce of strength. "Please . . . can we go now?"

"Totally. We're out of here."

eighteen

"Is your mom home?"

Now is *not* the time for any kind of parental conversation—no matter how chill Sarah Baker is.

"Don't worry, she's still at work."

Inside Zee's house, I make a beeline for the leather couch in the family room and curl up there. "Where did those come from?" I point at the two Starbucks drinks that materialize on the coffee table.

"You didn't even notice when we were in the drive-thru." Zaynab passes me a venti iced passion tea—my favorite. "Fatima, I need to know if he hurt you."

She folds her legs under her and sits on the floor, facing me. I've never seen her with such deep frown lines.

I suck in a breath and push it back out. "We . . . were both yelling, and . . ."

"FATIMA, you need to be straight with me. *Did he put his hands on you?*" She's focused on my every word and won't miss a thing.

Just tell her the truth.

"Zee, he didn't hit me. He wanted to talk, and he grabbed my arm—but I pulled away."

Her eyes are still narrowed, and I see conflict there. Then, softly: "Tell me everything."

Swallowing, I do. "I walked into the workout area . . . One of Raheem's clients was with him. She was touching him . . . Flirting for everyone to see. And he laughed. He touched her, too. He pushed some hair . . . behind her ear. He was all smiles until our eyes met. I ran and hid in the locker room and texted you."

My best friend inches forward. "He didn't try to explain?"

"No, he did. He followed me outside." I sip my iced tea but it's tasteless. "I wasn't interested in his excuses."

Zaynab stares out the large picture window into the backyard. "Has Raheem ever done this kind of shit before?"

I shake my head. "Maybe. But not to me."

Now she focuses in my direction. "Okay. This clinches it. It's *past* time for you to ask this guy about the lady and baby I saw him with. Or you can call off the engagement."

That's drastic. "Do you think I should?"

The refrigerator's ice maker disturbs the silence between us.

"Fatima, I've got an easy question for you."

I brace myself.

"Are you in love with him?"

Zee always asks the questions I'm not prepared to answer.

"It's important if the two of you are going to be *husband* and *wife*." I'm not sure Zee will ever approve of Raheem.

Which part should answer, my heart or my head?

"Our relationship was so smooth at the beginning." I drag in a breath. "It was perfect."

"Too perfect?" Zaynab suggests, her voice quiet.

"Maybe." I study her. "When did you get so wise?"

Zee laughs. "I was born old."

"Thanks for not leaving me stranded."

"Never." The fierceness in her eyes reinforces what I've always known. She'll always have my back.

I unwrap my hijab, then pull out my phone. I have no more energy to discuss this. *Redirection time.* "How are things between you and Amber? I like her, so don't screw it up."

My girl doesn't take the bait. "If you're hungry, we can order something. I'm getting a Pepsi. You want one?"

Before she runs into the kitchen, I raise my hand to stop her. "Zee, your vibe is off. What aren't you telling me?"

If my favorite couple is having issues, what hope even is there for me and Raheem?

Zaynab's gaze meets mine. "Amber doesn't want me to have to choose between being with her and being a part of the Muslim community. She can't stop thinking about the fucked-up stuff Imani said. I don't know how to convince her there's no choice to make."

"Do you want me to talk to her?"

"No."

I poke my lip out. "Why not? She might listen to me."

Zaynab ignores the question, gets up, and grabs two Pepsis from the fridge.

I glare at her until she comes back and sits on the couch. I wrestle both sodas away from her. "*Talk.*"

It's her turn.

"Fatima . . . I really like Amber. She's an amazing girlfriend. I want to be with her, no question. You know, since the fifth grade, my mom's always told me to only make friends with kids who will accept me, bitchy attitude and all. I keep my circle of Muslim friends small on purpose. Whether Amber and I are together or not, that isn't changing." She grabs a Pepsi out of my hand. "Don't worry about me. You have enough drama in your life."

"I always have room for your drama. Let's talk about it more later. But first, yeah, there's even more mess to share." I reach for my duffel bag, unzip it, and pull out the Target bag. I drop it in front of her on the coffee table.

"What the Hell is this?"

Silence. It's a gut-wrenching struggle to keep my hope from turning into despair.

"Is this for *you*?"

I want to explain, to say more than nothing, but I can't. Without warning, tears stream down my face. I wipe my cheeks with my palm and nod.

The ugly truth is out.

The longer Zaynab stays silent, the deeper I sink into internal quicksand. I hold my breath for as long as I can before pain forces a sob out of me.

"Shit."

My shoulders hunch over, bringing my chin to my chest. "What the Hell does this say about me?"

Zaynab gives me a minute. "You need to explain this to me. When did you two agree to do this?"

I clear my throat and meet her gaze. "We didn't . . . It just sorta happened at the Harris family home."

"Ha. You know that's not how that works. How did you even end up at his place?"

"He wanted me to see it."

"I see." She takes a swig of soda. "Do you love him?"

That question again.

"According to my mom, any girl would be happy to be matched with him. He's handsome, respectful, and from a good family. Raheem is every Muslim parents' dream."

"That's *not* the same as love."

"It could be the start." I know how naive I sound. "I don't know. I thought I did."

Zaynab forces out a fake cough. "It doesn't hurt he's rich enough to keep you in a professional chef's kitchen for the rest of your life."

I gulp down some Pepsi, the sugary drink giving me a dose of energy. "I have no idea how much money they have—I'm trying not to think about it. It scares me. They control people with it. And they'll expect me to change how I dress, who my friends are . . . who I am."

I remember the exact nanosecond when my fiancé questioned my most precious relationship: my friendship with Zee.

"First things first." Zaynab holds up the Target bag. "What are you going to do about this?"

"Crawl into a corner and hide?"

Zee laughs at my lame joke. "You can't make any decisions if you don't know."

"Maybe I should wait a week? I might not need the test." I'm afraid of the truth and I know it.

"What, and drive yourself *and me* crazy until then? No way." Zee throws her arm around me. "Whatever the results, I'm here for you."

She's right. There's no other choice. But I couldn't do this alone. Thank God my best friend is here with me.

"Be back," I say, rising with the Target bag clenched in my

hand. My feet know the way to the downstairs bathroom. I head there before I can chicken out.

Behind the locked door, the lingering scent of Sarah's lavender incense doesn't calm me down. I open the test and read and reread the instructions. Nothing left to do but take it.

So I do. I pee on the stick and everything.

Three minutes crawl along before the results are ready. But it's double that time before I check the stick.

Relief sweeps over my entire body, followed by a pang of guilt.

I read the words *Not pregnant* for the millionth time and control the urge to scream until my voice gives out. But for some stupid reason, mind-numbing happiness never comes.

Remember: you slept with a guy without knowing enough about him.

Since it wasn't planned and my period is still late, I grab the second test off the granite bathroom counter and repeat the process. After two negative results, I finish up, gather all the evidence, stuff all of it back in the Target bag, triple-wash my hands, and escape out the door.

"Hey." Zaynab is sitting on the hardwood floor across from the bathroom.

My pulse is still out of control. I join her on the floor. "You're not going to be an aunt."

She clears her throat. "Did Raheem . . . use a condom? If he didn't, you've got to worry about STDs. Not just about having a kid."

Damn. Didn't remember everything else that could ruin my life.

I guess we don't have any personal boundaries. "Raheem didn't use one, but he's the only person I've had sex with." My words echo in the long, empty hallway.

"That's true . . . but what about him? Was this *his* first time?"

Neither one of us knows the answer to her question. But the baby at Gymboree might suggest it wasn't . . . if it actually *is* his.

It just can't be, though. Can it? Wouldn't someone have heard, have known—have warned my parents?

"When you were in there, I googled it, and stress can affect your period. Maybe that's why you're late." She grabs me in a rare long hug. "I hope it was worth all this trouble. Was the sex any good?"

"Zee, you didn't just ask me that!"

We both bust out laughing. We laugh and laugh until it's hard to catch my breath.

I scoot closer to her. "It was beautiful. We should've waited until after the *Walimah* but he was . . . he . . . well, the whole night was magical. Was it that way with you and Amber?"

We're side by side, but now I avoid eye contact with her.

"You won't believe me, but I'll tell you the truth." She goes quiet. "We've done stuff, but we've never done the deed."

A wave of nausea hits me. It's just me, then?

"You *haven't*?" I press my back against the wall. "Is there a reason why you haven't?"

Zaynab doesn't respond for such a long time, I nudge her with my elbow. "What do you want me to say? I got nervous. I'm not ready. And Amber is heading to California while I'm staying here in Albuquerque, so I thought . . . you know, maybe we were going to break up anyway, and I'd regret it. For now, we've agreed to wait—just to make sure we're going to make it as a couple. Doing the long-distance thing isn't easy."

I reach up and flip on the hallway light. "You're right, but you're both from Albuquerque and Amber's parents are here. It's not like she's leaving forever. Be honest: Do you think she's the one?"

She shrugs. "No clue. But if we're still together in a year—maybe."

"Fair. I slept with the first guy who ever told me 'I love you,' so don't listen to any relationship advice coming out of my mouth."

"Damn, he used the L-word!" says Zee with a whistle. "Do you think he meant it?'

"He keeps saying it's his job to take care of me and that after we're married, *we'll* decide how our lives will go." My chin drops. "Do I have a choice now? I'd better work it out with Mr. Harris, because if we break up, I'm used goods."

"What did you say?" The change in her tone is immediate.

"Do you want me to repeat it?" My butt is sore, so I shift my legs. *Why don't they have a carpet runner in this hallway?*

"You best friends with Imani now?" Zaynab wraps her arm around my shoulders. "Don't *ever* say that again. Is that how you think of yourself?"

Yes. No. Maybe. Sometimes.

"I'm not a take-chances-with-guys kind of girl." I chew the inside of my cheek. "But when I'm around him, my brain shuts off and I do stupid things."

She nods. "Is Raheem acting different around you? Like . . . you know . . . post-coitus?"

"Do you count 'being okay with his client touching him at his job' as different?"

My best friend and I get up from the floor, and she hides the pregnancy tests in the bottom of the kitchen trash. A buzzing is coming from my phone, so I pick it up and answer the call.

"*As-salaamu alaykum,* Ma."

"*Wa alaykum as salaam,* Fatima. You need to come home. Your dad told me Raheem is coming over tonight and wants to talk to all of us."

Oh no. "Did he say why?"

"That's all I know. Please be on your way in five minutes."

"Okay, I heard you. InshaALLAH, be there soon."

I end the call and report back to Zaynab. "Raheem called my dad and asked if he could come over tonight. Mr. Harris always gets what he wants, so my mom says I should come home right now."

"Let me get my keys."

As Zee's green Mini Cooper speeds across the city, I suspect I'm racing toward a firing squad.

My past choices may have written my future for me.

nineteen

Zaynab drops me off at the pedestrian gate of my complex, and I promise to text her after Raheem leaves. My footsteps make quick work of the distance to my front door. For a few seconds, I glance up at the calm night sky full of bright stars, wishing for that kind of peace.

And then I rush into the house.

"MashaALLAH, you're home! Raheem just arrived." Ma's fuming with irritation. The scent of lemon furniture polish remains in the air—a nod to her stress-cleaning.

Nowhere to hide now. My fiancé sits in the living room with my dad. I follow behind my mother.

"*As-salaamu alaykum*, Sister Sharifa and Fatima." Raheem stands when we enter. His arms are overflowing with roses. "These are for each of you." He hands my mom a dozen peach roses, then gives me an arrangement of white roses.

My fiancé knows how to charm my mom. But I'm less impressed.

"*Wa alaykum as salaam*," Mom gushes. "These are beautiful. Thank you." Noticing the scowl consuming my face, she says, "Let me take all the flowers in the kitchen. Adam, will you help me?"

My dad's gaze travels from me to Raheem. "I'll be back." He takes my arrangement and I lose sight of him.

"Thanks for the roses," I say without cracking a smile.

Raheem stuffs his hands into the pockets of his jeans, his gaze fixed on the carpet under my feet. "I know you're upset. I am sorry about what happened today."

The image of his hand tucking the client's hair behind her ear is fresh in my mind. I hold onto my resentment. And his betrayal.

He takes a step closer. "Have you told your parents what happened at the gym?"

My palms grow damp. "No. Why would I?"

The twitching around his eye vanishes. "Good. Fatima, we need to clear the air if we're ever going to set a wedding date. Please, sit."

He motions for me to have a seat on the couch beside him. Too close for parental approval. Instead, I lower myself down, keeping a cushion between us. Any second I might burst from my skin.

My parents are back with the bouquets in vases, setting them on the coffee table.

"Brother Adam, Sister Sharifa, can you two stay here please?" Raheem's voice is surprisingly steady. "We need to talk to you."

Both my mom and dad give him their full attention. "Go on, Brother," my dad says.

"Before we can set a wedding date, I have to tell you what happened today at the gym." Raheem's calmness *has* to be an act. "I've already apologized to Fatima, but we think it's important for you to know why she's upset with me."

He never asked if I wanted my parents to know! We didn't agree to do this. Turning away, the only thing left for me to do is to count the rose petals in the flower arrangements in front of me.

Dad focuses on me. "Are you okay, Fatima?"

"Not really." Me smiling isn't happening.

For the first time, Raheem flinches. He hesitates before admitting, "When Fatima came into the workout area today, she witnessed one of my female clients touching me."

Clasping my hands together in my lap, I wait for the excuses to come.

My mom is quick to take his side. "I'm sure you did something about it, Raheem."

"I did, Sister Sharifa. That client is a flirt and likes being the center of attention." He clears his throat. "After asking her to take her hands off of me, I tried to explain the situation to Fatima, but she ran into the women's locker room. We're talking about it now—in front of both of you."

My dad walks over to me and lays a hand on my shoulder. His presence soothes me.

"This wasn't the first time that particular client has acted like this," Raheem says, "but I've always ignored it, hoping she'd stop." He shifts his shoulders to face me. "I'm sorry, Fatima. I told my manager what happened, and the woman is being reassigned to a different trainer. If she continues this type of behavior, her membership will be canceled and she'll be barred from the gym."

My brain only picks up one thing he said. "This happened before? The same client?"

Of course it's my mom who jumps in to defend Raheem.

"Fatima, inshaALLAH your fiancé is going to be a lawyer. Raheem's going to be around beautiful women—from his coworkers to his clients." Like I don't know. "But he chose you. As long as you don't overreact, these situations can't cause problems between the two of you."

I'm the one who overreacted? My own mother is twisting the situation around! She doesn't know how Raheem acted about Brian, and I can't tell her. But I get it now—he's a *complete* hypocrite.

Red rage simmers in my gut.

If Zaynab was here, she'd side with me. But she's not, and no one else does. Right now, the home I've known my whole life is the last place I want to be.

You've got nowhere else to go.

Dad is next with his two cents. "I think you can find it in your heart to forgive Raheem, can't you? He apologized in front of me and your mom. He didn't have to do that, Fatima." My dad's defense of him settles a chill over my whole body.

A dull throb spreads across my forehead.

My mom's warped wisdom strikes again. "This is one of the reasons you'll always have to look your best being married to an attorney."

The flowers in front of me look a little more wilted than before. Out of habit, I suck in my stomach a bit.

I start a silent count to twenty, but before I can finish, my fiancé speaks up. "Sister Sharifa, please don't do that. I want to marry your daughter the way she is and that won't change after we're married."

He does? It won't? Every cell in my body wants to believe him, but I've spent my whole life never measuring up to my mom's high expectations. Why should I measure up to his?

Gymboree. The baby. Hair tucked behind a client's ear.

My dad claps Raheem on the back. "Thank you for telling us, Raheem. I expect you to learn from this. Understand how to handle uncomfortable situations better so they don't escalate. I don't want my Fatima hurt by anything like this."

My dad winks at me. I manage a small smile.

"I am sorry, Sunshine," Raheem says to me. I can't tell if his remorse is real. "From now on, I promise to communicate better, and to never give you any reason to question my commitment to you. Do you forgive me?"

His silky voice *almost* lulls me into a "yes." But no. I need to find the courage and ask him about what Zaynab saw—the mother and child. And should I tell him about the pregnancy test?

Everything is so messed up. I just want him to be the person he seemed to.

"I forgive you, Raheem." What else can I say when my parents have already made up their minds? "But there's something else I wanted to talk to you about."

His body relaxes. "I'm listening."

I run my hands down my thighs. "Your mom planned the whole engagement party and even bought my dress without telling me. That's not how I want our married life to be."

A shadow of worry passes over his face, but he smiles again.

"Sunshine, I'm her only child, who inshaALLAH is only getting married once." Raheem's tone has grown diplomatic. "Since you let my mother arrange the party, I promise you can plan the *Walimah* you want."

"That's very generous of you," my mother says. She gives me a death glare. "You've been so giving to our Fatima."

Raheem's grin deepens. "Well, I have something else for

Fatima. Just a small surprise." He takes a small envelope out of his shirt pocket and places it in my hand.

I wince. Presents are great, but I know now that love isn't for sale.

"You don't have to keep buying me things."

"Fatima Tate, you're the person I want and need by my side for the rest of our lives."

Torn, I stare at my gift.

"Sunshine, don't you want to see what's inside?"

My curiosity wins out. I slip a finger under the flap and open the envelope. From inside a shimmering silver lining, I pull out a Williams Sonoma gift card.

"This is too much, Raheem. I don't think I've ever spent five hundred dollars on anything. How did you know they have my favorite bakeware?"

He leans a little closer and whispers, "I told you we can't have secrets between us."

"Aren't you a lucky young lady?" Ma prods. "And since you're both here and Fatima is now in a good mood imagining kitchen supplies, there's something else I need to discuss with both of you."

This can't be good.

"Fatima, Raheem, I spoke with Sister Jameela earlier today, and we think the wedding should be at the end of the summer. That way it's before you start college, Fatima, and before you begin law school, Raheem."

I steel myself for a battle.

"Ma, where did this suggestion come from? Raheem and I haven't discussed a date yet." I turn to my usual ally. "Dad, are you part of this?"

"Graduating high school and getting ready for college is a lot to deal with without adding a *Walimah* on top of that . . . I'm not sure it's the best idea," he admits.

I don't deserve my wonderful father.

Of course my mother isn't done yet. "Fatima, what are you even waiting for? Raheem is one of the most eligible bachelors in our community. MashaALLAH, any Muslim young lady would be blessed to become his wife." She speaks like the discussion is over.

My fiancé reaches over and squeezes my hand. I hold my breath and hope he'll use his charm to get my mom to back down.

"It's a great idea," he says.

My hopes sink into the carpet. "You *agree* with her?" I swallow my disbelief.

Raheem inspects my parents' expressions. "This summer is the perfect time. You've already said yes to this marriage, and our parents approve, so there's nothing stopping us . . . unless you have a reason to wait longer." He dares me to contradict him. "Do you?"

It sounds like it's already been decided.

I can only think of one last objection. "Isn't it too last minute to plan our wedding? You'd need a venue, a caterer, flowers, and a ton of other stuff. I haven't even made up my mind what I want."

"InshaALLAH, it'll work out," Raheem says, as if he's planned weddings before. "Share all your ideas with my mom. She's an expert at parties and has a lot of connections. I'm sure she will help you with whatever you decide."

Translation: we're rich and people cater to us.

Translation: once you're a Harris, you'll understand.

My mom beams at my fiancé. "I'll leave it to you to convince my daughter."

"I'll try, Sister Sharifa." Raheem winks at me. "Sunshine. You should know I always get what I want."

With both families on board, I don't stand a chance.

My fate is sealed. Unless I follow my best friend's advice and find the courage to take back control. Somehow.

Time to find out the truth about Raheem. It's my last chance.

twenty

Zaynab merges her car into the Tramway Boulevard traffic, zooming in the direction of the Gymboree.

"You were only a few minutes late," says my partner in crime. "We should still be there on time. You didn't tell Raheem anything, did you?"

I turn my engagement ring. "Of course not. Do you think I'm crazy?"

"I think you deserve the truth."

"He might not be up to anything shady. Seriously, what if this lady and baby are family friends or something? Or cousins? He could just be driving them to the class and back."

"He could be," Zee repeats. I can taste her disbelief. "You keep saying that, but I'm not going for it." She glances at me. "It's already Wednesday. Are you sure you're ready for your engagement party in three days?"

The reminder isn't necessary. It's like there's a big countdown clock over my head.

Zaynab turns wide onto Academy Boulevard and I grip the armrest as she swerves into the left lane. "Easy on the gas!" I complain.

Ignoring me, she says, "You only have two hours between the

end of the baking competition and the start of the party, don't forget. So time will be super tight."

I know, I know.

"InshaALLAH, I'll make it work." My stomach churns thinking about it. "Get me to the convention center on time, let me stash my ball gown in your back seat, and help me get changed, then we should be able to get to the hotel on time for the reception. Easy, really. My chef's uniform will stay in the car and no one will find out."

Zee brings the Mini to a sudden halt. The seat belt cuts into my chest.

Her eyebrows lift sky high. "Isn't that his Lexus?"

I turn toward where Zaynab is pointing . . . and immediately sink down into the seat.

My best friend slips on a red University of New Mexico baseball cap and takes out her shades. Pitiful. Her disguise is the *worst*.

"Zee, you're crazy." I don't want to laugh, but I can't help it.

"This way he won't recognize me right away. So he won't see me coming if things get out of hand and I need to step in." She sticks out her chin. "I hope you're ready, Fatima—because there he is."

A curvy brunette strides out of the Gymboree, one of her hands planted on her hip, followed by Raheem. His expression as he stares at her is pure disgust.

And . . . my fiancé is holding a chubby baby. The baby is real. Very, very real.

"Is it time?" Zaynab asks.

Heart pounding, I sneak another peek at Raheem. "Are you coming with me?"

"Nope. I'll be right here if you need me. Watching."

This is it. Taking several quick breaths, I slide out of the car and force myself to walk over to my fiancé and the woman he's now having a heated argument with. With the blood rushing to my ears, I can't even hear them.

I count to ninety before Raheem sees me.

For a second, the world freezes.

"*Fatima?*" Panic covers his face. "What are you doing here?" The baby in his arms lets out a wail, and he rubs its back.

"A better question is what are *you* doing here, Raheem?" I demand, my mouth dry.

"Ah, I get it," interjects the brunette. The intensity of her glare could cut steel. "*You're* the chosen one." Pointing to my yellow diamond, she asks, "When's the wedding?"

"Fatima," Raheem says, his voice wavering. "This is Chloe."

Chloe sneers in my direction. She cracks her gum, dropping her backpack on the hood of a Honda Accord next to me. "Give him to me," she snaps at Raheem.

The baby in his arms has round cheeks and a head full of loose black curls.

"Sunshine," Raheem whispers, seeing me looking, "this is my son, Umar."

I knew it deep down in my soul. But hearing his casual confession takes my breath away.

I stare at him like he's a stranger—because that's what he is to me.

Raheem gives the baby to Chloe. Then he slides close to me and holds my hand for a second before I snatch it away. "Sunshine, we need to talk about this."

"Why . . . *why* would you keep this from me?"

He scans the parking lot before answering. "I'm not proud. But I had to know we were a sure thing first."

My anger ignites like baking powder. I could've been in the same boat as Chloe. And he didn't care!

"How many unprotected hookups have you had, Raheem?" I cry. "You never know—Umar could have a couple siblings around town!"

I can't *believe* he didn't use a condom when he's already gotten someone else pregnant. How selfish is he? How stupid am I?

Raheem's jaw stiffens. "I've made a few mistakes, but Umar isn't one of them."

"What about *me*?" My voice cracks. "Was I one of your mistakes?"

I don't know if I can handle the answer.

Not that he'd tell me the truth.

"Are we done with the drama, Raheem?" Chloe breaks in. "I have to get Umar to the babysitter's house before my shift at the hospital." She switches the baby to her other hip.

"I'm leaving," I tell my fiancé—or whatever he is.

Chloe smiles at me with a hint of approval. "Good for you."

"Wait, Fatima!" Raheem pleads. "Don't go."

"Be careful with this snake," Chloe warns me.

Fury flashes on Raheem's face, and he takes a step toward the mother of his child. "Don't forget you're talking about me to my future wife. You *know* what I can do to—"

"You can do *what*?" Chloe cuts him off. "Stop paying the court-ordered child support? If that happens, my lawyer will haul your ass back into court so fast it'll make your head spin." She releases a bitter laugh. "Or . . . I could always show up at one of those Friday prayers and make a scene. Oh, you don't like me threatening you? Tough shit." Chloe nods in my direction. "I'm not one of these little girls you're used to dealing with."

Raheem's hands curl into fists and he exhales through his nose. He grips my elbow—way too hard. "Let's go, Sunshine."

I glance between Chloe and Zaynab, who is now out of her car, watching the scene, ready to intercede.

"No," I say to Raheem. "I already have plans."

"We need to talk about this, Fatima. Tell Zaynab to leave!"

"There's nothing left to say, is there?" The dry heat around us is cold compared to the searing fire inside me.

Pulling me closer, Raheem whispers, "After our *recent activities*, I think we have plenty to discuss. So can you give me a chance to explain, please?"

That makes me pause.

Notifications erupt from the phone in my hand. No one has to tell me who they're from.

If you don't want to go with him, come back and we'll leave

If he tries to stop you, I'll hurt him

I'll key him in the face I swear

My hands are shaking. Raheem lets go of me. "Text her back. Tell her I'll drive you home."

"Why should I?"

"Think about what I just said."

My hands shake, but I manage to reply: I'll text u when I get home

YOUD BETTER, is her response. I DONT LIKE THIS

"Please get in, Fatima," Raheem says, his words sharp as he

guides me to his car. He holds the door open for me, like always, but the guy I called my Muslim Prince Charming isn't anything *close* to that. Raheem has a dark side. Darker than I ever dreamed of.

Whoever the Hell this guy is, I don't know him anymore.

Could be, I never did.

We drive in complete silence. Raheem stops at a small park a couple miles from my house. My heart is already a block of ice.

"Sunshine, I know you're shocked—but I need to explain. I'm sorry you found out this way."

I angle my body away from him. Raheem touches my shoulder. "Not that you'd know it from her tantrum today," he says, "but Chloe used to be nice. We met three years ago at UNM."

At this point, I'm not sure I care. "Why aren't you two together? Umar needs a father in his life."

Raheem takes a minute to answer. "Chloe and I want different things and neither one of us would compromise, so I ended the relationship. But I give her money every month to take care of my son."

That shit doesn't cut it. He better have more to say.

"Why didn't you tell me?" I pivot in his direction. "We slept together, but you couldn't tell me you had a *child*?" I clench my hands and keep them on my lap. "That could've been *me*."

Raheem winces, then straightens his shoulders. "Sunshine, you mean more to me than she ever did. We should've waited, but the more I learned about you, the deeper my interest in you became. And now that we know each other on every level, I'm convinced we should be together."

His pitiful explanation changes nothing. It's all about him—what he wants, what I can do for him.

"I want you to be the mother of all my future children."

And there it is.

Venom builds in my blood. I look at Raheem's chiseled face and soulful eyes, and for the first time I see them for what they are: a mask.

"I'm ready to go home now," is all I say.

"How did you know where I was, anyway?" Raheem asks, as if I didn't say anything. "Did your *best friend* see me? I bet it was her. Zaynab probably told you about Chloe and Umar. She should mind her own damn business."

"Zaynab has nothing to do with this. *You* were the one keeping a secret from me," I counter. "I want to go home NOW!"

Raheem leans in, super close to me. "You're my responsibility, and I think we should get some fresh air." He exits the car and comes around to open my door. "Let's go."

It's a command. He holds out his hand, but I scowl at him and step out on my own.

We find a picnic table and I sit down opposite him. The bright Albuquerque sun hides behind an ocean of clouds. At the edge of the park, I spot a toddler running between his parents; his angelic little smile hits me in the heart.

Something clicks.

"Does my dad even know?" It sounds like an accusation.

A sneer twists Raheem's face. "Sunshine, I'm not a fool. I didn't tell either one of your parents. Don't you think it's better you found out first?"

It was a stupid question. My dad admires my fiancé. If he knew the truth, he wouldn't.

Whatever spell Raheem cast over me has shattered. He's not handsome at all. I've discovered his true face.

"I thought I knew you."

His biceps flex as he puts his forearms on the picnic table. "What are you saying, Fatima?" His lips are flat.

"What I'm saying is that with all your other *responsibilities*, I don't think it's a good idea for us to get married."

Raheem slaps his hand down on the top of the picnic table. My flight response kicks in, and my eyes scan the area for the best way to run. "Do you think I will ever let you go?"

A cold shiver of dread passes through me. "What did you say?"

He folds his arms tight to his chest.

"So now I don't deserve an answer?" I shout, springing to my feet.

"Fatima, please lower your voice. I understand you're upset, but you can't make a life-changing decision when you're emotional. Think of the consequences."

I hold onto the edge of the picnic table. I've never been good at confrontation, and my hands are already shaking, but this is my *life*.

"Raheem, are you threatening me?"

"You're not thinking clearly," he replies. "Fatima, I want to marry you. I've been drawn to you since the day we met. Now that we're engaged, I simply won't allow a small disagreement to derail our future."

Part of me wants to crumple to the ground. But I don't. "Raheem, you have a child. That's not a 'little disagreement'—it's a huge deal. And you can't control me or what I do."

Without a hint of emotion, he stands. "Let's get you home. After you cool off, we'll talk about this again."

Dizzy from all his sudden changes—hot, cold, hot, cold—I trudge behind him to his car and get in. Pain throbs behind my eyes, a tension headache on the way.

Raheem reaches across and fastens my seat belt for me. His powerful hand clamps down on my forearm.

"Sunshine, you need to understand." Our gazes meet. "I was your first and I intend to be your only."

There's malice in those brown eyes. Raheem can *never* find out about the pregnancy scare.

"If you decide to do something stupid—calling off the wedding, or even trying to postpone it—I will confess to our parents we had sex. Are you ready for them to know? I should also talk to the *Imam* and get his guidance. How do you think they'd like that?"

"You'd be admitting your own guilt, too," I fire back.

His sinister grin gives me chills.

"You forget how patriarchal our masjid is. My part will be written off as a youthful indiscretion, but you'll have a tainted reputation. You'll never find another husband."

Raheem's threat hits a nerve. Zaynab's instinct about him was spot-on after all.

My hope for a happy life fades.

I can't hold back a stream of tears. "Fine . . . let's go ahead with the engagement."

His grip loosens, and I yank my arm out of his grasp. "I'm so glad you see things my way. Today's been tough for you, Sunshine." Raheem glides his thumb across my cheek. "But we can still be great together."

He leans back, putting the key in the ignition.

I shut my eyes and pretend to sleep on the drive back. Maybe, if I keep my eyes closed long enough, this daytime nightmare will end.

All I want to do is wake up.

twenty-one

When Sister Jameela asked me out to lunch, I knew it couldn't be good.

We sit at an outdoor café, staring at each other.

The wind blows her usual lavender perfume into my nostrils. My chest burns as I hold in a cough.

"I am glad you're here, Fatima," Jameela begins. "We need to discuss an important issue." Her piercing gaze tightens my shoulders.

"What did you want to talk about?" With the engagement party in twenty-four hours, my will to fight is nearing zero.

My future mother-in-law glances around us. "Raheem told me you've met Umar," she says, her voice low. "My son trusts you NOT to share his personal affairs with others in the community."

A puff of powdered sugar could knock me over. "You know about . . . about the baby?" I barely get the words out.

"Of course," Jameela snaps. Her tone tells me my place. "I make it my business to know *everything* about Raheem. That's why I was taken aback by his interest in you. I didn't see that coming."

Shit. *Does she know we slept together?* I take a risk. "You don't like me, do you?"

Her scowl says it all. "My opinion doesn't matter anymore. Raheem is determined to make you his wife, so it's my job to ensure you're an asset to him."

Make sure *I'm* an asset to *him?* This woman blows my mind.

"As long as you're a supportive spouse who puts his career first," she says, holding my gaze, "I'll be satisfied." Wow. Unbelievable. "After law school, Raheem will practice for a few years before he enters local politics."

For a moment I almost pity him—his mom has his life all planned out for him, too. Almost.

Jameela pauses, a smug smile growing on her face. "My son has a bright future, and I won't allow you to compromise that. You need to get accustomed to living under constant scrutiny, Fatima, and adhering to certain standards."

I'm not the one who's threatening his potential political career. I've only slept with one guy—her son.

Raheem is the one with a secret child.

But I bite my tongue. Jameela must interpret my silence as acceptance.

"It's difficult for young ladies to understand they have a duty to keep their husbands' secrets." She settles back in her chair, too casual for her stern warnings. "Remember, when you become a member of the Harris family, loyalty is expected."

This woman is crazy.

Daring to look right into her eyes, I say, "Having a pastry career is important to me—it's what I want to do. I care about that much, much more."

Her sly grin doesn't budge.

"Marrying into the Harris family has its privileges. You never having to work is one of them. After my death, it will also be your and Raheem's responsibility to secure our legacy by having children and raising them to continue everything my father started."

These expectations weigh on my shoulders like a fifty-pound bag of flour.

A waiter brings my vegetarian burger and sweet potato fries, then sets a shrimp stir-fry bowl down in front of my future mother-in-law. The sweet honey mustard aioli drips down my chin as I take a bite of my burger, but this conversation killed my appetite.

"Fatima, my son is a wonderful young man," she says, sudden threat lacing her voice. "Don't you agree?"

"I'm glad I've learned who Raheem is. Sometimes I think he's too good to be true."

Sister Jameela doesn't react to the contempt in my answer.

"InshaALLAH, you'll be devoted to him," she replies. "He needs a supportive, behind-the-scenes wife." After reaching over and patting my forearm, she adds, "Don't worry. I'll teach you how."

There's a roaring in my ears. I count the number of times she taps her finger against the table. At fifteen, my anger is more under control.

"Before I forget, Raheem asked me Wednesday evening if we could change the time of the party. The hotel wasn't booked, so it was no problem. I'll need you and your parents at the Sheraton by one o'clock now. I told your mom and she assured me you don't have anything scheduled that day."

Panic alarms begin wailing in the back of my mind. *Shut up and stay calm.*

My chance to compete in the final round is slipping away each moment I sit here, saying nothing. Thanks to my fiancé. He knew about the competition. He's taking it from me.

Lunch passes in a haze. Jameela drops all the details for the *Walimah* on me like tiny cuts to my skin: the classical orchestra she's hired, the important attorneys who RSVP'd to the engagement party, the gifts we should expect. I smile and nod when I should, but I'm outside of my body.

When Jameela drops me off at home, I mutter a quick thank-you and run out of the car. I rush through the pedestrian gate to the condo complex without glancing back.

My days are numbered here with my parents. Tomorrow's party is the beginning of me living under Raheem's control. His family's wealth and influence mean nothing to me. My freedom shouldn't have a price.

Not looking where I'm going, I barge into my dad.

"*As-salaamu alaykum*, Fatima!"

"*Wa alaykum as salaam.* What are you doing home from work so early?"

"You'll see, Squiggles." He has a twinkle in his eye and points to the driveway.

I go cold.

"Surprise!" Raheem shouts, all smiles. He stands beside a white Lexus SUV topped with a gigantic red bow.

My dad wraps his arm around my shoulders. "Are you shocked?" The joy on his face tugs at my indifference. I put one foot in front of the other and make my way to my fiancé. I force myself to ignore the smug look on his face.

The SUV's white paint is immaculate and its tinted windows will protect me from Albuquerque's 300+ days of sunshine.

"MashaALLAH, you shouldn't have spent this much money on me," I mumble, no excitement in my voice. "I don't even have a license yet."

Raheem gives me the key, his hand caressing mine in the exchange. "That's not a problem, Sunshine; your lessons start soon. Please don't worry about the cost of the car. I need my wife to have a safe vehicle when she's driving around town."

This is a bribe. No other word for it.

Raheem focuses his attention on my dad. "Brother Adam! Why don't the three of us get in and I'll show both of you some of the features?"

I ease into the passenger seat while my dad climbs into the back. My fiancé takes the key from me and fires up the engine. Without moving, he shows me how to use the backup camera and all the basic stuff—how to turn on the lights, how to adjust the seats.

"Do you have any questions, Sunshine?"

"No." I cling to my resolve. *Is this what Raheem thinks it will take for me to accept him?*

He cuts off the engine and hands me back the key.

"Fatima, Brother Adam, I've got to go meet my mom at an appointment." Pivoting toward me, he gives me a meaningful look and says, "InshaALLAH, see both of you tomorrow at the hotel. *As-salaamu alaykum.*" I don't miss the ultimatum beneath the words.

"*Wa alaykum as salaam,*" my dad and I say in unison.

After shaking my dad's hand and winking at me, Raheem leaves. He's still driving away when Dad takes my hand.

"Why the long face, Squiggles?"

Tell him.

It's a crazy idea. I can't. But I hate lying to him. A headache sprouts behind my eyes. "Nothing," I lie.

"Fatima." My father puts himself in my direct line of sight, his tone unusually stern. "I changed your diapers. I know when something's wrong."

"Ew, Dad. Can we not go there?" Drawing in a breath, I try to find my courage. "Don't you think all the expensive gifts are weird?"

Dad rubs the back of his neck. "You'll have to get used to it. The Harris family lives a different life than we do. InshaALLAH, you'll never have to worry about money."

The relief in his voice claws at my heart.

I dig the toe of my shoe into the ground. "How do they have so much, though?"

Dad coughs. "From what Raheem shared with me, his grandfather had an early interest in the tech industry. He invested in Microsoft and Apple in the '80s—we should all be so lucky."

Good for Raheem's grandfather, I guess. "It's still over the top."

Dad leans against me. "If you don't want that beautiful car, I'm more than happy to accept his gift, Squiggles." He gives my hand a tight squeeze. "InshaALLAH, you will always be taken care of."

I meet my father's eyes. Without an ounce of humor in my voice, I inform him, "You've always given me everything I need, Dad." I don't want him to doubt it.

There's a slight sheen to his eyes as he kisses my forehead.

Raheem thinks he can take away my chance to compete—my very dreams—and replace them with a car. That's one thing. But how can I disappoint my *father*, who's worked so hard for me, by walking away from this engagement—with a scarlet letter, no less?

My father guides me into the house and I head straight into my sanctuary: the kitchen.

I preheat the oven for cupcakes, then take out all the ingredients and make a basic yellow cake batter. Next I put liners in my cupcake pan and use an ice cream scoop to portion out my batter. Once the cupcakes are baked and cooling, I whip up some buttercream.

Raheem promised that once we were husband and wife, he'd support my dream of becoming a pastry chef. His promises are nothing but lies.

Like a robot, I fill one of my piping bags.

No one—not even Zee—knows I turned down my university acceptance. I was so sure Raheem would help me become a pastry chef.

As I frost the cupcakes (I'm making my best attempt at yellow roses), my racing heartbeat slows. Losing myself in the decorating zone brings me to a better place.

Without him, I'm on my own—no college, no culinary school, no good reputation. Becoming his wife is my only option.

He gets to steal my dream, and in return, he'll give me his name. An unfair trade.

twenty-two

The day of my engagement party I wake up for the predawn prayer covered in sweat.

I was in a doctor's office with Raheem. He had baby Umar in his arms. A nurse handed me a bottle of prenatal vitamins and congratulated me on our growing family.

A scream caught in my throat as I opened my eyes.

To clear my mind, I take a quick shower, then throw on an old tee and capris and add my floor-length prayer covering. I tiptoe into my loft area and manage to pray *Fajr* without tears running down my face. My head is cloudy from a lack of sleep, so I curl back onto my bed and close my eyes.

"Fatima, you need to get up." My mom's loud voice carries up the stairs. "Today's a special day and we have a ton to do before the party this afternoon."

I stagger to my feet and yank open the door. "Ma, I'm up. Give me some time to throw some water on my face and I'll be down."

Today is the beginning of the end of Fatima Tate and the start of Mrs. Raheem Harris.

My half-open eyes spot her smiling face at the bottom of the stairs. I groan. My phone rings so I plop down on my bed and swipe right to answer.

"Hello?" I answer, a gnawing in my gut.

"Fatima, this is Chloe, Raheem's ex-girlfriend." Her shoved-together words are barely understandable.

My brain can't process this.

Whispering, I demand, "How did you get my number?"

"From Raheem's phone last night while he played with Umar," she admits, the sentence tumbling out of her mouth. "Listen, I know he's probably told you terrible things about me, but we need to talk." A pause. "Can you meet me at Rolling Hills Park? It's important."

"That's near my house." I'm vague on purpose.

"Good, good. I can be there in thirty minutes. Does that work for you, Fatima?"

"Okay . . . See you then." I hang up, unease overtaking me. But I'm willing to hear her out. She knows Raheem even better than me—this could be big.

Five minutes later, clean and fresh, I join my mom in the kitchen. I'm not hungry, but I grab a couple strawberries, a piece of cantaloupe, and two slices of toast, not wanting to raise her suspicions.

"Ma, I'm walking to Rolling Hills Park after breakfast. I want to get in some exercise . . . alone." Hope she gets the hint.

To my surprise, my mom's lips turn in a smile. "That's a great idea. A brisk walk burns the most calories."

It takes a huge effort to suppress an eye roll.

After a few minutes of staring at my own food, Dad enters the kitchen and steals a strawberry off my plate. I pretend-pinch him.

My mom puts down her cup of peppermint tea. "Our daughter wants to walk to the park this morning by herself."

He winks at me. "It's a big day, Fatima. I think it's good for you to have some quiet time on your own."

That's settled, then. I grab my Hydro Flask out of the fridge, slip on a two-piece hijab, tuck my phone into one pocket and my keys into the other, and head out the door.

"InshaALLAH, I'll be home in an hour," I call back before they change their minds about giving me this small freedom.

Rushing out of the complex, I head left for two blocks. My Vans crunch the dry, brownish grass as I finally step off the sidewalk and into the park. I spot Chloe sitting on a bench.

She's alone. I exhale a couple times, then head in that direction.

"Hi, Fatima," she says, seeing me approach.

"Hey." The bright sky over us darkens a bit.

Chloe fixes her eyes on me. "Do you wanna sit?"

My stomach's a little queasy. I claim the other end of the bench.

"I'm sorry for calling you out of the blue." Her hands are balled up into fists.

"Okay." I'm not sure what else to say.

She glances over my shoulder, then scans the park. She's on edge. *What's happening?*

"Did you tell Raheem you were meeting me?" she asks.

Now I'm squirming in my seat. "No . . . no. I didn't even tell my parents. Why did you need to talk to me today?"

Chloe nods, her shoulders relaxing. "Good." But she doesn't answer my question. "Good," she repeats.

"Where's Umar?" I ask.

"He's with his dad." Chloe tucks one knee beneath her chin, resting her foot on the edge of the bench. She could pass for a teenager. Too young to be co-parenting with Raheem.

In fact . . . Chloe kinda looks like me.

Her eyes round as she continues. "Fatima, I needed to talk to you woman-to-woman. To beg you not to go along with Raheem's plan. Umar is all I have."

I have no idea what she's talking about. "What plan?"

"Please don't pretend. After you two are married, he'll seek full custody of our son—you know that. But I'm Umar's mother. Not you." Her eyes sear me. "I'll fight you two with everything I have."

Furious despair radiates off her, shimmering in the arid June air.

"You don't understand, Chloe. I didn't—"

"Most months, Raheem only comes by twice. But now he wants to raise him?"

Twice? What I just heard is unbelievable. My fingers squeeze the life out of my Hydro Flask.

"Chloe," I begin, "I didn't know about any of this. I only found out Umar existed three days ago."

She's quiet for a while—I hope she believes me.

Finally, she curses under her breath. "That's typical Raheem behavior. He doesn't care what anyone else wants. It's always about him." Chloe turns, confronting me face-to-face. "Trust me, Fatima, if Raheem has to choose between what's good for him and what's good for you—he'll pick himself every time."

The park spins around us.

"You need to be careful with him," she goes on. "He's got a nasty temper, and once someone's on his bad side . . . it comes out."

I take a shaky sip from my water bottle. "Are you scared of him?" The next question is hard to ask, but I have to. "Did he ever . . . hit you?"

She hesitates for a moment. "No, but I worry about Umar."

"You think he's a danger to his own son?" I blurt out. "He's just a baby."

"Please don't repeat this—but the late Mr. Harris used to beat Raheem when he was a child." Chloe lowers her voice even further. "By ten years old, your fiancé had learned how to follow every one of his father's rules. He learned to never talk back. I'm sure he expects the same of Umar.

"I didn't plan to get pregnant, Fatima, but once I did, the ugly side of him appeared. The Harris family is ruthless in business and in life. Jameela offered to buy me a house and a brand-new car if I'd sign away my parental rights."

"I'm so, so sorry," I breathe. "That's fucked up."

"Accept gifts from people like that and they'll try to control you. I take the court-ordered child support and nothing more." Chloe crosses her arms over her chest. "I don't want anything else from them. He is my son!" Her agitation is justified.

Chloe's strength and determination humble me.

"I'd never want to take Umar away from you," I say. "I swear."

She nods, believing me, I think. "Why are you marrying Raheem? After everything I've said, what kind of man do you think he is?"

Water pools in my eyes. "My parents think he's great," I offer. Boy, do I sound lame. "To be honest, Chloe, I have my doubts . . . but . . . you know how he is. Raheem will stop at nothing for us to become husband and wife. He wants me. He'll get me."

Chloe puts her dark brown hair into a ponytail and secures it with a scrunchie from the front pocket of her jean shorts. "Girl, please. Tell him to screw himself and call it off. I don't know much about Islamic marriages, but you can say no, can't you?"

I use my palms to wipe my eyes before the tears flow. "I have a choice, but there's other stuff to worry about."

She doesn't know it's not that easy. Raheem's blackmail threat is real.

Chloe rubs the back of her neck. "Fatima, you're too young and too cute to marry someone you don't want to. Do you think you can't find someone better? Did he tell you that?" Before I can answer, she mutters, "*Asshole.*"

My lips flicker into an involuntary smile. She reminds me a lot of Zaynab right now. Her strength convinces me to take a chance.

"It's not that. If I don't go through with becoming his wife, my entire family will suffer—I can't be responsible for that." My limbs tremble as the unbearable weight of *the secret* bears down on me. "Besides, my parents have never had anything close to the wealth of the Harris family. That kind of security for me is super important to them."

After running my unsteady hands down my lap, I blow out a ragged breath. "If I call off or postpone the wedding, Raheem's threatening to tell my mom and dad we already slept together."

Her eyes widen. Then she asks the one question I don't want to answer: "Is that true?"

An avalanche of shame crushes me. "Yes."

"Now I get it." Chloe puts a hand on my shoulder. "Sex outside of marriage in your religion isn't allowed. Your situation sucks."

I should've known she'd understand. I'm so grateful for her lack of judgment.

"If people in my community find out, our reputations would

be ruined," I admit, hearing the panic in my own voice. "My dad's an active member of our masjid, and my actions would put that in jeopardy."

Chloe runs her index finger along the top of the park bench. "So your fiancé has real ammunition against you. Shit."

We've both been burned by the same guy.

"When did Raheem tell you about his father?" A fly buzzes around my head, but I swat it away. Nothing will make me leave this bench. I have to know everything.

"Last year when I was pregnant. He's afraid of turning into his dad—a control freak who showed his son very little love. But honestly, a control freak is what he is."

I'm afraid. What kind of father would Raheem be to our children?

Chloe checks her phone, then stuffs it back in her pocket. "I'm sorry I accused you of plotting with Raheem to take my son away from me. I understand now that you won't help him with that." Her voice cracks. "Fatima, don't get lured in by the fancy parties and all the wealth. It's not worth it."

Raheem shared more intimate details about his life with her than with me. Much more. In some ways, he's closer to her and always will be—she's the mother of his child.

Did he love her? Am I the acceptable bride? The consolation prize?

Chloe gets up. "I told him I'd be home by eleven o'clock. Do you need a ride?"

"It's not far. I'm okay with walking."

"Be careful, Fatima. Let's make sure to pray for each other."

"Okay." Can't hurt.

As soon as she leaves, I cover my face with my hands. My head's spinning. Once it stops, I stand, straighten, and force one foot in front of the other.

No tears fall—they're all used up.

twenty-three

I'm wearing the floor-length gown Sister Jameela bought me. Taking my time, I apply some mascara and a little pale pink lip gloss. Only when my future mother-in-law suggested the makeup did my mother give in.

Must be nice to always get what you want.

Having the Harris last name has all the advantages . . . But I want none of it.

Running my fingers down my arms, I want to hate my dress but can't. The burgundy satin is butter-soft, while the lace bodice and sleeves are light and not scratchy. The gold necklace that belonged to Raheem's grandmother is under the cream *shayla*-style hijab wrapped around my head.

My reflection in the bathroom mirror doesn't show the sadness seeping from my pores. The privileged life I'm being forced into will be a facade.

I leave my bedroom in the three-inch heels Jameela expects me to wear. Each slow step down the stairs maims any sliver of hope I have left.

My dad whistles. "MashaALLAH, Fatima, you'll be the belle of the ball! I think I'm underdressed." He won't be: his white knee-length *thobe* with black piping down the sleeves and black dress pants is fine.

I laugh. "Dad, you didn't need to rent a tux for the engagement party."

"This delivery came for you." He hands me a red box.

"Who's this from?" Instead of waiting for an answer, I take the card out of the envelope attached to the box and read it.

Can't wait to see you tonight, Sunshine.

The smile on my dad's face isn't contagious. Even when my fingers trace the elegant writing on my present, I can't think of a bright side to my situation.

"Fatima, you seem . . ." He stops talking as my mom joins us.

"What's that?" Her gleeful voice reaches me as I open the box, revealing a dozen chocolate-covered strawberries. A sour taste fills my mouth.

"MashaALLAH," my mom exclaims. "You're so blessed your fiancé likes to spoil you."

This is the worst.

My dad gives me one of his famous bear hugs. "Are you okay?" he whispers in my ear.

"Don't worry," I breathe. "I'm okay."

If only it were true.

An hour later, I gasp as I step inside the swanky hotel ballroom.

The burgundy tablecloths are the exact shade of my dress, while each place setting is marked by a crisp, white linen napkin. Sparkly gold is everywhere: the napkin rings, the sashes on top of the chair covers, even the material hanging down from the ceiling.

My mom takes my hand and brings me close. "This is gorgeous. I can't imagine how fancy your *Walimah* will be."

I force myself to keep a blank expression. "Ma, please don't remind me. I'm nervous enough already."

Scanning the room and the elongated dessert table, the tall cake at its center grabs my attention. Around that masterpiece is a ring of red velvet cupcakes, my future mother-in-law's favorite. Raheem's German chocolate cake is there, too.

My mom must have followed my gaze because she pulls me toward the sweets. "Fatima, you can't tell me *this* doesn't bring a smile to your face."

The cake in front of me is huge: three tiers, each decorated with white buttercream and a crimson collar. A cascade of burgundy fondant roses half covers the intricate swirls etched onto the frosting. I hope the inside has a layer of raspberry jam.

Congratulations Raheem & Fatima is piped on the bottom layer.

It takes my breath away. How can such a beautiful creation mean the end of my dreams, of the life I wanted for myself?

"I'll be back, Fatima," my mom says as my dad slides up beside me. She disappears through the ballroom's double doors.

"It's going to be a large party. You okay with that, sweetie?" he asks.

I shrug. "It's not like I have a choice."

He squeezes my hand. "Learning to pick your battles is important."

"*As-salaamu alaykum*, Fatima. Brother Adam." Sister Jameela's loud greeting interrupts this quiet moment with my dad.

We both pivot and face Raheem's mother as she approaches, a hotel employee on her heels. The poor lady, with panicked eyes and messy hair, must have been at Sister Jameela's mercy all day.

"*Wa alaykum as salaam*," Dad and I say in unison.

Before I'm forced to back up to avoid a collision, Sister Jameela stops and holds her hand over her heart. "MashaALLAH, Fatima, that dress is gorgeous on you. Raheem will be so pleased." She nods at my dad. "They make a beautiful couple."

He beams. "My daughter's always been the apple of my eye." He winks at me. "Now, Jameela, where's that son of yours? I need a few minutes with him."

She glances over her shoulder. "He's on the phone in the parking lot." She turns and points to the hotel employee right behind us. "Can you please take Mr. Tate to find my son? Then make sure the kitchen staff understands the changes I need made to the coffee bar."

The woman, wearing a director of catering name tag, smiles at the suggestion and waves my dad forward. "If you'd follow me, Mr. Tate, this way." She races away from the whirlwind that is Raheem's mother.

"*As-salaamu alaykum*, Jameela." My mom is back, giving me the chance to slip out of the decked-out ballroom.

I rush down a hall to escape into a women's bathroom, going into the first stall and shutting the door tight.

Just breathe.

When my pulse stops racing, I leave the small space and stand in front of the sink, warm water running over my hands. I dry them, then rewrap my shimmery hijab and step out to face the evening again.

You can do this.

As I approach the open ballroom double doors, Raheem is waiting for me.

"*Salaam*, Fatima."

His tailored black suit and bright white dress shirt fit him like a glove. His burgundy tie matches my gown. (Jeez, his mom covered every detail.) Raheem's eyes sparkle, and his perfect smile completes the perfect facade.

"*Wa alaykum as salaam.*" My greeting couldn't be any shorter or more impersonal. His smile falters.

Glancing behind Raheem, I catch more than a few hotel staff members busy setting up more tables.

"MashaALLAH, you're so beautiful, Sunshine." Raheem leans into my personal space, his breath tickling my ear. "I wish this was our *Walimah* so we could leave here as husband and wife."

The hint of sandalwood in his cologne gives me flashbacks of our night in his bedroom. I can't help but wonder if that was part of his plan—to push me toward this very moment, ready or not. My palms grow damp.

I take two steps backward. "We don't always get what we want."

Before Raheem layers on more useless compliments, Sister Jameela appears at his side. "Here the two of you are!" she says, a deep stress line on her forehead. "The photographer wants to take a few pictures of both families before the guests arrive."

Photos? A permanent reminder of *today*? No thank you.

Zaynab walking through the door closest to the north parking answers my prayers. I make a beeline for her.

"Fatima?" my fiancé calls from behind me. "The pictures!"

I throw myself onto Zee, wrapping my arms around her. "I'm so glad you're here," I whisper, a quiver in my voice.

She hugs me back. "I told you I'd be here early."

With precision, I keep Zaynab between me and Raheem. I grab her hand and pull her into the ballroom, away from him and his mother.

"You weren't lying," she says, taking in the decorations, table settings, and massive dessert display. "Homeboy's family is loaded."

My parents are standing next to a banquet table by the dance floor; they both wave us over. "*As-salaamu alaykum*, Zaynab," they greet her as we join them.

"*Wa alaykum as salaam*, Sister Sharifa, Brother Adam."

"Do you want to be in the pictures with us, Zaynab?" my dad asks. "You're practically Fatima's sister."

"Thanks, but no. I'm just here to give moral support."

Raheem and Sister Jameela join us.

My future husband clears his throat, a smirk growing on his face. "Fatima, our moms suggested we get our marriage license next week. What do you think?"

The question is a punch to the gut.

Keeping my face blank takes everything I have. "We talked about August. Our *Kitab* and *Walimah* wouldn't be for two months."

My mom pats my shoulder. "Fatima, you two would go to the Bernalillo county clerk's office downtown to get your New Mexico marriage license. You'd still live at home until after your wedding party."

A rush of cold sweeps across my body. I grab Zee's hand.

I can't fake it another second. Some honesty slips out. "I'm not sure about this."

Raheem's ability to keep a straight face is better than mine. "What aren't you sure about? Your mother just told you nothing would change until after our *Walimah*—it's not a big thing."

My dad turns to me. "If next week is too soon, you two could wait a bit."

Dad senses something is wrong—I know it. But even he doesn't get it.

My heart is pounding. A slow flood of simmering anger bubbles up inside me.

"It's not about next week." I draw in a big breath, squeezing my best friend's hand hard for support. "I'm having doubts about getting married at all."

Keep going.

Everyone's finally listening.

My mom buries her face in her hands, but in the blink of an eye she recovers. "Why? He asked and you said yes. Don't you like the yellow diamond engagement ring and the expensive car he bought you?"

Raheem turns, addressing my dad. "Brother Adam, can you and I talk alone?"

But my father's steeled jaw tells me he's not having it. "It's too late for that. We're all staying here until this is resolved. Fatima, why are you uncomfortable with this?"

Zaynab squeezes my hand, too.

Sister Jameela glances at me, pity written on her face. "Dear, it's normal to be nervous. Happens to every bride-to-be."

"Fatima, she's right. I was almost sick to my stomach the day your dad and I got married." I should've expected my mom's dismissal of my feelings, but DAMN. It still hurts.

With my inner strife about to boil over, taking a risk is my only option. I know this isn't right. I can't go forward.

Breathe!

Speak!

"I'm having second thoughts because I want no part in Raheem seeking full custody of his son after we're married. It's cruel to the mother."

Everyone freezes. I absorb both of my parents' stiff postures.

"Or do you *want* me to go along with that?" I can't help my voice getting louder and louder.

The quiet, gentle, fun-loving Adam Tate who raised me vanishes. In his place, a seething man pivots and yells at my fiancé. "*Is what my daughter said true?* If it is, you'd better explain why the *Hell* we weren't told about this!"

I'm a jittery mess.

My mom whispers into my dad's ear, but he waves away her words. "Not this time, Sharifa."

Raheem refuses to turn his head in my direction. "Brother, it is my fault. I wanted to make sure this relationship would work out before sharing that personal detail with your family. Your daughter only found out a few days ago."

His calm, steady voice dares me to punch him.

His mom addresses me, her fake smile still in place. "Is that what's troubling you, Fatima? Don't worry. He hasn't made a final decision—and even if he goes forward with it, it wouldn't be for a few years."

My mouth falls open at her malice.

I shake my head. "Sister Jameela, you don't get it. I'll *never* agree to raise Umar. Chloe is his mother—not me." Pivoting toward Raheem, I ask, "Why aren't you marrying her, Raheem?" A quick draw of breath and I add, "Did she turn you down?"

Without saying a word, his sneer tells me my suspicion might be true.

His mother's pointed gaze burns my flesh. "She refuses to raise my grandson as a Muslim. Raheem has every right to expect that." The venom behind her smile disgusts me.

"Your son wasn't concerned with Chloe's religion when that adorable baby was conceived," I snap. "So why is he now?"

"How dare you judge him! Their relationship was a mistake, but now that Umar is here, we're making sure he's provided for." Once she's done waving her finger in my face, she plants her hands on her hips. "Shame on you for not supporting Raheem!"

Sister Jameela can't even admit what her son wants is wrong.

One of the ballroom doors opens, and a man carrying a tripod and an oversized camera bag comes in. Raheem's mom darts toward him to stop him coming closer.

My fiancé clears his throat. "This situation is all my fault, Brother Adam."

The hard lines around my dad's mouth don't budge.

To my surprise, words fly out of me. "Even if I forgive you for lying to me and my parents, why would you take the son you say you love away from his mother?"

Raheem winces.

Gotta love the sting a direct question can produce.

"My relationship with Chloe was wrong . . . but her pregnancy changed me. I was in the room when Umar was born, and I called the *Adhan* in his ear. My son needs to grow up with our traditions, but she doesn't agree."

Dad's face turns a deep shade of red.

Every one of Raheem's excuses is pathetic.

"There's more to being a father than whispering the call to prayer in your newborn's ear," I state, without a drop of emotion. "Mine's the best, and you're nothing like him. Never will be."

My fiancé's always-in-control attitude starts to crumble. His eyes bulge, and his gaze moves from person to person: me, Dad, Ma, Zee. Sweat dots his forehead.

The engagement party officially starts in thirty minutes.

It takes all my willpower to keep my voice steady. "To make this easy for both of us, Raheem, I've decided to call off the engagement."

Something in the air around us shifts.

The guy I used to think of as my Muslim Prince Charming doesn't flinch, but his jaw clenches tight. "You should reconsider."

I pull the yellow diamond off my finger, lean in close, and drop it into my ex-fiancé's hand. "No. This belongs to you."

Can it really be this easy? Just like that, I'm free?

"I should be surprised, but I'm not." He pockets the returned ring. "You're not cut out for life as my wife if you can't handle small disagreements."

Zaynab laughs out loud.

Raheem's snicker tells me he's not done. "Just curious, Fatima: Do your parents know our history? Did you tell them how we met? How well we know each other?"

A lump forms in my throat. The hidden meaning behind his questions is clear.

He smirks, and I have no idea why I ever thought he had a nice smile. But he's wrong if he still thinks he can keep me in a relationship I don't want anymore. I'll accept the consequences instead of the gilded cage.

"Are you sure you don't want to reconsider?" he presses.

Shame burns my insides, but I shake my head.

"Brother Adam, Sister Sharifa, the truth is your daughter and I met last year at the Shared Table. We agreed not to tell you, but we spent a lot of time together, and we texted every day. We were dating. And we have another secret."

I brace myself.

"Last Saturday night, after Fatima made it into the final round of the baking competition you forbade her from entering, we ended up at my house. We had sex that night."

My mom gasps louder than she ever has before. An invisible rope pulls at me, wrenching my soul half out of my body.

"But I love your daughter and I'm willing to forget this tantrum if she puts the ring back on and agrees to get legally married next week."

The arrogance! I can't tolerate it. I won't tolerate it!

"You're *blackmailing* me into marrying you—you realize that, right?" I was so wrong about this guy—I get it now. "You're not a good man."

"Your whole family should be thanking me!" Raheem counters. "Who's going to want you now?" His hateful tone is new—and disgusting.

A vein in my dad's neck is bulging, but my mom puts a hand on his shoulder. "Adam, we should go. He's not worth it," she pleads with him.

Dad hesitates. "Raheem is the worst kind of hypocrite, Sharifa."

"You're out of control, Mr. Tate. I thought you were better than this," Sister Jameela scolds, returning and standing very close to her son.

But Mrs. Harris is irrelevant now. I no longer care what she thinks.

It's now or never to make this final.

"Who I do or don't end up with isn't your business anymore." I take the new Lexus key fob from my bag and I toss it onto the floor at Raheem's feet. "I won't be needing this."

Zaynab pulls at my arm. "Let's get the Hell out of here."

My former fiancé still thinks he can win. "The *Imam* should be here soon. We should sit and discuss this with him. I'm willing. Are you, Fatima?"

Pushing a pang of embarrassment down, I stand tall. "Fine with me. Should we talk about how you're trying to force me to go through with the engagement? Or perhaps we could discuss your plan to rip your infant son from his loving mother?"

I glare at him until he looks away.

My best friend squeezes my hand again. "Fatima, come on. Let's book it. There's still time to get you to the competition's final round if we go right now!"

For a second, I'm not sure what to do. But after one last glance at the dessert table, I hike up my dress and follow her out of the hotel. We don't just walk—once we're out of the ballroom, we're laughing and running and holding hands, rushing down the hall to the parking lot. I'm free.

The baking competition is something Raheem Harris won't take away from me.

twenty-four

We're in Zaynab's Mini Cooper and speeding downtown.

"I can't believe you brought my stuff with you!" My chef's uniform, pressed and clean, is in her back seat, alongside my baking tool caddy.

She's weaving in and out of the Saturday afternoon traffic on I-40. "Why? Your best friend couldn't hope there'd be a way for you to compete?"

I'm so grateful for this small miracle.

But there's another issue. "Zee, I've barely practiced at all since Sister Jameela changed the time of the engagement party. I figured there was no point. Any cake I make today won't be good enough. A final *gift* from Raheem!"

She lays on her horn and merges onto I-25 South. "He's a jerk and a loser, but you can't think about that asshole right now! Just pray we get you to the convention center on time."

I recite every *du'a* I remember from Islamic Sunday school until we get there. Zaynab pulls into the first empty spot and we race through the parking garage and into the building. I make it to the registration table, gasping for air.

"Hi!" I force out, wheezing. "I'm Fatima . . ."

The lady shoves my badge at me. "I know who you are, Miss

Tate. Since you're so late, you only have six minutes to be in the Zia Room in your chef's uniform. I'll let the judges know our last finalist has just arrived."

"Thanks." I'm not sure she heard my whisper. I'll ignore her tone for a chance to compete.

Zaynab and I sprint into the bathroom.

I only take one step into the stall before I slide the evening gown down my body. Next, my best friend shoves a pile of clothes at me. I slip into my white T-shirt, black-and-white checkered pants, and chef's coat. As soon as I'm dressed, wrap my white hijab around my head, and step into my closed-toe shoes, Zaynab pushes me toward the exit.

"Go!" she shouts. "I'll put your clothes and heels in your bag. I've got your phone. You need to get in there and work some baking magic!"

"Thanks!" My best friend is amazing, and she's right.

My focus needs to be on my bake. I speed walk into the Zia Room and am surprised that the other four finalists are still there.

"Nice of you to join us, Miss Tate. If you're lucky enough to be accepted into a culinary program, don't make being late a habit. Your instructors will always notice." Chef Erica's criticism stings. "I'll be right back. Cross your fingers we'll be starting the competition soon."

The moment she's gone, Brian rushes over to me. "What the Hell happened? Did you stay up late practicing and oversleep?"

My fingers grip my tool caddy harder. "I wish it were that simple. Why aren't we starting yet?"

Alicia and the other two teenagers in the room are huddled

together in a private conversation. I turn my back to them and concentrate on Brian's friendly face.

"Today is your lucky day," he says. "Only two ovens are working, so we've been waiting while a maintenance person fixes the rest of them." My baking buddy pushes up his sleeves.

Lucky isn't really the word to describe today. A random memory of the mess at the hotel sneaks up on me, but I push it away.

Chef Erica returns in a flash.

"Student bakers, I need to go over a couple things with you for the final round. Remember, each of you will have two and a half hours to bake and decorate your entries. Please *pace* yourselves," she insists. "When you get to your stations, check that you have all your ingredients. If anything is missing, raise your hand and one of the volunteers will help you."

Sounds easy enough.

"None of the judges is expecting perfection today. We've already tasted your first two desserts and can't wait to be wowed by your cakes. Let's head into the ballroom!"

My fingers tremble, going over recipes in my head. Brian turns and wraps his arm around my shoulders, giving me a quick side hug.

Color me surprised.

"Don't worry about the cameras," he says. "They're from the local KOB station. And forget these other bakers. As long as one of us wins the top spot, I'll be happy."

I'm queasy and tempted to bolt for the exit, but I manage a thumbs-up. Getting an innocent hug from him helps.

We follow Chef Erica into the ballroom and find our stations. Every seat in the first ten rows is taken.

"Welcome to the final round of this year's Teen Baking Championship. Today we have asked the finalists to bake and decorate two-tiered cakes. We'll be judging the students' creativity and how well they use either fondant or buttercream in their designs. Taste will count for fifty percent of the scores. I would like to thank all of the sponsors . . ."

I couldn't concentrate on the rest of Chef Erica's speech if I wanted to. Instead, I check my mini fridge and the ingredients on the counter. Everything needed to make my orange cake with ginger buttercream is here. A couple of the spectators keep turning to the back of the room. I stretch my neck and catch sight of a TV crew with its big beefy camera on a tripod.

Oh great, another reason to be stressed. *Good thing baking relaxes me.*

I hear the last thing Chef says as she finishes her speech.

"The time to start baking is now."

Showtime!

I preheat my oven, then start by greasing then flouring my two eight-inch cake pans. A circle of parchment paper goes in each next. Once the flour, baking powder, baking soda, and salt are sifted and combined in a separate bowl, I add my softened butter and sugar to the stand mixer.

It whips for four minutes.

After scraping down the inside of the bowl, I add the rest of my wet ingredients. The last step is adding the dry ingredients in three stages. Now that the batter is done, I pour half of it into both cake pans and get them into the oven.

My eyes search out my best friend in the audience. She shoots me a thumbs-up.

Get back in the baking zone, Fatima.

Frosting time. I put sugar and egg whites in a stainless-steel mixing bowl, then rest the bowl on top of a pot of simmering water. I whisk the mixture together until the thermometer tells me it's reached 165 degrees. Only then do I transfer the mixture into the stand mixer's bowl and let the paddle attachment do its magic. Adding in chunks of butter comes next.

Once the vanilla extract and orange zest are blended in, my Swiss meringue buttercream is almost done. After a small breakfast and no lunch, adrenaline is pushing me to finish.

In a small container, I stir together a few tablespoons of frosting and a few drops of a soft gel food coloring. When it's deep orange, I reincorporate the colored frosting back into the rest of my buttercream.

Stashing the bowl in the fridge, I take my cake layers out of the oven.

While they cool on a wire rack, I sneak a peek at my competition. Brian is closest to me, and his layers are cooling while he's making his frosting.

Getting back to my own baking station, I turn each layer out onto a wire rack. It takes me ten minutes to clean up my area and now it's time to decorate. I grab my buttercream from the fridge.

"Student bakers, there's only thirty minutes remaining in the final round. Your cakes should be out of the oven by now."

Chef Erica's words light a spark inside me.

Since there's no time for a crumb coat, this won't be my best work, but I pull my shoulders back and keep going. As long as my decorations get done, I'll be satisfied.

I trim both layers with a serrated knife and when they're both as flat as I can make them, it's time to start the hardest part of baking for me. With the cake stand in front of me, I spread a dollop of buttercream in the middle of it and lay the first layer down. I fill a piping bag with my frosting and cover the top of the base layer. After smoothing it with my offset spatula, I repeat the process with the second layer.

Dots of frosting cover the backs of my hands, but there's no time to stop.

When the top and the sides are coated, I take my cake scraper and with a gentle touch, run it along the side to smooth out the buttercream. I scrape then turn, over and over again until I'm convinced it's an even layer of frosting. Changing to the star tip on my piping bag, I make small stars around the bottom of my cake and change it again to make a rosette border on the top.

There's just enough time for me to switch to the small, round piping tip and draw swirls along the top of the cake.

"Bakers, please place your finished cakes in the designated area of your workbenches in the next five minutes."

Chef Erica's announcement gets me out of my baking trance.

I step back and turn the cake stand in super-slow circles, dotting each swirl with a couple of light orange sugar pearls. With no time to do anything else, I blow out two long breaths and place my decorated cake, secure on its stand, on the platter at the end of my workbench.

And, just like that, the competition is over.

When every surface of my baking station is spotless and my stuff is back in my tool caddy, I turn and catch Brian mumbling to himself.

His cake is covered with light blue frosting, small and large turquoise fondant ribbons along the sides and the top. It's beautiful. My gaze wanders and I see Alicia's amazing checkerboard fondant decorations.

"Now that the final round is complete, I would like to thank our five finalists for their beautifully decorated cakes. Bakers, you can either wait in the Zia Room or remain with your families in the seating area. I'll return to let everyone know when we have made our decision.

As soon as Chef Erica steps away, I get more attention than I want.

"Fatima! Fatima!"

I hear my parents' booming voices over all the noise.

For a brief second, I'm too shocked to move. They're yelling from the back of the room. I rush to the last row of seats.

"Ma, why are you so loud? You didn't have to sit this far back. Zaynab's in the second row." My underarms dampen with sweat. "I'm sorry about what happened at the . . ."

She puts a finger to her lips. "Fatima, I'm not happy you lied, but we'll have plenty of time to talk at home. For now, I want to know how your cake turned out."

For a moment, I'm simply too stunned to speak.

My dad walks toward me and wraps me in his bear hug.

"I can't breathe!" I squeak.

He lets go. "How did your baking go?"

My heart warms, because neither of them wants to discuss Raheem or the situation at the hotel—only my baking. "The taste should be okay; I used the same recipe as the cupcakes I just made. My decorations were kinda basic, though. Some of the finalists did fancier stuff than me."

"Those orange cupcakes were delicious. If the judges don't like them, there's something wrong with their taste buds." My dad's voice is so loud, a couple other spectators standing a few feet away from us gawk at him.

"*Dad,*" I whisper. "Other people can hear you."

He nudges me with his elbow. "It's fine. We don't want them to be surprised when you win first place."

My mom's eyes are glassy, but she's not saying much.

I blow out a deep breath. "Dad, I don't want to be overconfident. Making it to the final round is amazing enough."

In double the time it takes me to make my favorite cream cheese frosting, Chef Erica walks to the front while a volunteer rolls a workbench beside her. I count five medals and certificates, plus a tall trophy.

"Good afternoon. Can I have all five finalists come and stand up here with me?"

Here goes.

My legs are jelly, and being on display sucks, but I manage to line up beside the other teenage bakers. My parents move up and now share the row with Zaynab.

"I'd like to thank all of our CNM culinary student volunteers for their hard work, and Williams Sonoma for sponsoring the entire competition in addition to donating gift cards for each of our high school finalists," Chef Erica begins. "A huge thanks to the Culinary Institute of America, whose culinary program in California is flying out our grand-prize winner and a parent to their campus to learn from their professional pastry chefs."

I raise my head. My dad holds up his crossed fingers, so I refocus on the floor in front of me.

Grinning, Chef Erica continues, "We have a surprise. As an additional prize, if any of our five finalists apply and are accepted into CNM's culinary program, they will each receive a $200 bookstore credit to use toward the cost of their uniforms and tools."

The audience cheers.

"Our fifth-place winner is Katie . . ." Chef Erica announces.

"Our fourth-place winner is Mateo . . ."

My heart is pounding so loud in my chest it's hard to hear.

"Our third-place winner is Alicia . . ."

She shuffles toward Chef Erica, a fake smile plastered on her face.

Forcing my body still is tough since all I want to do is jump up and down.

It's down to me and Brian. I lock my knees so my legs don't give out.

"Our second-place winner is . . . Fatima Tate—who also had the cleanest baking station throughout all three rounds."

The sudden applause from my family drowns out all other sounds.

Forcing myself to put one foot in front of the other, I accept my certificate, silver medal, and sealed envelope in a daze. As soon as I'm back in my spot, a small three-person section of the audience chants my name.

"Our grand-prize winner of the Teen Baking Championship is Brian Aguilar of Las Cruces, New Mexico!"

We all clap for an entire minute. It's deafening. I'm disappointed, but I'm also truly happy for him.

"The other two judges and I would like to acknowledge all the students who applied and competed this year, and their families,"

Chef Erica tells the crowd. "We hope to hold another great competition next year."

I give Brian a quick side hug—just like he gave me—before an older woman with long gray hair steals him away.

Zaynab rushes me, a cheesy grin covering her face. "I knew you could do it! Congrats! Next stop, whatever culinary program you want!" She nods towards my parents, still in their seats, but staring at us. "I'll take your dress home and you can get it whenever. If you never want to see it again, let me know and I'll donate it to Goodwill."

My best friend is the best.

"You don't have to go," I plead with her. "My dad's going to want to celebrate. You should come over and eat with us."

Zee shakes her head. "Thanks, but I'm not trying to be there when the three of you rehash what happened with the asshole."

After a quick hug, she leaves, and I head over to my parents.

"Great job, Fatima. The judges know talent when they taste it." My mom hasn't yelled once. She might actually forgive me for lying to her.

"I'm so proud of you!" My dad's joy is contagious. "You did an amazing job without any formal training."

I love this man.

"Excuse me. Fatima, are these your parents?" Chef Erica joins us, her steps muffled by the mini celebrations around us.

"Y-yes! Mom and Dad, this is Erica Newsome. She's the head executive pastry chef of CNM's culinary department." I gulp down some air. "This is Adam and Sharifa Tate, Chef."

"I wanted to thank both of you for allowing your daughter to compete. Fatima is a gifted student with a natural talent like I have rarely seen. I expect great things from her in the future." Chef Erica tilts her head in my direction. "Miss Tate, you missed the current deadline for entry into the CIA. But if you decide to apply for the next one in a few months, I'd be happy to write you a letter of recommendation."

She deserves a hug, so I give her one. "Thank you so much, Chef."

"You're very welcome. It was nice meeting both of you," she says to my parents.

I don't think my dad's chest can puff up another centimeter. "It was great to meet you, too."

Putting his arm around me, he says, "Now! Let's go celebrate, Squiggles. Where do you want to eat?"

"Anywhere." I plant a kiss on his cheek.

Today didn't go the way I expected. My engagement is over and my secret was exposed, but my parents are still in my corner.

I may not have won first place, but my future is full of hope again.

twenty-five

By the time we are back home and finish *Maghrib* prayer, my stomach is full of food from my favorite Pakistani restaurant. I could eat their butter chicken every day.

I fold up our prayer rugs and stash them in the hall closet.

"Fatima, can I ask you a question?" Both of my parents are sitting on the couch, but it's my mom asking.

After claiming the loveseat, I lock my ankles in front of me before nodding.

"Why didn't you tell me or your dad about Raheem's behavior? Did you think we wouldn't believe you?" Her jumbled rush of words worries me: she doesn't usually speak so fast.

I study the ceiling above us. "No, it's just . . . I was scared. He saw the birthmark above my belly button—no way to lie about that—so I knew he could prove what he said. I didn't know how either of you would react, so I kept my mouth shut."

My mom isn't done yet. "I'm confused. What did his son even have to do with that?"

I blow out a stream of nervous energy. "After I found out about Umar, we argued. When I admitted my doubts about our relationship, Raheem *flipped*. Like. Freaked. *Out.* He said if I called off our engagement—or even tried to postpone our wedding—he'd expose our secret to both of you and everyone at the Islamic Center."

"And . . ." she urges.

"And his ex-girlfriend Chloe called me to talk not long after that. She told me Raheem's plan to seek full custody of his son after we were married, and she warned me not to trust him. I knew then I couldn't go through with it."

I pray she understands.

"Fatima, please look at me." I don't miss the sadness in her eyes. My heart is ready to break into tiny pieces.

"Ma . . . do you hate me?"

"As your mom, hearing how much you went through by yourself is upsetting, yes. You didn't think you could ask for my help." She gets up and rushes over to me, embracing me. "Fatima, don't you know how much I love you?"

She kisses my forehead before hurrying into the master bedroom.

"Dad, is Mom okay? She just, um . . . ran off."

He pats the cushion next to him. "Come here." I uncurl my legs and move. "Do I have your full attention?" His solemn tone tells me he's serious.

"Yes."

Nothing prepares me for the intensity in his eyes. "Your mom doesn't want you to see her cry. You know we struggled financially when we were first married, and we both thought if you married Raheem, life would be much easier for you."

"But an easier life isn't worth it if I'm miserable. Aren't you disappointed in me?"

"You're my daughter, our only blessing from *ALLAH*, and I failed to protect you. Raheem tried to force you to go through with the marriage. You didn't deserve any of his manipulations."

I fiddle with the cuff of my sleeve. "Do you think he ever loved me?"

My dad tilts his head. "When did he tell you that?"

I can't answer that question, so I don't.

My dad isn't finished. "Raheem Harris has never loved anyone or anything other than himself and his bank account. If that's how he treats the mother of his child, you never had a chance. He pretended to be a good person with a good character. We were all fooled by him."

"Can you ever forgive me?" I reach for my dad and melt into his hug.

"I can't think of one thing you could do that I wouldn't forgive." After a few minutes, he releases me. "Is there anything you need me to handle? Do you have anything of his I can return to Sister Jameela? Raheem deserves to have me smack that condescending smirk off his face, but I promised your mom I wouldn't."

The fierceness in his eyes makes me tremble. *Damn, he's not joking.*

My heart pounds like a jackhammer in my chest. "Dad, did you fight Raheem after I ran out of the ballroom?"

The question hangs in the air, unanswered, long enough for me to wonder if he's going to answer it.

"Fatima, most of the time I'm sensible. I wanted to—but I didn't hit him. Right after the two of you left, I stepped away from Raheem. Your mom and I went to Satellite Coffee." He sighs. "We were still there when Zaynab texted me and told me where you were."

I rub my eyes but can't hold back a yawn. A deep exhaustion grips me.

"Before you go to sleep, I need you to consider talking to someone," my dad suggests. "You've been through a lot in the past few months. Think about it."

I press my fingers against my lips.

I can't go upstairs without asking one last thing. "Are you mad at me for entering the competition without your permission?"

"Fatima, you can't face every situation alone." My dad holds my face in his hands. "Promise me you'll never be afraid to confide in us again. We're a family and your mom and I love you. I know part of this is my fault. I'd never want you to go through with a wedding to any man who's blackmailing you to be his wife."

A single tear runs down my cheek. "I love you."

He wipes away the tear. "Not as much as I love you. Go get some rest."

Two weeks later, I'm in our kitchen surrounded by buttercream, mixing bowls, cups, spoons, and the two half-sheet cakes I made yesterday.

My dad's inspecting my progress. "Daughter, why do I have to wait until tonight for a piece of your cake? One of the benefits of having a future pastry chef in the family should be desserts on demand."

He's lucky I don't launch a glob of frosting at him. "Dad, what's right in front of you?"

I've been baking for two days—he can't possibly miss the four dozen vanilla cupcakes on wire racks. "InshaALLAH, thirty-six of them are for Zaynab's party today, so I'm keeping the other twelve here. As soon as I frost them, they're all yours."

"I'm not sharing them," my dad confesses to me.

I shrug. "That's between you and your wife."

His deep belly laugh reminds me I'm home. Well and truly home. My mom comes out of the master bedroom. "*What's between your dad and me?*"

I tilt my head toward the cupcakes.

"Oh no you don't, Adam Tate! I'm leaving for my twelve-hour shift at the hospital. You better save me at least two." Her stern expression doesn't last very long. She's already laughing.

And so am I.

My parents are so happy together. One day, inshaALLAH, I'll be in a relationship like theirs. But right now, I have a cake to decorate.

"Before I go, Fatima, I need to know your decision about schools. Which one did you choose?" The encouraging gleam in my mom's eye is something I never thought I'd see.

My dad slaps the table in a rhythmic beat. I lift my eyebrows at him. "It's my drumroll," he explains.

I had a speech ready, but I can't remember a single word. "The Culinary Institute of America's campus is amazing. Brian's already set up his visit for next month," I start, sort of rambling. "He'll end up there. He's a great baker, and a great friend. But I've decided to stay here and go to CNM. It's local and it won't cost a ton of money. Their lottery scholarship covers almost all my tuition."

My parents exchange frowns.

"But you said New Mexico was too small and you wanted to study in a bigger city. Did you change your mind?" my mom prods.

"We don't mind if you stay here for school, of course," my dad adds.

I grab my mom's lunch tote and water bottle from the fridge.

Handing them to her, I explain. "If I stay here and get my associate's in culinary studies, I'll be able to save money and apply to the Le Cordon Bleu program in Ottawa. Chef Erica thinks I should consider the one in Paris, but I'm not sure about studying so far from home."

My mom gives me a quick hug. "Sounds like a fantastic plan. Don't you agree, Adam?"

"Of course it is. Our daughter is one smart cookie." He winks at me. "Speaking of, do we have any of those chocolate chip cookie bars left?"

"Dad!"

"I guess we should cancel our family road trip to California. Since you're not going there."

"I have a better idea, Ma. Denver is closer and we could spend the weekend." I have it all planned out in my head. "There's an IKEA outside the city and . . ."

She grins. "InshaALLAH, we'll talk about it before I go to work tomorrow."

My budget can't afford Williams Sonoma anymore. But IKEA works for me.

"Fatima, are you sure you're okay if I meet some brothers for coffee after *Isha* prayer? I won't be back until late tonight." My dad is too cute. "I could come straight home from work to be here with you."

"I'm fine being home by myself." I gesture around the kitchen. "I have to finish decorating Zaynab's cake and all these cupcakes before her party tonight."

Dad gathers his keys and tucks his wallet in his back pocket. "And you're okay with going to the graduation party by yourself?"

"You worry enough for both of us," I tell him.

My mom chimes in. "You don't have to go to the party if you're not ready. I'm sure Sarah would come pick up the desserts."

"I need both of you to listen to me." My words bring them face-to-face with me. "You've got to stop treating me like I'm fragile. Some days will be better than others, and today is a great one. Missing this party isn't an option. I love you both, and inshaALLAH, I'll be fine."

It's midafternoon when I pull into the driveway beside Zee's Mini Cooper, my blaring horn disturbing the quiet street. Thirty-six cupcakes in three carriers line the back seat.

My best friend bangs on my window, a frown across her beautiful face. I push the button and the glass slides down.

"Sis! Your horn scared the Hell out of me. Why didn't you ring the doorbell?"

I turn off my car and step out. "My cakes need the air conditioning. And I need help carrying them." I unlock the trunk. "Did you clear space in the fridge?"

"What about the special, beautiful, wonderful cake you made for *me*?"

"I made a special, beautiful, wonderful cake for you *and* Amber. Remember her?" I lift the full sheet pan out of the trunk and walk at a snail's pace into the house. When I get to the kitchen, Amber is pulling stuff out of the fridge to make room.

"Hi, Fatima! I made space for it."

My BFF leans over my shoulder to get a glimpse of the two-tiered sheet cake before I slide it onto the shelf and close the doors. "Nice work. You know I'll be putting a couple slices away for later."

She hasn't changed.

Once the cupcakes are tucked away in the fridge, too, I can breathe again. "Zee, I asked you last night to clean out the refrigerator! Why was your girlfriend doing it when I got here?" I fold my arms across my chest.

Zee slumps onto the closest barstool. "When would I have time? My mother's lost it. I've scrubbed, vacuumed, and dusted every surface in this whole place. Why do we live in a four-bedroom house anyway? It's only the two of us."

I snort. She wouldn't last two days with my mom.

I scan the kitchen, catching a glimpse of party balloons outside in the backyard. "Where is your mom? I parked in her space."

Amber rubs Zaynab's back. "Don't mind Grumpy here. You know she hates housework. Miss Baker went to the grocery store to get more ice."

"Don't let her hear you call her that. Since I met this one in fifth grade"—I point to Zee—"she's made me call her Sarah."

The two of them exchange weird looks.

"What?" Now I want to know.

Amber clears her throat twice. "Your girl here doesn't want me to say anything, but I can't help it. Are you okay, Fatima? Like, really okay? Breaking up with your fiancé had to be difficult. Do you want to talk about it?"

Her concern brings me joy. "It was hard. But it would've been worse to go ahead."

Zaynab nudges her girlfriend's shoulder, but Amber keeps talking. "Is it true he bought you a brand-new Lexus?"

I have no reason not to answer her question. "I'm not a saint or anything, so yes, the gifts he bought impressed me—at first. But when I got to know him, that changed. His money wouldn't have solved our problems." A fleeting wave of sadness hits me—not for him, but for the person he pretends to be.

Amber comes around the kitchen island and wraps her arms around me for a few seconds. "I'm here if you ever need an ear."

"Thank you." I squeeze her, staring out the large picture window at the blue sky.

"Babe, can you go outside and help my mother? I think she bought, like, twenty bags of ice," Zaynab asks.

"Sure! I'll be right back."

When it's just the two of us, my best friend won't stop watching me. A minute passes and I've had enough. "*What?* What's up?"

"We're alone. You can admit if you're not okay."

I have no reason not to be. The corners of my mouth inch up. "InshaALLAH, once my culinary program starts and I'm baking all the time, I'll think about him less and less. Today is a good day."

All of a sudden, Zee walks through the family room, yanks open the back door, and grins. Beyoncé's "Single Ladies" booms out of the speakers in the garden. Now she's dancing, imitating the moves from the iconic video.

"What are you *doing*?"

"You can't tell?"

I grin at her. "But you're not single."

"Amber won't mind if I'm just helping my best friend celebrate."

The party hasn't started yet, but the song's bass pushes me to join her. We move our bodies to the addictive beat, and when it ends we're crying from laughter, sprawled across the grass.

I survived to bake another day. My life. My decision.

The future belongs to me.

Easy Chocolate Fudge

Yields: 3 dozen pieces

Ingredients
2 cups semisweet chocolate
1 can sweetened condensed milk
1 teaspoon vanilla extract
1 cup chopped pecans (optional)

Method
1. Preheat the oven to 325°F. Put the pecans on a baking tray and toast them for 5 to 7 minutes.
2. Spray an 8- or 9-inch pan with cooking spray. Then line it with parchment paper.
3. Combine chocolate and condensed milk in a heavy-bottom, medium-sized saucepan. Warm it over the lowest heat. Stir continuously until it's smooth and the chocolate is completely melted.
4. Remove from heat then stir in the pecans and vanilla.
5. Spread mixture evenly into the prepared baking pan. Refrigerate for at least 2 hours or until firm.
6. Use a large flipping spatula to help you lift the fudge out of the pan.
7. Remove the parchment paper from the fudge. Then cut the fudge into pieces.

Blueberry Orange Scones

Yields: 12 scones

Ingredients

For Scones:
  1 cup fresh blueberries
  3 cups all-purpose flour
  ⅓ cup sugar
  Orange zest from 2 oranges
  1 tablespoon baking powder
  1 teaspoon salt
  1 teaspoon ground cinnamon
  10 tablespoons unsalted butter, chilled
  1 large egg
  1-⅔ cups heavy cream

For Egg Wash:
  1 large egg, beaten

For Glaze:
  1 cup powdered sugar
  ¼ cup orange juice

Method
1. Position the oven rack in the center and preheat the oven to 350°F. Line a baking sheet with parchment paper or a silicone baking mat.
2. Sift the flour, sugar, baking powder, cinnamon, and salt in a large bowl.
3. Cube your butter and add it to the flour mixture. Toss the pieces in flour and then start smashing and rubbing between your palms and breaking the cubes apart with your fingers

until the butter has mostly disappeared into the floury mix. (This can also be done with 4 to 5 pulses in a food processor.)

4. Add the orange zest to the butter-flour mixture.
5. In a small bowl, combine the egg and heavy cream and whisk until thoroughly combined.
6. Toss the blueberries into the flour with your hands.
7. Add the cream mixture to the bowl with the dry ingredients and fold with a rubber spatula (or your hands) until it all comes together into a soft, slightly moist dough. Do not overmix.
8. Lightly flour your work surface, then place the dough on top of it. Dust the dough with a little flour.

Triangle Scone Method: Divide the dough into 2 equal parts and pat each piece with your hand into a flat round about 3/4-inch thick. Cut each round into 6 wedges with a floured knife or metal bench knife.

Square Scone Method: Use the rolling pin to roll the dough out to a 3/4-inch-thick rectangle. Using a sharp floured knife or metal bench knife, cut the dough into 12 2-1/2-to-3-inch squares.

9. Place the scones at least 1 inch apart on the prepared baking sheet.
10. Whisk the remaining egg in a small bowl. Using a pastry brush, lightly brush the tops of the scones with the egg wash. Bake for 20 to 25 minutes, or until golden brown around the edges and cooked through, rotating the pan halfway through the baking time.
11. Transfer the scones to a cooling rack and let them cool completely.
12. While the scones are cooling, make the glaze.
13. Sift the powdered sugar into a bowl. Add the orange juice. Whisk until smooth.
14. When the scones have cooled long enough that they won't melt the glaze, spoon the glaze over the tops of the scones, letting it drip off the sides, then serve.

Flaky Pie Dough

Yields: 2 9-inch crusts (one top and one bottom crust)

Ingredients

2-¾ cups all-purpose flour
1-½ teaspoons sea salt
¼ teaspoon baking powder
1 cup unsalted butter, chilled, cut into ¼-inch cubes
½ cup water, cold (as much needed)
2 teaspoons apple cider vinegar

Method

1. Sift the dry ingredients together in a mixing bowl.
2. Add the cold butter pieces to the bowl. With a paddle, or by hand, mix the butter into the dry ingredients. Mix until the butter resembles small peas.
3. Add the apple cider vinegar to the cold water.
4. Slowly add the wet ingredients. Starting with ¼ cup, mix the water in with a spatula, then add the rest of the water. *
5. You should be able to press it into a mass with your hands.
6. Remove the dough from the bowl and press it into a ball. Use a knife and a cutting board to cut the dough into 2 equal-sized pieces.
7. Flatten each ball into a disk. Wrap them each tightly in plastic wrap and refrigerate for at least 20 minutes.**
8. Roll out the bottom crust to about 12 inches across. Try to keep it in a circular shape.
9. Place dough into 9-inch pie plate. Fold over the edge of the dough and tuck it into the edge of the pie plate.

*Add the water slowly and pay attention. The dough should just barely stick together. You can always add more but you can't take it away.

**Can be made ahead of time and kept in the refrigerator overnight.

Apple Pie Filling

Yields: 1 pie filling

Ingredients
1 pound Granny Smith apples
1 cup sugar
½ tablespoon lemon juice
½ tablespoon vanilla extract
2 tablespoons all-purpose flour
¾ tablespoon ground cinnamon
2 pinches salt
1 large egg

Method
1. Line a 9-inch pie pan with pie dough.
2. Peel, core, and thinly slice your apples. Place them in a large bowl.
3. Toss the apples with lemon juice, sugar, and vanilla.
4. Sift your flour, salt, and cinnamon into the apples. Toss the apple mixture until mixed well.
5. After you put your pie filling in, roll out the second disk of dough to about 9-½ inches across. Place it on top of the filled pie. Use a fork to seal the top crust to the bottom crust.
6. Crack the egg into a bowl and mix it. Then take a pastry brush and lightly brush egg wash on the top crust.
7. Get a sharp knife and cut 2-½ inch vents into the pie crust. This will help the steam inside the pie escape.
8. Line a cookie sheet with parchment paper or foil. Place the pie on lined cookie sheet. This will catch the drips and make cleaning easier.
9. Bake at 375°F until juices are thick and overflowing. Bake for about 1 hour and 20 minutes.
10. Let the pie rest for at least 1 hour before serving.